Relentless:
Redeemed Series Book 1

Relentless:
Redeemed Series Book 1

Patricia Haley and Gracie Hill

www.urbanchristianonline.com

Urban Books, LLC
97 N18th Street
Wyandanch, NY 11798

Relentless: Redeemed Series Book 1

ISBN 13: 978-1-60162-678-3
ISBN 10: 1-60162-678-9

First Trade Paperback Printing November 2014
Printed in the United States of America

10 9 8 7 6 5 4 3 2 1

*This is a work of fiction. Any references or similarities
to actual events, real people, living or dead, or to real
locales are intended to give the novel a sense of reality.
Any similarity in other names, characters, places, and
incidents is entirely coincidental.*

Distributed by Kensington Corp.
Submit Wholesale Orders to:
Kensington Publishing Corp.
C/O Penguin Group (USA) Inc.
Attention: Order Processing
405 Murray Hill Parkway
East Rutherford, NJ 07073-2316
Phone: 1-800-526-0275
Fax: 1-800-227-9604

Relentless:
Redeemed Series Book 1

by

Patricia Haley and Gracie Hill

Relentless is also available as an eBook

Also by **Patricia Haley**

Mitchell Family Drama Series
(Listed in story line order)

Anointed

Betrayed

Chosen

Destined

Broken

Humbled

Also by **Gracie Hill**

Where the Brothers At?

Sorrows of the Heart

The Kitchen Beautician

Saved, Sanctified and Keeping My Secret

Patricia dedicates Relentless *to the memories of three beloved father-figures who were supportive, encouraging, loving, and faithful men of God.*

Deacon Robert (Bob) Thomas, Jr.: (1928–2013)
Uncle Clifton (Cliff) Tennin, Jr.: (1930–2014)
William Ronald (Pop) Fisher: (1943–2014)

Gracie dedicates Relentless *to those who have storms raging in their lives and are still wounded by past hurts which prevent them from being whole.*

The winds of adversity will change.
God can calm the tempest storms in your life.

*On that day a great persecution broke out
against the church . . . he dragged off
men and women and put them in prison.*

—Acts 8:1, 3

Chapter 1

Adrenaline surged. There wasn't any greater satisfaction than hearing the jury foreman belting out the
verdict, "We find in favor of the plaintiff." The sum of
the judgment didn't quench Attorney Maxwell's legal
thirst; although $12 million wasn't bad for a day's work
in court. Best news was that there were plenty more cases
to come. So long as corruption continued slithering into
the church, he'd be a man on a mission. Anticipating the
battles he'd get to fight sent exhilaration surfing through
his body that he could ride indefinitely.

Maxwell saw the wave of reporters waiting on the
courthouse steps as the bright spring sunlight refused to
be hidden. He jiggled the knot on his tie and straightened
his Armani suit coat, which didn't need much help. It
always fit perfectly, as expected, consistent with the rest
of the life he'd carefully and purposefully crafted. "Are
you ready to face the crowd?" Maxwell asked his client.

She grabbed his arm, shaking. "Do we have to go out
there? Now that we've won, I just want to get out of here."

Absolutely not was what he should have told her, but
there was no need for further convincing. He'd proven
that his plan worked best. She was walking out with a civil
case victory against the almighty Reverend Morgan, the
so-called anointed leader of one of the largest ministries
in the tri-state area. Whatever he was supposed to be,
reverend, minister, doctor, or bishop, the well-deserved
label of being a bona fide predator could also be added

to his bio. No way was Maxwell going to pass up a prime opportunity to shout their victory over the airwaves. He'd send a message to the other perpetrators. There would be no rest as long as Maxwell Montgomery was alive and breathing. Churches were on notice and they'd better take him serious.

He expeditiously ushered his client toward the door. She gave some resistance, which didn't deter his movement. Six months ago she was deemed a fired disgruntled employee who was raising false allegations against one of the most prestigious ministers in Philadelphia. He kept pulling her toward the door, with the media closing in. Thanks to him her inappropriate interaction with Reverend Morgan had been legitimized. It was no longer her fault, and on top of it, she was going to get $12 million, less his 40 percent cut. Far as he was concerned, she didn't get a say in how the rest of the day was going to play out. He forcefully pushed the door open leading from the courthouse and braced against the gust of wind.

The clicking sound of cameras, microphones shoved near his face, onlookers lining the steps, and incoherent chants equaled mayhem for most. But, the controlled chaos was a work of beauty to Maxwell. His client was squeezing his arm so tightly that he had to peel a few of her fingers back to loosen the grip.

"Do you feel vindicated?" one reporter blurted out.

As his client stammered, Maxwell jumped in. Microphones homed in. "Justice was rendered today. The past six months have been a pure nightmare for my client. Her reputation has been maligned. She's been hounded by church members simply because she was willing to come forward and expose the truth. She should be praised for her courage, not demonized, and today is the first step toward her getting back to a normal life."

"Were you really expecting to win such a substantial settlement from a church?" One reporter asked.

"It's the only fair outcome; doesn't matter if it's the church or the Vatican, wrong is wrong, and we have the court of law to right those wrongs," Maxwell echoed, fueled with satisfaction.

"Do you see this as an indictment against religion?"

"No one is above the law." Maxwell broke the grip his client had and raised his arm. He knew which network had the largest viewing audience and intentionally pointed his finger directly into their camera and said, "I'm serving notice to the corrupt leaders out there. If you think the church is going to save you, you're sadly mistaken. I'm coming for you and you and you." Maxwell was charged, ready to sail out of the crowd and whisk back to his office to start the next case. He reclaimed his client and began maneuvering through the crowd.

"Attorney Maxwell, is that a threat to all local clergymen?" a reporter asked.

Maxwell screeched to a stop. "I don't make threats, only promises."

"How many more lives are you going to ruin?" a voice shouted from the crowd. The mob was thick and Maxwell couldn't see who was speaking. "You have ruined my family and our church." As the woman got louder, it was like a pebble rippling in a pond. The crowd backed up and the media swarmed to her. "Who do you think you are, God?"

She was a distance away, at the bottom of the steps, but Maxwell could see her clearly. It was Minister Morgan's wife, the one he'd just beaten in court. He couldn't understand why she was making a scene. She should have crawled out the courthouse's back door in humiliation like her husband, glad that this had only been a civil case and not a criminal trial. Instead of accepting the jury's decision, she wanted to go another round with Maxwell in front of the media. Even if he wanted to cut her a break, she wasn't leaving him much choice coming at him in front of a crowd. He had to be swift and set precedence. Otherwise others might make the same mistake in the future of trying to undermine his mission of exposing bad church leaders.

"I'm not the guilty one here," he said burning his gaze into hers. He laid his palm onto his chest. "I can appreciate the outrage. We should all be outraged at the behavior we heard about earlier in the courtroom. If more citizens would turn their outrage into action, perhaps we wouldn't have to rely on the court to solve church matters. Until that day comes, here we stand." His blood was pumping, faster and faster. This was his platform and he was poised to capitalize, using the very words that his religious mockers glibly uttered from their pulpits every Sunday. It was a language they understood. "As a society, we can't let leaders of any kind abuse their power and take advantage of people. The Bible says to expel the wicked man from among you." He let his gaze slide back from the Reverend's wife to the camera all along maintaining intense control while letting each word resonate. "I did my job. I sought justice for a victim." Maxwell interlocked his arm with his client's. The message had more oomph with the victim standing nearby. "Your husband isn't above the law as we've seen in this courtroom today."

"You went after him for no reason. You're working for the devil, and God is going to punish you."

Maxwell grinned and straightened his tie once again, reveling in the label. He'd grown accustomed to the routine. The church leader did something inappropriate, his wife and congregation stood by him to the bitter end like cows being herded off the cliff. That's the way it had been for his family twenty-six years ago when they were driven off the cliff and not much had changed.

"Maybe God will." He chuckled. "But today your husband was the only one punished for his actions." Maxwell stepped firmly down the stairs, satisfied until he heard another voice.

"You hurt my father. You're a bad man," the little boy said clinging to his crying mother and burying his face into her side.

Insults fueled Maxwell's resolve. It confirmed that he was disrupting his opponent's peace of mind, the first step in bringing them down. He was fully prepared to attack the reverend's wife if for no other reason than being ignorant to her husband's dealing. His mother and father had been ignorant to the fraudulent tactics of their pastor and no one gave them a break when it came to their sentencing. No mercy had been granted to them back then and none would come now for these people. But the boy was an unexpected factor. *Who brings a child to court* he wondered?

For a split second, Maxwell was emotionally dragged back to the tiny town outside of Philadelphia where his security had been snatched away at age twelve, probably a few years older than the pastor's son standing in front of him. At least Reverend Morgan wasn't headed to prison; at least not yet, not like Maxwell's father had. Maxwell shook off the nostalgia and hunched his shoulders as he pierced through the crowd, refusing to let anyone or anything curb his zeal, not even a little boy sobbing for his father. The little boy didn't realize it now, but he'd be all right. Maxwell was proof of it. He'd survived while his father served time for fraudulent activity in the church. If his father had done the crime, maybe Maxwell would have been at peace with the outcome. The truth was that his father was only guilty of stupidity resulting from staying loyal to a crooked preacher and naively taking the rap for his transgressions. Maxwell rebelled. Those memories weren't going to suck him into a funk. He pushed ahead having regained full control of his surroundings, eager to get to his office.

Suddenly there was a thumping sensation smothered by oohs and aahs. The air felt light and the sky hypnotic. He seemed to be floating to the ground. Screams and a bunch of chatter faded out. Maxwell could see the people crowding around him. Every action was in slow motion. He wasn't sure but guessed that this must be what peace felt like, being oblivious to pain, shielded from the chatter, naysayers, and circumstances. Maxwell's thoughts crashed back to reality wielding a powerful headache with it, as he was instantly jerked out of the clouds of euphoria. He placed the palm of his hand against his forehead, pressing in and feeling the coolness right above his eyebrow. He didn't need to see the blood to know it was there.

"Attorney Maxwell, are you okay?" his client asked, bending down to pick up the rock lying on the ground. "Did anyone see who threw the rock?"

No one responded.

A flurry of cameras clicking, tapes rolling, and microphones poking into his face wasn't as well received this time. Maxwell tried standing, refusing to be caught on TV in a weakened state. He would regain composure and show the assailant and everybody else how indestructible he was. Not even a boulder, let alone a rock the size of a ball of yarn, could shut him up. He placed his bloody palm on the ground and pushed up to stand. Halfway up his legs buckled, sending him crashing to the ground. Aahs radiated in the crowd.

"Call 911," his client screamed out, staying by her attorney's side.

"No, I'm good, just give me a minute. I'm fine," Maxwell protested, wishing it were true.

A reporter crammed a microphone within inches of his mouth. "Are you going to press charges?"

"Are you going to wage a civil suit against the person who assaulted you?" another reporter asked drawing a few pockets of laughter from the crowd.

Unwilling to accept defeat, Maxwell was determined to stand. He made repeated attempts with each ending in failure and landing him smack on the ground. It was a position he'd spent his entire adult life avoiding.

Chapter 2

A constant throbbing felt as if someone was banging a hammer against his head. The ringing sensation was an alarming reminder of the cowardly attack. Maxwell massaged his temples hoping to eliminate any feeling, a feat he'd become the master at doing.

"I see you're finally awake," a nurse said entering the room holding a chart. "Quite a bump on the head you have there." Maxwell mumbled in response but apparently not loud enough to interrupt the chatterbox as she kept talking. "Let's see how you're doing here," she said, shoving a thermometer into his mouth and wrapping the blood pressure cuff around his forearm. She paused with her incessant gibberish until the blood pressure cuff loosened, indicating the test was complete. There was a small chance the nurse wasn't a nuisance, but the pain surging inside his skull magnified light and noise, converting both to sources of extreme irritation.

"It's a little bump." Maxwell touched the spot and quickly withdrew his hand while wincing. "Trust me, I've been through worse than this," he stated trying to overshadow the effects of his intermittent whacks of pain.

"Maybe so, but any type of trauma to the head can be serious for someone your age. I'm guessing that you're, what, about fifty-five or fifty-six, right?" she asked studying his face and jotting on the chart.

"What?" he blurted. Thoughts swirled. His sight was fuzzy but he wasn't the blind one in the room if she guessed him to be fifty-five. "I'm only thirty-nine," he demanded not sure if the tone was a result of anger, embarrassment, or simple shock. He was a pit bull in the courtroom, bowing to no one in defeat or fear. Yet, he felt vulnerable lying in the bed listening to this nurse, not even five feet tall, summing up his existence. He felt naked and tugged at the sheet slightly.

"Oh, I'm sorry. After working in the hospital for twenty-five years, I'm usually pretty good at guessing a person's age."

The nurse was unaware of the current she'd sent raging through Maxwell.

Initially shaken, his confidence kicked in allowing him to erase the low-grade vulnerability. He was invincible, had to be. He wasn't going to toss aside years of hard work, literally thousands of legal hours because a blind old nurse made him temporarily question his mortality. Thirty-nine or fifty-five didn't make a difference. What-ever number of days he had left would be spent doing what he did best.

"Any blurriness or nausea?"

"None of that. When can I get out of here?"

The nurse looked over the chart. "I'm not sure what your doctor wants to do. I know we're keeping you overnight, and we'll know more when the doctor checks on you in the morning."

"I don't need to stay overnight. Like I said, it's just a little bump." He couldn't let some coward blindside him with a rock and believe it had made an impact other than driving him harder.

"You have a concussion. So, we'd better keep you for observation. Better safe than sorry is what I always say."

As far as Maxwell was concerned, she'd already said plenty. He rolled over, no longer facing the nurse. "I'll wait until the morning, but that's it. I'm going home regardless of what the doctor says."

"You'll be glad you stayed, Mr. Montgomery."

He heard her exiting the room, leaving him with his pride and a mound of memories. Hush swept across the room. Maxwell reflected on the mob of reporters at the courthouse earlier, angry church members, and other people who had no interest in the case beyond curiosity. Not everybody was going to appreciate his efforts, a fact he could live with as long as restitution was being served. He could say that his determination to seek justice was based on a deep-seated humanitarian desire to rescue victims, ones who didn't have the ability to stand up against the slew of religious giants, but that would be a lie.

He let his eyes roam around the hospital room before rolling over onto his back and staring toward the ceiling. Emptiness filled the space, a stark contrast to the scene surrounding him earlier. Even his great legal mind wasn't able to explain away the obvious. There was no one at his side, no one doting on him. He was alone. He rubbed the bandage above his eye and shook off the slightest bit of despair. There was no time for pity, no tolerance for weakness. His convicted father had taught him that much. Shake it off. Get healthy. More work was the cure.

The phone rang, startling Maxwell into consciousness. Scanning the small room, it took a second to figure out where he was. He searched around the bed for his cell phone with no success. He suspected it must be in his suit jacket, which was out of arm's reach. He rolled over ready to ignore the noise until it stopped temporarily and then began again. Finally he realized the ringing was coming from the phone resting on the nightstand situated off to the side. The volume seemed to get louder, with each ring intensifying the throbbing in his head. Irritated he snatched the receiver determined to keep the conversation short. "This is Maxwell," he said without softening the edge in his tone. *The person on the other end should get the message quickly.*

"Paul, it's Christine."

He didn't respond. His sister was the last person he expected to be on the call. It had been at least a year since they'd last spoken.

"Are you okay?" she asked.

"I'm good," he said, intentionally not elaborating.

"I was watching the news and saw you drop to the ground. They played it over and over. I've been frantic trying to find out what happened to you," she said speaking very rapidly. "Mom is worried to death too. You should call and let her know you're okay." There was no reason to reply. She knew that wasn't an option for him. "You are okay, aren't you? I mean really okay?"

"I'm fine."

"So, why are you in the hospital?"

"Ah, don't worry about that. I'll be out of here tomorrow morning, no big deal. Getting hit by a rock isn't going to put me out of commission. I have a pretty thick skull."

"That's true." Her tone was lighter.

"How did you know I was here?"

"Oh my goodness, that's a long story. I called the news station. They told me the name of the ambulance company who took you to the hospital, and I called them to find out where they'd taken you. I've been on the phone all afternoon making at least thirty calls."

"I'm surprised the ambulance company gave you the name of this hospital. That's violating a patient's privacy."

"Don't worry; I'm not going to stalk you; although if it were left up to our mother, she'd have me rush over there to check on you."

"No need to do that." Maxwell gently rubbed his forehead.

"Don't worry, I'm only joking, at least partially. I'm not going to bother you unless it's an emergency." Exactly what Maxwell wanted to hear. "But, Paul, I am concerned about you and what you're doing with the churches. It seems really dangerous, and we're worried about you."

The edge which had softened in his tone was sharpening again. Twenty-two years and she was still calling him Paul. The day he received the letter confirming his full scholarship to college, he'd walked out of the tiny apartment in Chester, PA, leaving behind respect for his parents, any support that they might be willing to give, and his name. Spending the last three months of high school in a shelter was one of the best decisions he'd ever made, except the part about having to leave his little sister. Christine was as much of a victim during their childhood as he'd been, but she was grown now and too connected to their parents to have a meaningful relationship with him. Distance had to be maintained. "Can you please call me Maxwell, please?" he requested firmly, refusing to mask his agitation.

"I'm so sorry. I know you've told me over and over but I just forget sometimes. I'm sorry."

Maxwell gained no satisfaction in berating his sister. The stabbing edge of his words penetrated his hard interior, softening his tone again. "Don't waste your time worrying about me."

"Well, you can't stop us from worrying. You might not talk to us, and you might not want to see us, but you can't stop us from caring about you. You're the only brother I have, and like it or not, I love you."

Maxwell's head began hurting again. He didn't want to get into an emotional back and forth with his sister. The call was civil and ready for closure; best to leave something to talk about next year. "Like I said, don't worry about me. I can take care of myself. I always have,"

Maxwell insisted, knowing she understood every bit of what he was saying and not saying. "I'm getting tired. I better let you go."

"Sure, sure, I'm glad to know you're going to be all right. I'll let Mom know." He figured the call was over until Christine called out, "Maxwell, there's something else I need to tell you."

"What; is there something wrong with Tyree?" He sat up in the bed, pushing past his headache. "What's wrong? Tell me," he asked, anxious, almost demanding an answer.

"No, no, there's nothing wrong with Tyree. Your nephew is perfectly fine for a six-year-old. I would let you speak to him, but he's at school."

Maxwell drew in a deep breath and sighed with relief. "If he ever needs anything, I hope you'll let me know."

"You know I will, but honestly this isn't about Tyree. It's Dad."

Maxwell's headache intensified, seeming to come at full force. He wanted to get off the phone. "Christine, my head is killing me. I better go."

"But, he's not doing well. We think it's cancer."

Maxwell didn't hesitate. "My head really is killing me. I have to go."

"Wait, do you want me to give Mom or Dad a message from you?"

"Tell my nephew hello for me, and I won't forget his birthday in a few months."

"But you sent him plenty last Christmas. He doesn't need anything else."

"Who's talking about need? Every now and then it's all about what we want." He'd wanted his old room back, the one he had before his parents lost their house and crammed them into a two-bedroom apartment. Being forced to share a room with his little sister was a sobering reminder of how gullible his parents had been and how they'd let the church ruin their family.

"Thanks for the call and take care of yourself."

"You too, and remember that I'm praying for you," she said ending the conversation.

Maxwell adjusted his head on the pillow. Chester was only twenty miles from Philadelphia, but it might as well have been 20,000 miles away. As long as the crushing memories of his past lived in that town, he didn't plan on returning. He closed his eyes and rested. Tomorrow would come quickly and so too would his burning desire to get cracking on the next case, perhaps the largest of his career—Greater Metropolitan. Years in the making, he was finally ready to take a stab at the great Bishop Ellis Jones, the man responsible for destroying his family. Vindication was the way and Maxwell was excited. The anticipation ushered him to sleep.

Chapter 3

His release couldn't come fast enough. Spending another night stuck in the hospital was absurd. A second night wasn't an option. As soon as the doctor told him he was free to go and the nurse handed him a filled prescription for pain, Maxwell had dashed from the hospital glad to catch the last remaining hour of daylight. A short cab ride and he was driving from the courthouse parking garage. He should probably go home he thought, gently massaging his temple. The notion was fleeting. Maxwell was barreling down the street before the notion could fully form into a slight possibility, let alone action. Instead, Maxwell whipped his Porsche 911 into the reserved parking space, stopping inches from the M. M. sign. Late Saturday afternoon, the parking lot was practically empty. *Perfect;* he could go inside and regroup. Space and privacy was what he yearned and his office was the ideal oasis.

Maxwell was out of sorts having found his cell phone with a dead battery. He couldn't get any calls or messages, causing him to be agitated. He'd poke around his receptionist's desk to see if there were any messages left for him. There was bound to be a stack from Nicole. If his sister had tracked him down in the hospital, he figured Nicole would make the same effort in reaching him. He didn't want anyone swooning over him. Keeping love at least an arm's length away from his heart worked and Nicole understood. She'd allowed him the space he required for going on two years. Fear had a way of skewing perspectives though. His mishap at the courthouse was bound to get her all worked up and worried about him. He figured that's what companions did. Fourteen- and fifteen-hour days didn't leave much time for dating. So, he based her reaction purely on what seemed logical. He was poised to tell her he was okay and not to worry. He ruffled a few papers on his receptionist's desk and didn't find any messages, not from Nicole, not from other clients offering concern, from no one.

He lingered at the desk for a moment. His eyes moved around the room noting its emptiness and the solitude that mocked him. Refusing to play the victim, Maxwell toughened up and went into his office. It was the room where dreams came true for the weak and retribution was realized for him. Entering his sanctuary was the boost he needed. A few sharp pains here and there and a little blurriness was the only lingering reminder of his recent attack. Couple of days and that would be gone but the troubles strapped to Reverend Morgan weren't going away as quickly, not after the reverend lost his case yesterday. Neither would those of Bishop Jones once Maxwell orchestrated his due justice.

He plopped into his chair and extracted the files from his lower right side drawer. They were waiting on his arrival. He opened the folder feeling revived, alive. The absence of Nicole's call was hurled out of his mind. His heart was entangled in only one love affair and that was his commitment to making hypocritical leaders account-able. Dusk would soon be rolling in and night would quickly follow. Maxwell didn't mind. Working most of the night in total submersion was the best medication for his mild headache.

***

Hustling through the airport was commonplace. Shuttle service, freezing hotel rooms, lavish dinners eaten alone night after night was the reality Nicole knew, one she acknowledged without resistance. Becoming senior consulting manager was the reward, an achievement she'd sacrificed her personal life to earn and graciously accepted. She flipped the magazine pages, hastily without recalling a single image or story title. She checked her watch repeatedly, each time with only two or three minutes having elapsed.

Maxwell continued crashing her sanity. On any other occasion his memory would be shoved into her bag, surfacing when her plane landed at Philadelphia International. Today images of him couldn't be suppressed. Hearing the news about his attack yesterday stirred her in a way she hadn't felt before. She pulled out her phone, wanting to call him again, but how could she? The two calls she placed earlier today and the one last evening were sufficient. That's what she'd have to keep telling herself. She knew he'd return the call if and when he was ready. That's how they worked: no stressful relationship business, no commitment, and no issues. It was the way Maxwell wanted it. Nicole began flipping the pages again checking her watch. It was what she wanted too, she guessed.

"Flight number 467 for Philadelphia now boarding at Gate 41," the departure gate attendant announced.

Nicole gathered her belongings, trying to shake off her uneasiness. Restlessness in the pit of her abdomen would not go away. She stuffed the magazine into the front pocket of her shoulder bag and snatched up her Starbucks cup. "Our Executive Platinum guests are welcomed to board." Nicole walked briskly toward the door, ready to hop on board and sleep away her jitters, hoping to land refreshed after the red-eye flight.

"Mommy, can we go now?" the little girl asked the lady standing near Nicole.

"No, dear, that's for people who fly all the time and don't get to go home very much."

Nicole shortened her strides. Someone from behind asked if she was in line. "Uh, no, go ahead," Nicole said, pretending to search for something in her bag as she stepped aside to let the other passengers go ahead, those with the distinction of having racked up 100,000 air miles in a year, the equivalent of about twenty round trips from one coast to the other. She fumbled in the bag until all platinum and even gold members had boarded. Families were next, a category she didn't plan on joining too soon. At least that's how she'd felt, particularly with a shot at making partner in the firm being squarely within her grasp.

"Excuse me, miss, are you in line?" another mother asked who had been standing nearby holding a baby.

"No, you can go ahead," Nicole said taking a few steps back. Her first-class seat wasn't going anywhere. She'd wait and board with the final group. Standing slightly off to the side gave her a view she hadn't seen before. She was always in the front of a line, never having to wait near or sit by families. For those few minutes, she watched the mother in line with her children. From a distance, the view was more endearing than she'd imagined. But it was from a distance, the place she'd always preferred. Suddenly, making partner didn't seem as electrifying but it was all she had. She stepped in line with boarding pass in hand. There was no need to fret. She was only thirty and had plenty of time to obtain it all: another promotion or two and a family. Nicole glanced at her phone again hoping for a call; none came. She strolled down the Jetway, certain Maxwell was okay. He had to be.

Chapter 4

Nicole tapped away at the keys on her laptop as the dim light shadowed her space. She'd caught a nap right after they'd left Los Angeles around ten-thirty. Four and a half hours into the flight, she was wide awake. The other people around her were sleeping, including the mother and baby sitting across the aisle. Admittedly, Nicole was perturbed when she boarded the plane. She sat in first class for a reason, and spending an overnight flight near a crying baby wasn't going to work. Surprisingly, the baby had done very well. Nicole continued typing, stopping to read the screen. She pressed the call button overhead.

Shortly, the flight attendant came to the seat. "How can I help you?" she asked reaching to turn off the lit button.

"Could you please bring me a cup of coffee, with two sugars?"

The attendant returned immediately with the hot cup. Right after she set the cup down, the plane dipped. The liquid jiggled in the cup a little. Flying constantly, Nicole had adjusted to moments of turbulence. A few dips here and there came with the territory. She went back to typing. The plane dropped again, this time spilling coffee into the cup holder. People began stirring. The baby across the aisle woke up and peered around. Nicole made eye contact as the baby began cooing. Nicole released a smile, intrigued.

"Ladies and gentlemen, we're coming into a rough patch of weather flying over Ohio. I'm going to ask everyone to please take your seats and secure your seat belts. It may be a little bumpy, but we'll do everything we can to make the ride as comfortable as possible," the voice blared over the intercom.

Before the pilot could finish, the plane dropped like a roller coaster. "Oh," Nicole exclaimed as the plane took a dip, splashing coffee onto her leg and burning the skin underneath her pants. She snatched a couple of napkins lying on the armrest and patted the coffee spots. The baby began crying. Cabin lights were turned on and everybody in first class seemed to be sitting up in their seats. She refused to panic. The baby was wailing now. Screams from the rear of the plane could be heard all the way up to first class. Nicole sat back in her seat, with arms braced and hands clutched around the ends of the armrests. Once she realized the motion wasn't going to stop, fear set in. Panic clicked into high gear. What if the plane was damaged in the storm and couldn't land? She couldn't stop thinking about Maxwell. Plenty of what-if scenarios took over. Her heart raced. The plane shook like the sides were going to blow off followed by a drop. It felt like she had fallen several stories. Nicole jumped in her seat as the overhead air masks came down. "Oh my God," Nicole yelled, not caring who heard. She wasn't a spiritual person but if God was listening it couldn't hurt to call Him for help. Maybe she should have gone to church more often. Maybe then she would have learned how to pray. She gripped the armrest tighter and squeezed her eyelids shut.

"This is your captain speaking. Please stay in your seats and remain calm." Screaming and moans drowned out the captain as the plane continued dipping and rising. "The air masks have automatically released as a precaution, but the cabin pressure is stable. I repeat; this is only a precaution."

Nobody seemed to be paying attention to what he was saying. He was secure behind the cockpit security door and couldn't see or hear the chaos in the cabin. "Flight attendants, I'm asking for you to stay seated too. We're going to climb higher and try to find a smoother elevation. When we're at a safe cruising level, I'll turn off the seat belt sign."

Nicole winced. She didn't care about a silly seat belt sign. Didn't he know the plane was about to crash?

The mother across the aisle cradled the baby girl until her cries dissipated to a whimper. Reflecting on the vacant seat next to her, Nicole was empty. If she were to die at this very minute, who would care? Would there be anyone crying themselves to sleep because she was gone? Not Maxwell. He'd surely attend her memorial service at 11:00 a.m. and be in the office by 12:30, not having enough time to join the procession going to the cemetery. There was no one she could think of, and the revelation caused her to tear up. Water droplets filled her eyelids as she stared at the little girl. Maybe there was more to life than her career. She pulled a tissue from her purse and dabbed her eyelids. The plane was settling down as her anxiety escalated.

"Ladies and gentlemen, this is your captain again. I have good news and bad news." Sighs flowed throughout the plane. "Good news is that we're out of the storm. The bad news is that we'll have to make a brief stopover in Pittsburgh. The FAA requires us to have the air cups restored before continuing the flight. We'll be on the ground in about thirty minutes." Chattering abounded. "Hopefully, the service crew will get us back in the air quickly, and we'll get you to Philadelphia as soon as we can."

Nicole advanced her watch three hours to 5:45 and relaxed. She would soon be safe on the ground and able

to call Maxwell. Forget about the layover. She planned to
rent a car and make the five-hour drive in four. She and
Maxwell needed to talk, and it couldn't wait.

Chapter 5

Papers and folders consumed the king-sized bed, with Maxwell scrunched near the edge. The sharp pitch of his alarm clock sounded off. Maxwell rolled over and stretched out his long arms turning off the piercing noise that told him to get up if he was going to be out of the house and on the jogging path by six o'clock. He made his way to the master bathroom, turned on the light and right away bent over one of the sinks, allowing the faucet's cool water to pool into his hands. He buried his head into his hands, careful of the tender scar over his right eye. He gently touched the spot and immediately pulled away. There wasn't a benefit to be gained in dwelling on his wound. Pushing forward, staying focused was the best way to handle pain.

He raked the hairbrush over his short smooth strands of hair that lay in place without much effort. A few minutes later he'd returned to his bedroom dressed and almost ready to go.

Maxwell was still surprised Nicole hadn't called but wasn't going to dwell on it. He put on his running shoes and started lacing them up. Each time he drove the shoe string through an eyelet, he thought about a church on his list. As much as he tried to maintain control, Greater Metropolitan continued to dominate his priorities. He couldn't let emotions force him to act hastily. Each brick had to be laid at the precise instant in order to build this wall of destruction he'd envisioned for the bishop. Standing up straight, he scooped up his keys and cell phone from the dark cherry wood dresser and out the front door he marched waging a strategic battle in his mind.

Maxwell eased down his cobblestone driveway and started with a slow jog. If he could just block out the low-grade headache until he could take some meds later, then his day would be off to a good start. Half a mile later he was running alongside the riverfront in Fairmount Park catching random glimpses of the Philadelphia skyline as it poked through the lines of trees. The sound of oar blades slicing into the cool water as a rowing team maneuvered by was the only noise giving life to the park. The crisp morning breeze calmed Maxwell as the streaks of light belonging to a new day continued parting the darkness. Several greetings were tossed his way from a couple of ladies. Once he turned to give his delayed response, they had long passed. It was a good thing no crimes were being committed in the vicinity, because he wouldn't have been able to describe any significant details.

Ironically he was known for having impeccable recollection. He recalled details from as far back as two years old, going to church, sleeping in his big-boy bed, watching *Sesame Street* on TV every morning. That was the extent of his good times. The last five years in his parents' house he wished to forget. As his foot hit the pavement, he reflected on the past, forcing him to run faster, attempting to pound out the images. He quickly returned his focus to the path before him and picked up his pace, determined to lay out his plan for the day and shove out haunting memories. As much as he tried, Maxwell couldn't stop thinking about the day his father went to prison and the real perpetrator hadn't suffered a single day of inconvenience. Maxwell had often wondered how Bishop Jones's children would have turned out had their father gotten locked up and left them broke and struggling. Maxwell would never know the answer to his longstanding question. He slowed a bit, feeling in control of his emotions. This time when a lady passed and said hello, he responded without hesitation.

When he turned around at the 2.5 mile marker, Maxwell felt a quick, sharp pain shoot through his right eye. He shook his head but didn't break a stride. He finished up his normal five-mile run with not quite the same vigor as he'd started. Pain or past wouldn't hinder him from anything he set his mind to do. Dragging up his driveway, he stopped at the front steps to stretch out his legs. He looked down at his watch; 7:30 a.m., right on time. He shoved open the heavy wooden door. The Sunday morning preachers would be starting soon, and he wasn't going to miss any of the performances.

Two pain tablets and a bottle of water commanded attention as soon as Maxwell got inside. After chasing the pills down with an entire sixteen-ounce bottle of water, the remote control and his sixty-five-inch HD TV would be his refuge. He dropped onto the sofa and settled into the corner, kicking his left shoe off and then the right; another day, another battle. Maxwell wielded his remote control at the TV and pressed the power button. A big voice bellowed from the small man standing in the pulpit challenging his audience to trust God in all things. The plea filled the room, riding the waves of a crystal-clear surround sound system. Maxwell listened and watched intently. He followed the preacher's hand gestures, the way he moved, walking up close to the edge of the podium. Shouts of "Amen" mounted as people jumped out of their seats, yelling like they were at a football game. The cameras panned the room showcasing the lively crowd of people committed to this pastor, supporting him, encouraging him, and trusting him. Maxwell shook his head and snorted out an airy humph as the pastor extended his right hand toward the people and began praying.

Maxwell scooted to the edge of his seat and began counting backward from five, becoming more animated with each number. When he reached number one, Maxwell shouted falling back into the seat and cackling as the minister appealed for donations. "Right on time," he whispered glancing at his watch again. He picked up a legal pad from the glass table in front of him and moved the church up on his list from number thirty-two to eighteen. The bigger the audience, the bigger Maxwell's interest.

The doorbell caused him to pause. A bit sluggish, he didn't rush to the door. The bell rang several more times before he could get it answered. The only person he was remotely expecting was Nicole. Wasn't like her to show up without calling, but with his recent attack, she might have been out of sorts. He cracked the door open and sighed.

"Mr. Montgomery, I'm a little early. I hope it's okay." The elderly lady adjusted the glasses on the bridge of her nose.

Maxwell leaned against the door. "I forgot you were coming today."

"Oh, I'm sorry. Is this a bad time?"

"Of course not, come on in," he said rubbing his head and stepping aside. "It's not you. I simply forgot that you're cleaning today."

"Eight o'clock every Wednesday and Sunday morning for the past ten years," she said standing in the entrance. "Honestly I don't know why you have me come twice a week. Your house is never messy." She headed into the kitchen.

Maxwell reclaimed his seat on the couch, placing his feet on top of the table and crossing them at the ankles.

She was right. He didn't need the house cleaned, but he knew more about her background than she realized. She'd worked hard to put two children through college years ago as a single mother. Tragically one died from colon cancer and another in a car accident. She didn't have much money or family left for support. With three more years left before she could get social security benefits, he wanted to keep helping her. $300 twice a week wasn't a fortune for him but seemed to help her tremendously. As long as she wanted to work for him, she had a job.

Moments later she reemerged from the kitchen tying on her apron. "I heard about what happened to you, and I was just sick about it. That's the main reason I wanted to get here early, to make sure you were okay."

"Nothing a pain pill can't cure," he responded, intentionally downplaying the incident. Friday was history, and the sooner he got back to routine, everyone else could too.

Chapter 6

The morning crept along as Maxwell found himself precisely where he had to be. Surfing the channels, he'd caught several TV ministries. He moved down the East Coast, starting with New Jersey, Delaware, and Baltimore, making his last stop in Philadelphia. He'd missed a few minutes of the 7:00 a.m. slot while talking with his cleaning lady, but not a second of the prime slot was to be compromised. Channel 17 offered the last sermon on his tour for the day.

There he was, big and breathing hard. The thick voice of Bishop Jones pulled Maxwell forward on the sofa as he snatched his feet down from the table and planted his elbows into his thighs. A plump belly and a head of gray hair was evidence that the bishop had aged, but the voice and that glare in his eyes hadn't diminished in twenty years.

"Praise God, and I am pleased that you are sharing this Sunday morning worship service with me. Whether you're here in the audience or sitting in your living room, you're sure to be blessed by today's message. Stand to your feet," the bishop urged, lifting both palms toward the ceiling, "and let's honor God in prayer."

Maxwell ignored his ringing phone calling to him from the kitchen.

"Mr. Montgomery, do you want me to answer the phone?" the cleaning lady shouted from the kitchen.

"That's okay, just let it ring. They can leave a message," he responded without relinquishing the stare he had locked on the television. Maxwell couldn't sit idle as his aggravation rose. The bishop's swagger in the pulpit stirred his anger. The image was like an instant replay for Maxwell since he had witnessed it so often as a child. He even remembered seeing his father's wide eyes filled with admiration and hunger for the next words out this man's mouth.

Maxwell didn't hear the words Bishop Jones laced with his prayer. He gave his attention to the words spoken in a different place and life, back when his family attended the bishop's ministry. Back when it was a tiny little church in Chester headed by a young Pastor Jones, long before the title of Bishop crawled in front of the man's name. The phone rang again. Maxwell still didn't answer, but he did break through the time warp to hear the closing prayer.

"I encourage you to rebuke Satan in every aspect of your life. He will attempt to destroy you and prevent God's Word from being heard here today. But God's Word is powerful and will not return unto him void in Jesus' name. Amen."

"Whoooo," Maxwell yelled.

"Mr. Montgomery, are you all right in there?" the cleaning lady called out.

Partially embarrassed, Maxwell responded, assuring her there wasn't a problem. She wasn't a religious woman, which was one of the key considerations that led him into hiring her. The fact that she was willing to clean on a Sunday was a bonus. Growing up, his parents didn't let him do any work on Sunday. It was deemed God's day of rest in the Montgomery household and not a floor was going to be swept, not a shirt ironed, or a dish cooked. If his work wasn't done by 10:00 p.m. Saturday night, he had to wait until Monday morning. Since he left their house, he'd worked practically every Sunday since. Anybody working for him had to be willing to work on Sunday or find another employer, no exceptions.

He didn't want to frighten his cleaning lady by getting too caught up in the TV ministries but harnessing his disdain at home was difficult. It was his sanctuary. Home and his office were the only places where he could freely release his pent-up anger.

Maxwell redirected his attention to Bishop Jones who was shifting into a high-preaching gear, spewing scriptures and moving around the podium. His heavy voice was tossed at every listening ear. "We must have self-control and allow God to lead us." He paused to wipe the sweat that was pouring from his forehead, face, and neck.

Maxwell pointed his index finger at the TV screen. Then he wrote down several things he wanted to investigate regarding the bishop and Greater Metropolitan. The foundation that he would build his case on had to be solid. After circling tax fraud, ethics violations, financial mismanagement, infidelity, and a few other standard improprieties that Maxwell had his investigator delving into, he reviewed the list. His gaze moved left to right over each detail he'd noted, each pastor's name and their church. Drawing a big red circle around Greater Metropolitan and the bishop's name, his conviction strengthened. Pushing the pen down hard into the legal pad, slowly, he drew another red circle around Greater Metropolitan, sealing his commitment to giving the bishop what he deserved.

The thunderous roar of applauses snatched Maxwell's attention back toward the screen. "Praise God, we've had a dynamic service rooted in the Lord this morning. Before I close today, I want to ask for your prayers regarding an upcoming project that I'm very passionate about. In just two days, this coming Tuesday, local ministers, community leaders, the mayor, the school superintendent, the chief of police, and I will come together in a joint collaboration. We will meet to develop a much-needed strategy on how to reduce gun violence and increase jobs and educational opportunities for neighborhoods most at risk in Philadelphia."

The room erupted into shouts and applauses as the camera zoomed in on a woman in the front row. She was bent over in her seat. Her face was buried into her hands as she sobbed. The bishop looked over at her just as a lady sitting next to her wrapped the woman up in an embrace. "Sister Hinton, I know you are grieving over the recent death of your son who was killed in a drive-by shooting. We're committed to preserving families here, and we share in your loss. We're praying for God to encourage your heart and give you the peace that only He can."

Watching the bishop intensely, Maxwell had heard plenty. He tapped his hand quietly on the chair, snatched up the remote, and flipped through the channels. He didn't want his cleaning lady to think he was crazy. He was fiery mad but completely sane. He had to be in order to accomplish what he had planned. After a series of clicks he landed on ESPN settling for some sports highlights. He fidgeted in the seat, repeatedly bumping the remote against the chair. The taste of victory tugged at him, ferociously tugging at him. It was the glue that had kept him in his seat Sunday after Sunday. He anxiously flipped back to Channel 17 drawn like an addict. Landing on his channel, he settled briefly until the donation appeal roared in.

"This ministry needs you. I need you, and if you sow into the kingdom, God will bless you in return. We must be reminded that everything we have belongs to the Lord for He is the one who gave it to us." Amens abounded.

Maxwell gently massaged his right temple feeling the cool air pass his lips as he inhaled. Thoughts pounded his head from the inside out. Years ago felt like yesterday. Every now and then he'd get an unexpected whiff of poverty and hopelessness, an old familiar smell in his nostrils. Maxwell panned the room, slower this time. A sudden wave of heat engulfed his body getting him on his feet. He took two steps away from the sofa, looking around the living room, beyond the fireplace. He peered into the open formal dining room, taking in the furniture, paintings, cathedral ceilings, and sculptures that didn't have a match anywhere else in the world. Maxwell bit down hard on his bottom lip. Where were the bishop and God when he was washing dishes in that grimy fast food dive, mowing lawns, tutoring, eating Ramen noodles for breakfast, lunch, and dinner, while applying for every possible scholarship he could get his hands on? Not God, not the bishop, and certainly not Paul Montgomery Sr. did a single thing to help him get here. That's why they stayed on one side of life and he was planted on the other.

For eight months he'd watched the bishop's Sunday morning sermons, taking notes, figuring out what to look for, and waiting for him to slip up. Maxwell had spent a small fortune on an investigator. He was certain the investment was going to pay off. With his eyes narrowed and teeth clenched, he picked up the remote control and pressed down on the power button silencing the bishop.

"I'll be in my bedroom," he called out to the cleaning lady as she worked in the kitchen.

"That's fine with me," she shouted in return, coming to the front staircase. "I can clean your room last."

"Ah, don't worry about my room. Clean whatever you like and make it a short day for yourself."

"Thank you, Mr. Montgomery, but you know I'm not going to cheat you on the cleaning. You pay me a good rate, and I'm going to give you the full cleaning."

He wasn't going to argue. It was bound to be one fight he'd lose, one loss he'd gladly take. "Suit yourself," he said not the least bit irritated. Actually, she was as close as he was going to get to a mother figure and there was a slight comfort for him.

Maxwell crossed the threshold into his bedroom, pulling the T-shirt over his head. He couldn't count the how often his father had told him to put God first and to love and support the pastor and the church. Shaking his head, Maxwell let go of a muffled laugh. He peeled off his shorts and socks, stepped into the shower, and pressed the palms of his hands into the shower wall. The hot water beat down onto his back. It was in that private space and time when he allowed himself to feel the heaviness of his journey and the loneliness it mandated.

Chapter 7

Maxwell wrapped a thick towel around his waist and wiped the steamy fog from the mirror. He rubbed the left side of his face and then the right. His reflection, the one that used to call him Paul, had long been silenced. Painting his face with shaving cream didn't help him escape the features that belonged to his dad: a small nose, thin face, dark brown eyes that were deep and serious, and a slight dimple that framed his chin. Not every memory from his childhood was worth discarding but the scarce good ones weren't worth sifting through the whole lot.

Warm water washed away the remnant of any shaving cream left behind. He dried his face and slapped on $175-an-ounce aftershave which stung like bees. The twinge of pain helped him shake off a past that he could not change. The phone rang in Maxwell's bedroom. It was a reminder of a slew of calls he'd ignored while watching the programs earlier downstairs. He didn't react immediately, hoping for a break. Just as he was settling down, the phone began ringing again. He knew the cleaning lady wasn't going to answer. So, unless he got it, the calls would continue until he either snapped or unplugged the house phone and powered off his cell. He moaned.

Couldn't he have one morning of uninterrupted peace? He wasn't greedy. He didn't need the whole day, just a few hours. Before he could answer, the cell phone rang. The shrilling sound ate at him. Whoever was calling better have a really good reason for hounding him. He secured the towel tighter around his waist and let his feet sink into the plush carpeted pathway leading to the phone lying on his nightstand. A greeting fell out of his mouth hurriedly as he scooped the phone up before it could ring again.

"Paul, I'm worried to death about you. Are you all right?" Her voice was seasoned with age and concern.

"I'm fine, Mom." His resolve emptied out of him like water spiraling down a drain.

"I tried calling you a few times earlier this morning, but I didn't get an answer." He kept quiet. It was best. "I would have called before today but Christine felt you needed your rest and I should wait. But, I knew that really meant you didn't want to talk to me." The silence was deafening. After a few pregnant seconds, his mom asked, "Paul, are you there?"

Maxwell pulled the phone from his ear, rubbing his wrinkled brow; he took in a slow breath. With a bitter taste of frustration he responded. "It's Maxwell, not Paul. Maxwell!"

He didn't have to wait for her response. It came through the phone wrapped in sincerity but with a firm assurance. "Your father and I named you Paul. That is your name, and you cannot change who you are. Only God can do that." Her voice softened. "We love you; you can't change that either. I love you. You're my son, and no matter what you do or how you treat me, I will always love you and care about what happens to you."

Walking away from the bed and toward the window, Maxwell gripped the phone tighter. "I've got to go."

"Okay, son, but I'm praying that you will forgive your father. He did what he felt to be right. His loyalty to Pastor Jones might have been misplaced but not because it was wrong to support our pastor. I know people lost some money."

Maxwell interrupted, unable to let her downplay the depths of his father's egregious error. "People lost a lot of money trusting in the pastor's Ponzi scheme."

"Well yes, you are right, but that was over twenty-five years ago. We have got to let the past go and move on, son, or it will keep you from enjoying your life now."

"I'm only doing all right for myself and if it means bringing a bunch of criminal and religious shysters to justice, then that will be icing on the cake."

"Be careful, son, about persecuting people. Let God be the judge. That's not for us to do."

Maxwell wasn't interested in another sermon. "I have to go."

"Well, take care of yourself. I love you."

"Good-bye," were the only words he allowed to pass his lips. He gingerly touched the sore spot over his eye with his fingertips and gave his attention over to getting dressed, moving around the room, and pushing his mother's words and the sound of her voice out of his head. Just as he opened the double doors of his walk-in closet his phone rang again. Looking over his shoulder at the phone, Maxwell hesitated before answering it. His mother should have known that two calls in one day were too much. He didn't want to hear any more of her admonishment, but flat out ignoring her call was a level of disrespect he wouldn't entertain. He snatched up the phone making a proclamation through gritted teeth and pinched lips: "Maxwell speaking."

"You won't believe what just happened to me. I could have died. I could have died this morning." Nicole's frantic voice jumped over the phone line.

"What's wrong? Calm down and tell me."

"My flight from Los Angeles flew into a storm this morning. Rain was crashing into the plane like boulders. It was thundering and lightning," she rattled off with her words racing. "The weather was so bad. The plane kept hitting pockets of turbulence that felt like it was falling out the sky," she said with each word spoken fast and some high pitched. "I've never been so scared," she cried out.

Maxwell was unprepared for Nicole's emotional state. She was tough, always in control, his equal. Hearing her fall apart put him on edge, a position he didn't embrace well. "Are you okay? Where are you now?"

"I'm okay now, I guess. We had an emergency stopover in Pittsburg."

"How long before you take off for Philadelphia?"

"I have no idea when they're taking off, but for sure I won't be on that plane or any other one, not today. I rented a car, and I'm driving to Philadelphia."

"You know that's about five or six hours. Are you sure that's what you want to do?"

He knew Nicole was all about business, always taking the most direct approach to problems. She didn't like wasting time. He didn't either. That's one of the reasons they worked. Her throwing away time on a long road trip surprised him.

"I'm already on the road. I tried calling you earlier, but I didn't get an answer. I figured you were out running."

Maxwell thought about the surge of calls. He didn't bother telling Nicole he'd intentionally ignored the noise earlier. He felt badly about missing her call but couldn't do anything about it. "Where are you now?"

"I pulled off at a rest stop for a few minutes, long enough to get some coffee and to call you again."

"Nicole, I don't know what to say. I'm glad you're okay," he stammered. "Is there anything I can do for you from here?"

"Actually, there is. I need to see you as soon as I can. I should be home around two o'clock."

"No problem, call me when you get in town. We can grab lunch."

Hearing Maxwell's voice soothed her anxiety. The calming effect coming from having someone out there who cared was what she needed. "I'll call you as soon as I get into the city. I'm looking forward to seeing you." Nicole ended the call and looked down at her diamond watch, the one she'd rewarded herself with when her income hit the six-figure bracket several years ago. She would drive as fast as she could without having an accident or getting a ticket. Nicole wanted to get home quickly and for once it wasn't because she wanted to get a head start on the next work project.

Chapter 8

Maxwell dwelled on the anxiousness in both his mother's and Nicole's voices, causing him to be distracted his entire way into the office. Slightly irritated, he was slipping and didn't appreciate the angst. He'd mastered the ability to keep distance between his emotions and actions. He kept his feelings in check, and there was no room in his world to let others disrupt his focus. Nicole and his mother didn't warrant an exception. He tossed their worries out and zipped toward the parking garage, placing his energy where it belonged.

Prepared to do battle, he dialed the number for his private investigator, restored to the frame of mind where he had to be. "Garrett, it's Maxwell here. I'm going to need your help. Are you free?"

"I am. What do you need?"

"Not over the phone; meet me at my office in twenty minutes." Maxwell glanced at his Rolex.

"Gotcha."

There were only two people on earth Maxwell trusted. His private investigator was one. They'd worked together for years, shared confidences that could easily land them into morality court. They coasted along the fringes of criminality but never crossed the well-established line he'd figuratively drawn. Maxwell wasn't necessarily proud of tactics he'd used in tackling the churches, but guilt wasn't a fruit he tasted. There was no place to second-guess his actions. He believed what he believed and did what he did. So long as he didn't break the law and get caught, he was justified.

Twenty minutes later he was unlocking the door to his practice while juggling a small box of files. Five modest offices, not counting his expansive personal one, a conference room, reception area, and coffee break room summed up the suite. Besides his receptionist, paralegal, and occasional intern, the office was mainly underutilized. Spending the extra money for unused space might have been a detriment for someone else but not Maxwell. Despising the way he grew up, Maxwell was set on never being cramped again.

He entered his office, appreciating the quiet that consistently resounded on Sundays. This was his favorite workday with no phone calls and nobody traipsing around the office. It was just him left alone with his plans. He set the box down and peered out the window to take in the city view.

"Knock, knock," Garrett said poking his head into the open doorway, startling Maxwell.

"Come on in, man."

"Do you want me to close the door?"

"No, we should be okay. I'm not expecting any of those holy rollers to show up around here today," he said, chuckling. "Except us heathens." He erupted into a full roar of laughter as he took his seat.

Garrett stepped in and took a seat, laughing too. "That's the good news. They help keep you in business, which keeps me in business. So, it's all good," Garrett said rearing back in the seat. "What's going on? Your urgent call has me intrigued."

That's what Maxwell appreciated about his rapport with his investigator. There wasn't a need to dance around the topic; get right to the point, unfiltered. "Look here, I have to jumpstart this business with Greater

Metropolitan. Man, I really need to fire this up," he said jabbing his fists into the air repeatedly, ending with a right uppercut. "I feel like things are happening with that church and I don't have a grip on it." He grabbed both arms of his chair. "It's time to shake things up."

"I'm ready; let's go. Just tell me what you want me to do."

Maxwell stroked his hand across his head. "Well for starters, I hear they're having a community forum gathering at the church Tuesday to address gun violence."

"All right that's a good thing."

"No, no, man," Maxwell said shaking his hands in midair. "You know Jones is up to something."

"You think so? I mean it sounds like a legitimate cause."

"Oh come on, man, you've been in the game long enough. You know there's always a gimmick with these cats. You know the drill by now," Maxwell said flailing his arms into the air. "Their rhetoric sounds good, compels the congregation, gets them fired up emotionally, paralyzing their sense of logic, and then bam, that's when they go in for the kill."

"Cash money time," Garrett said, chiming in unison with Maxwell. "They've mastered the art of digging into those pockets."

"With the long arm of grace at the other end of their benevolence basket," Maxwell added, coming around the desk to give Garrett a high five. They chuckled on a bit longer.

"Ca-ching, ca-ching."

"Now you're talking like the seasoned professional I know you are," Maxwell told Garrett. "See why we have to get cracking? I don't know exactly what Jones is up to, but we can't let him pull a fast one on us."

"I hear you."

Maxwell stepped back to the window. "We have to get in on this meeting. The mayor is going to be there."

"Which means security will be tight."

"True, but we've always been able to get around those baby roadblocks." Garrett nodded several times and grinned. Maxwell continued, "Let me know the damage, and I'll get it to you tonight." Maxwell didn't recall exactly how much money was in his home safe, but typically the cost of doing business with the local security detail or a political official hovered between $2,000 and $5,000. He kept cash on hand, which erased a paper trail. If he was ever charged with bribery, there wouldn't be any evidence. Maxwell was too careful to get caught, which was why he always made sure Garrett made the contact, leaving him clean. There would never be a withdrawal from any of his money accounts that matched the timing or amount of a bribe.

"Let me go make a few calls and see what I can do."

"Good. We need a confirmation, today. I can't miss that meeting Tuesday."

"Here's another idea. It is a community forum. Why not call the bishop and ask him directly if you can attend? He might go for it," Garrett suggested.

"Yeah, right; asking Jones for anything would be my last resort, and I do mean last resort. Besides, I'm not interested in the public meeting that they'll do for the media. I want to be included in the backroom conversations that are either already in play or soon will be. That's what I want."

"Gotcha, I'm on it."

"You can use one of the empty offices to save time."

"That'll work," Garrett said preparing to leave Maxwell's office.

"Oh, and I'm sure you'll be using your throwaway phone and not the one in this office."

Garrett grinned. Maxwell thought so, but taking precautions made the difference between freedom and doing five to seven years in federal prison. He didn't visit inmates in prison let alone envision a personal stay. Garrett understood and didn't seem to take any offense.

The ball was rolling. Maxwell's heart was pumping, rapidly. He was charged and on a high. The throbbing pain above his eye had numbed after he'd swallowed a couple of pain pills. He plucked the accordion file from the box labeled SENIOR. The title was intentionally set so as not to stir interest in a random person stumbling upon the file. To Maxwell, the code was the constant motivation he yearned. "Senior" stood for Paul Montgomery Sr., the man who let the lives of four people go to shambles in order to prove his loyalty to Jones. Both the bishop and Senior deserved the fallout, even if it was two decades later.

Hours passed. Maxwell had moved to the conference room where he could spread out the papers and use the white board.

Garrett poked his head into the room. "Did you know your cell phone has been ringing in your office?"

Maxwell glanced up at the clock. Two-thirty. "Thanks, man." Maxwell whisked to his office. Five missed calls from Nicole. He had her on the line. "Hey, are you in town?"

"Yes, I made really good time on the road, no traffic. I've been home for about an hour. I've called you several times."

"Sorry about that. I'm working on an important case. Something came up, and I'm swamped."

"We're still going to lunch, right?"

Maxwell peered quickly at his watch and then directed his gaze out the window. "I really need to take a rain check if it's okay with you." He was in a productive mode and didn't want to lose the energy.

"No, it can't wait. I told you this morning I have to see you. What could have become so urgent in a few hours?"

He didn't expect her response. Usually there was no problem when either had to cancel a date. "I didn't realize you'd react this way."

"What way?"

"Emotional when this is about business."

"I'm not being emotional, Maxwell. How dare you discount me as some out-of-control emotional woman?"

"I didn't say that."

"You didn't have to. Geez, Maxwell. You know me better than this. I deserve more from you."

He wasn't a relationship expert but was pretty certain that no matter what he said, it wasn't going to be right. So, he opted to listen.

"I told you in no uncertain terms that my life was in jeopardy this morning. I was legitimately shaken up, and the best you can do is tell me you can't meet with me because of business? Well thanks a lot."

Her fury roared.

Maxwell wasn't moved. She was incorrect. He didn't owe her anything. The relationship had always been mutually beneficial. However, she was right on one front. Maxwell could show more compassion. "I can't make lunch, and that's the truth. But, I will make sure we get to do dinner." It would be tight, but he wanted to offer her the support she clearly craved. After all, it wasn't her fault about the awkward timing.

"Don't go out of your way for me."

He heard the anger and responded, "Nicole, I apologize."

"For what?"

"For being a jerk. I'm sorry," he said leaning one palm on his desk. "You were in a serious situation, and I should have been a better friend."

"It's like you don't care."

"And that's not true."

"Fine, I guess."

"Good, I'll pick you up around nine for a late dinner."

"Maxwell, that's too late. If you're serious about caring, pick me up earlier or don't pick me up at all."

"All right, I'll be there at seven-thirty."

"Make it seven," she said before ending the call.

He rubbed the back of his neck. Why did the plane incident have to happen today, the worse time possible? Between Nicole and Bishop Jones, the rest of his day and night were taken leaving zilch for him. He massaged his aching temples. There was too much pressuring him. Something was going to have to give, and it most certainly wasn't going to be his priorities.

Chapter 9

Tension wasn't averted. Maxwell had arrived at Nicole's fifteen minutes late. It took ten minutes of pleading to get her to open the door, let alone join him for dinner. He didn't bother explaining to her that Jones and the Greater Metropolitan case had sucked every second out of his afternoon. Maxwell didn't bother going further in telling Nicole he had another five hours of work left tonight. She wasn't interested in his reason for breaking a promise; that he was sure. After a long-winded apology and lots of begging, she agreed to go out with him.

Hopefully they could keep the date to two hours, leaving him time to finish his work and grab three or four hours of sleep. By using a few favors and spreading a little money around, he was expecting a spot in the closed-door meeting scheduled for 9:00 a.m. on Tuesday. According to what Garrett told him, the bishop didn't know Maxwell was going to be present. That alone was worth the money spent, and warranted his stellar preparation. Every second between now and Tuesday had to be used wisely if he was to fully capitalize on the meeting.

Maxwell whipped into a parking space next to a man who was walking around to the passenger side of his car.

"Nice Porsche," a man said as he walked by holding the hand of a pregnant woman.

Maxwell acknowledged the compliment as he pulled open Nicole's door. She planted her stylish designer shoes on the ground and climbed out.

Nicole saw the couple too as a longing stirred within. She yearned to step into Maxwell's familiar embrace, allow him to hold her tightly, and squeeze the tension from her body. Her anger hadn't completely released its hold. So, instead she tugged at the knot in his tie as if it needed straightening. The gesture wasn't a hug, but she was close enough to take in a hint of his cologne and give him her intense wanting eyes.

"You good?" he asked her.

"Yes, but I'm still a little shaken up from this morning," she answered letting her hand slide down the length of his tie as she stepped away and let him reclaim his personal space.

"Well, you're safely on the ground now."

Nicole wondered what Maxwell would be doing if she hadn't landed safely. Would he go to her condo to be near her things in an effort to feel close to her? Would tears fill his eyes? Would he be inconsolable? She couldn't provide a confident answer, which widened the crack of emptiness in her that began forming on the plane.

Standing inside the restaurant waiting to be seated, Nicole noticed the pregnant woman rubbing her stomach and the man gently massaging the valley of her back. The woman spurted out, "Ouch, that hurt. This baby is really starting to kick hard." The man smiled and placed his hand on the woman's stomach.

Nicole looked at Maxwell who hadn't noticed anything but the screen on his phone. "Can we have dinner without letting work intrude?" she demanded feeling her anger rising again. Whenever they met for dinner or spent meaningful time together, work intruded. She'd never objected in the past. Today needed to be different for Nicole. They were seated quickly by a waiter who handed them menus, briefed them on the chef's specials, and laid napkins across their laps. Nicole opened her menu, but her eyes roamed, drinking in the large room, couples holding hands, crystal chandeliers dancing with colorful prisms of light, and the pearl white baby grand piano serenading the crowd. Peering at the menu, food wasn't really the source of her hunger.

Three well-manicured fingernails latched onto the top of Maxwell's menu, pulling it down and revealing the urgency in her eyes. "I'd like to talk to you." She waited for his gaze of affirmation, which he never gave.

"Sure, just one quick minute."

The waiter returned with two sparkling glasses of water and a small dish of lemon slices. "Have you made selections for the evening?"

"Not yet," Nicole replied.

"No problem, take your time. Let me know if you have any questions."

Then the wine steward came to the table. Maxwell took a quick sip from his water glass. "I'll take a bottle of your white wine."

"Sir, we have a nice selection here," the steward said holding out a wine list.

"Surprise me," Maxwell responded.

"My pleasure, sir," the steward said and left.

Once Nicole and Maxwell were alone, he surrendered his attention. "Now, I'm listening. What's up?" he asked with his gaze locked on her.

Nicole leaned forward slightly, admitting, "I just can't let go of what happened on that plane." Her voice was soft, almost weak; definitely not her typical "I'm in charge" air. She knew it and made no apologies. "It was like something in a movie."

The steward returned and set two glasses in front of the couple. Then he poured a sip. Maxwell sampled the wine, savoring it in his mouth a couple of seconds before swallowing. He gave the thumbs-up and both glasses were filled.

Nicole anxiously waited for the steward to hurry up and go away. She'd been interrupted too many times today. She had to get her story out before imploding. She sipped the wine hoping it would mellow her anxiety. Finally spirits were flowing and the wine steward was gone. They were alone again.

"What were you saying?"

Nicole pressed her fingertips into her chest just above her left breast. "I was scared! I wanted to hold on to someone, but there was no one there for me. The seat next to me was empty."

Maxwell handed Nicole the glass of wine sitting in front of her. "Relax, drink this."

She took a sip, peering at him over the rim of the glass. "I've never experienced anything so unnerving in my life. Things like that make you think." Taking in a slow, cleansing breath, she sat back and rested her forearms on the table. "When I finally got home, I dreamt the plane had actually crashed and there were no survivors. It was so real. I could see myself hovering in the air." She took a gulp of the wine. "I could have died." Maxwell fidgeted, but it didn't give her pause. She had to share her heart. "I had to question what I'm doing with my life."

"Oh come on, Nicole," Maxwell said beckoning for the waiter. "You can't let one situation get you so rattled. It's over, you're safe, and that's the end of it."

Maybe yesterday, she would have agreed. "It's not so simple." The waiter approached the table forcing her to wait before continuing. As soon as they placed their order, Nicole snatched Maxwell's attention back into their conversation. "I'm serious. I'm not sure I like what I see in my life. I went off to college at seventeen, graduated early, and put all my energy into building a career. I've never been married and don't have any children."

"But you're doing what it is you want to do. You get to travel and set your own course. Think about it," he said leaning in toward the table. "Look at where you are. Do you know how long it takes most people to get anywhere near making partner? Years and years, if ever. Look at you," he said filling his wine glass.

"Maxwell, that's what I'm saying. Don't you get it? I don't think my career is enough anymore. I want more. In my dream, I felt like I had missed something. But it was too late to change anything." Nicole turned in her chair, crossed her legs, and looked down at her designer shoes, which didn't seem as satisfying as compared to last week. Her outlook had to change.

"It's okay. The plane, the dream, all of it is enough to make you a little uneasy," Maxwell reached for her hand.

She withdrew her hand from the table, refusing to be dismissed with his superficial concern. "Maxwell, where is our relationship going? Where do you see us two years from now? Will we still be dating, engaged, married with children, or what?" She threw her left arm over the back of her chair, brushed the waves of hair from her face, and with a stern staring assault, she challenged Maxwell for an answer.

"What's with the melodrama? We've been going along with things the way they are between us for some while now. Neither of us put any pressure on the other, nothing really serious, just getting together when it works." Maxwell thumbed his fingers on the table and let his glances shift to and fro.

Nicole stared past Maxwell at the couple sitting across from them. What sounded like joy in their voices and pleasure in the laughter floated across the room. "I know it's a cliché, but life is short: goals, success, being able to drive the best cars and having material things are all good. But, having someone to share those things with, a partner for life, is what I think I want." Honestly, Nicole couldn't recall the chemistry with Maxwell ever being completely fulfilling. Her thoughts and gazes lingered with the couple. She was unable to stop staring. The intensity and effervescence of their relationship was intoxicating. She wanted what they had—love.

"Nicole, Nicole." Maxwell quietly tapped on the table with his knuckles. "You can't possibly be telling me your career is no longer the most important entity in your life."

"That's exactly what I'm saying."

"Yeah, right."

She laid her warm palm on top of Maxwell's hand. A passionless smile and her wide eyelids partnered with her voice to say, "People change. I don't want to roll over in bed at night to an empty spot anymore. And I think I'd like to have children, maybe one or two." Nicole withdrew her hand, pressed her lips together hard and released a newly acquainted truth. "I want to be in love with someone and to share my life with a person. I want all of it, not just a fragment." She sipped the wine as a lump of emotion clutched at her throat, making it difficult to will away the tears burning across the ridge of her eyelids. Nicole pulled both hands down into her lap and exhaled, feeling the cool air pass her lips.

Maxwell rubbed his temple with his index and middle fingers. "My head is starting to hurt. Let's pick up this conversation later." He desperately wanted to take a pain pill but resisted. Nothing would ever control him, especially not a drug.

Their waiter sliced into the thick air surrounding the table as he served food and poured them both another glass of wine. Nicole took a long, slow drink then traced the rim of her glass with her index finger as her gaze latched onto Maxwell. Dinner wrapped up before dessert was served. She didn't bother complaining. Maxwell had gotten what he wanted, an evening on his terms. Nicole inhaled a dose of restraint struggling to control the myriad of feelings rumbling. Maxwell hadn't heard her heart. He wasn't connecting with how she felt. Nicole wasn't sure if he was incapable or just didn't want to.

Chapter 10

Maxwell arrived at his office early Monday. Sleep couldn't bind him to his bed. Not even the tension-laced drive to Nicole's or the unexpected door she'd slammed in his face last night would interrupt his mission today. His focus was completely wrapped around being prepared if Garrett was able to get him an invite to Jones's conference. He poured himself over pages and pages of notes he'd taken over the months. He was determined to come up with an angle, a clue that would point him in the right direction. If he could get the invite, he'd be able to set things in motion and watch the effect.

Maxwell reached into his desk drawer for a marker to use on his white board. He needed to see how the puzzle pieces were fitting together. A jovial face glared up at him. The five-by-seven of his nephew tugged at his heart, reminding him there was family he cared about. Yet Maxwell wouldn't let those ties keep him from his journey, the one he had to travel alone. The boy's honey-colored eyes, full cheeks, and toothy smile reminded Maxwell of his sister. His ringing cell phone snapped him back to task. He shoved the picture to the rear of his drawer, grabbed the marker and went to the coat rack by the window.

Quickly pulling his cell phone from the jacket of his suit coat, he eagerly answered. "Garrett, tell me you've got good news."

"Do I ever let you down? Everything is set. You can expect a call this morning."

"Yes." Maxwell clenched his fist and shook it in the air. "I don't know what you did or who you talked to. Don't need to know. Good job as always."

"I'll catch up with you later," Garrett said and ended the call.

With his right hand pressed against the thick glass and his left shoved into his pants pocket, Maxwell watched the people down below meandering along the sidewalk and the cars moving toward their destinations. A sardonic grin crawled across Maxwell's lips. Gloating, he walked back to his desk, gathered up the cluster of papers, and moved to his round table next to the white board. A light knock on his door followed by a soft voice and a head full of thick curls peered through the partially opened doorway.

"Mr. Montgomery, the mayor is on line one," Sonya announced, doubling as a paralegal and administrative assistant for the firm.

"Thanks! I'll take it." Sonya nodded and closed his office door. Four smooth paces and Maxwell was standing at his desk. He placed his hand on the receiver, gripped it tightly, pushed out a grunt, and went into character. "Good morning, Mayor."

"Mr. Montgomery, thank you for taking my call. I know you're very busy. So, I'll get right to the point. I would appreciate it if you could attend a nine a.m. community meeting tomorrow here at City Hall. There will be some key city officials and clergymen in attendance. Our goal is to reduce the mounting gun violence in the city and build alliances with at-risk youths." Maxwell stared straight ahead envisioning the mayor's meeting. "I apologize for the late invitation. However, your legal expertise and insight could be very beneficial to our overall objective."

Maxwell suppressed the laughter rumbling in his throat. He continued with the surprised facade. "Absolutely, Mayor, I wouldn't want to miss something so desperately needed. And the fact that you are including clergymen will certainly add value to the meeting." Maxwell was charged by the notion of having a flock of ministers feeling awkward in his presence. He gave the mayor a lively, "I will see you there." Maxwell hung up with a newly motivated drive that thrust him to the white board. For the next few hours he sifted through papers, lined up questions, and mapped out a course of action for blindsiding Bishop Jones.

The afternoon had sliced away the early morning haze and Maxwell hadn't left his office. It didn't seem like Sonya could quell her curiosity about the mayor's call any longer. For the second time today, she knocked on Maxwell's door and entered without being directed to do so. "Mr. Montgomery. I'm checking to see if you would like me to order you some lunch? You didn't even have your coffee this morning."

Without glancing in her direction, he responded, "I'm fine, thanks. I've got a lot of work to do today, and I don't want to stop right now."

"Did you need me to do anything for you based on the mayor's call earlier?"

Suddenly, he looked up from the paper he was holding. "Oh, yes, you can cancel my appointments for tomorrow. Clear my calendar. I will be out most of the day." She left with him intentionally giving her no additional information.

Maxwell got up from the table and added another item to his list on the white board. Considering the number of young folks at Jones's church, he wondered how many of them had been arrested, incarcerated, or had gang affiliations. What had Jones done to help steer any of them in the right direction? Had he bailed any of the young men out of jail? Had he mentored any of them? Had he put any of the federal funds to good use, those specifically earmarked for helping at-risk youth? Maxwell snapped his fingers and pointed to the list in front of him, thinking that might be an effective line of questions to toss at Jones and the other ministers. Drawing upon guilt instead of blood would be his strategy.

He called Garrett to work another miracle and get answers before the meeting. It would cost more money. Maxwell didn't care. Every dollar spent was deemed a wise investment.

Chapter 11

Maxwell took anxious strides as he walked up the steps of the city hall building, his eyes scoping out every minister and politician he recognized. A barrage of oohs and aahs forced him to turn around and see just what commanded the crowd's attention. The shiny black automobile held onlookers captive. It was elegant, big, and bold. The taunting chrome grille accented the car's sleek body along with the signature crafted rims. It was unmistakably a top-of-the-line Mercedes, and there was no confusion about who the owner was.

Bishop Jones stepped out of the car, pulled at the lapels of his suit jacket with both hands, and plastered a wide grin onto his face. Walking away, he turned to aim his key ring at the luxury vehicle. The car's alarm engaged, sounding off with some sort of customized trumpet and saxophone blended melody. The bishop supposedly relied on God for other conveniences. Maxwell wondered why a man as holy as the bishop professed to be wasn't trusting God to watch over his mighty fine vehicle.

"Bishop, how are you? God sure is blessing you," were just a few of the greetings he received.

Jones shook hands and puffed out, "Praise the Lord," repeatedly as he moved toward the courthouse.

At a faster pace, Maxwell continued up the steps with the intent of making a noticeable entrance into the meeting while intentionally avoiding the bishop outside.

The conference room was packed with those whose voices sang out in conversation to pass the time, waiting for the meeting to start. Maxwell and his determination entered, being announced with every step as the heel of his shoe struck the floor. At least three clergymen were robbed of their voices when they recognized Maxwell. He watched one minister stop in midsentence and latch onto him with a cringing stare; just the effect he wanted to have. They knew who he was and feared why he was there.

Maxwell claimed the last open seat on his side of the long table, reared back in the high-back leather chair, and pulled a gold engraved pen from his jacket pocket. Now the show could begin. He was ready, sitting in the premium seat near the head of the table. He was a little more than an arm's length away from where he expected Jones to sit. There were a few nods and several glances directed his way but no one shook his hand or welcomed him to the table of community concern. Maxwell didn't care as he drank in the familiar faces. There was no mask to hide their trepidation with a civil attorney who held a near-perfect win record sitting among them. Confident, Maxwell made visual contact with anyone who was willing to accept his challenge. In his mind only the guilty would have no peace. He smirked.

Jones's wide body filled the doorway as he paraded into the room flanked by the mayor. Jones sat at the head of the table while the mayor walked down to the other end shaking hands as he passed. Wiping his forehead with a monogram handkerchief, Jones shifted left to right, perhaps to prevent his body from spilling over both sides of the chair. A gust of cologne sat at the table with him. Maxwell brushed his index finger under his nose floating a wide-eyed glance at Jones.

"Good morning and thank you for being here," Jones began. "We're here today with a joint mission. We all want to identify a plan of action that will help young men who are at risk as well as reduce the gun violence that is robbing our children of their livelihood. We can no longer allow our streets to be war zones with our children enlisted as soldiers."

Maxwell's gaze rolled around the long table assessing the attentive group. He flashed back to the picture of the Last Supper that hung on his living room wall as a child. Half hearing what Jones was saying, he noticed the bobbing heads, scribbling pens, and the occasional amen that one or two men couldn't refrain from spurting out. All of them were caught up in the spell that Jones cast with his thick, melodious voice. He promised to make a difference in the community by trading opportunities for headstones.

Maxwell squinted, lowered his head slightly, and homed in on Jones, jumping in on the heels of his last words. "Bishop Jones, your interest is commendable; in fact, I applaud your efforts here today."

Jones turned his head toward Maxwell; his thick eyebrows sank down under the weight of the wrinkles that creased his forehead.

"You have one of the largest followings in Philadelphia, and I believe you have a large group of young people in your congregation." Maxwell studied the blank stares of those near him but wasn't deterred. "I'd like to ask a few questions about the success of programs you have underway." A response wasn't immediate which promoted Maxwell to continue tinkering with the subject. "You've surely managed some youth outreach programs that have already been successful. How many youth have received GEDs through your federally funded 'Not Too Late to Learn' program? How many moved from failing grades to passing grades after participating in the 'Afterschool Home Work Club' hosted at Greater Metropolitan?"

Piercing stares crawled across the table and onto Maxwell like leeches desiring his blood. He didn't flinch a bit. Maxwell was pretty sure Jones's intense demeanor was sculpted by the thoughts tumbling around in his head while he grasped for quick answers that would keep him from looking ineffective. Maxwell didn't need Jones to toss out numbers. He knew the answer to each question. He was sure the community would be interested, too, especially since Community Development Block Grant funds and Federal Faith Based Initiative funds were awarded based on taxpayers' money.

Jones leaned forward with his right forearm pressed into the table and his left hand anchored to the arm of his chair. "Are you questioning the church's motive and commitment to community change?"

Maxwell decided to let Jones off the cross. It wasn't his intent to persecute him publicly just yet. He only wanted to sow a few seeds. "Not at all, Bishop; I'm sure those programs were successful and the money put to good use." Maxwell could taste his own unsavory lie. "We should consider some of the best practices that you implemented and use them as a stepping stone toward the objective of our meeting."

Maxwell began to paint with a broader stroke of his brush. Commanding the room, he pulled everyone in, and he continued with his previous line of questioning. "How many young men have you bailed out of jail and put into mentoring programs? How many young gang members have you invited to the church to settle a turf war with a rival gang? How many drug dealers have you tried to help get a job? Have any of us done enough?" Maxwell included himself to disguise his covert mission. "These are questions each of us should ask ourselves. Our

at-risk youth aren't going to stop doing what they're doing. They're not going to stop making poor choices until
they have alternatives."

The thick aroma of contempt and unrest in the room
dissolved, allowing Maxwell to witness fewer pinched
foreheads and several men relax in their chairs.

"I knew you would have some valuable input, Mr.
Montgomery," the mayor said. "We should all accept
some level of accountability for what's wrong in our
communities. And we all must share in the responsibility
to steer our youth down positive pathways and identify
ways to derail those who are already on a locomotive
headed toward destruction. What you've said is a great
segue into a strategy that Bishop Jones and I have been
discussing for several weeks now." The mayor stretched
his hand out toward Jones and nodded his head for him
to have the floor again.

A calm satisfaction washed over Maxwell, much like
when he finished an opening statement in court. He
settled into his chair, twirled it slightly to the left, and
locked in his line of vision on Jones. He picked up his pen
ready to take notes. Maxwell didn't want to miss a single
word that fell out of Jones's mouth. His very words could
possibly be used as a wrecking ball later.

The meeting drew to a close after a half day of discussion. Maxwell's time was premium at $1,000 an hour,
although most of his money came from contingency
payments after his client won a case. He gladly offered
his services pro bono this morning. If asked, he would
have easily stayed another four hours. His ax had been
sharpened. Notification had been duly served to his
adversaries. Every crooked clergyman under his foot was
subject to be crushed at his whim. That's how he felt, and
if they didn't realize it, shame on them.

Maxwell gathered his belongings and prepared to exit as quietly as he'd entered the room. The mayor approached him extending additional gratitude for Maxwell's participation and an invitation to sit in on follow-up sessions. He gladly accepted, pleased that the other meetings wouldn't cost him any money. The investment he'd made with Garrett was already paying dividends.

"Excuse me, Mr. Montgomery," Maxwell heard someone say. He looked up to find a slightly familiar face but the name didn't readily come forward. "I'm Pastor Renaldo Harris."

"That's right, you're at Faith Temple." Maxwell recalled the young face. It was the local minister from one of the mega churches on his watch list. Harris hadn't officially made the top priority list like the bishop, but Maxwell was sure his time would come. He was a prime candidate pastoring a mega church with lots of money coming in. "I've seen several of your commercials," Maxwell said.

"Good to hear. We try to reach the people through every available media," Harris said with a certain confidence that made Maxwell take notice.

If it had been anyone else, except someone in that meeting room, Maxwell would have interpreted the tone as one of sincerity. But, not with that pack of wolves. Oh no, he wasn't that naive. Harris had a racket and when Faith Temple moved up on the hit list, Maxwell would find out what it was.

"I won't take up any more of your time, Mr. Montgomery. I just wanted to officially introduce myself and to let you know that your ideas were on point regarding the youth programs. I believe there's quite a bit we can do together to bring these programs to fruition much quicker than we discussed here today." The pastor reached into the pocket of his suit and pulled out a business card.

"When you get a chance, please give me a call. I'd love to talk more." He handed Maxwell the card and followed with a firm handshake. "Feel free to give me a call or, better yet, stop by one of our services. We have a service Saturday evening at six and two on Sunday, eight in the morning for the early risers and a second one at eleven. I hope to see you soon."

Maxwell didn't know quite how to take Harris. Because Faith Temple wasn't in his crosshairs, there wasn't much immediate ammunition he had available. A few quick background checks in the past hadn't revealed anything meaningful and had annoyed Maxwell. As curious as he was about Harris and what he might be up to, he couldn't get sidetracked. Philadelphia public enemy number one was Bishop Ellis Jones. That was the prize and no distractions could veer Maxwell off course. It had taken decades to sit at the seat of judgment and be within arm's length of the bishop. Maxwell wasn't about to lose ground now. Harris would have to wait in line like the rest of the lowly so-called holy men scampering from the room. He continued gathering his belongings and didn't extend any other courtesies. Hypocrisy wasn't his style. There may have been one or two men in the room who he respected, maybe, but as far as he was concerned it wasn't likely. He briefly contemplated the odds of having integrity in a room lined with preachers and politicians. For Maxwell, each group was corrupt and in need of neutralization. He decided to give the politicians a free pass. They could keep lying, stealing, cheating, and defrauding the people. Maybe one day, when all the ministers had been banned to the outer edges of the earth, and he had another lifetime to live, then perhaps he would start on them. Until then, he'd tackle one priority at a time. He'd learned from the mistakes of others over the years to only handle one venomous snake at a time. If he got too cocky and tried handling several simultaneously, he was likely to get bitten.

Losing wasn't an option in a battle where he'd dedicated his entire adulthood to winning. There was only one acceptable outcome—total annihilation with no exceptions. Glancing around the room, he was committed and on track. He left the room thoroughly satisfied.

Chapter 12

A day faded into a week without an ounce of enthusiasm seeping from Maxwell's veins. His continued vigor compelled him to open the leather-bound planner on his desk. He pressed up and down on top of an ink pen, counting the clicking noises it made with each down stroke of his thumb. Maxwell drew a red X through dates. It was the eighth consecutive mark he'd made since beginning the arduous task of tracking the number of days it would take to bring Jones down. Each red X represented a crack in Jones's foundation that would soon crumble and fall down around him, leveling his naive and adoring community. Maxwell's disgust warmed. It couldn't be soon enough for him. He was eager for folks to look beyond the layers of lies and tailor-made suits to see clearly the man in front of them.

The longer Maxwell stared at the page, the more it seemed to bleed with a sea of red that stared at him in defeat. The alarm on his PDA demanded his attention. He pushed a button to silence it. Fueled by his self-imposed 11:00 a.m. appointment, excitement streamed through him pushing Maxwell to his feet. He'd gotten to the office earlier than usual determined to get some work done before leaving so early in the day. He had time to go over his precision-crafted lines once again before taking off.

Maxwell tapped twice on a page in the day planner with his index finger and closed it. He walked to the far side of the office and stepped into his private bathroom.

Standing in front of the full-length mirror, he fidgeted with the knot in his tie. He scrutinized his tall frame from head to toe determined to look stylish but not overstated. Gaudy watches and bright suits had no place in his wardrobe. Looking at his reflection, he repeated the lines he'd drafted for presenting his youth proposal to the bishop, paying close attention to the rise and fall of his voice and the expression on his face. He ran through the lines repeatedly. The delivery had to be perfect and the message clear, sincere. Satisfied with the last run-through, he was now off to set a challenge in motion.

He bolted from the bathroom, grabbed his suit jacket and took an extra few minutes to get it on perfectly, readjusting his shirt sleeves, cuff links, and tie again. Not a thread could be out of place. His meeting was too important to be overshadowed by a wardrobe malfunction. He hustled to the door, and then stopped. He'd forgotten something. He went to his desk to pluck out an envelope and a small sheet of paper from the top drawer. He opened a box in the drawer and counted out $860, leaving it practically empty except for fifteen bucks. It didn't matter. He'd taken cash from his pocket in the past to cover the bill. Hatred was a heavy load to bear. Holding the hospital bill in his hand, admittedly there were instances when it had to take a rest.

Maxwell rushed from his office and stopped at Sonya's desk. "I'll be gone until three." He handed her cash. She looked befuddled. He stuffed the bill inside the envelope and gave it to her. "Can you please take care of this for me? It's ready to go, but I don't have time to get a money order or to address the envelope."

"Is it the same one we've used before?"

"Yep, the hospital and not the house address."

"Then I have it."

"But, I need it in the mail today." He took a step and then turned to say, "Oh, and please don't use a return address."

"I know, I know," she chimed, waving him off.

He walked away looking down at his watch.

Maxwell maneuvered the expressway like a race track zipping in and out; slicing between cars that didn't have the high-performance engine that a Porsche offered. He pressed a button and warm sunlight invaded the car along with the cool wind that whisked inside. He went over his lines again, regulating the infliction in his voice. As he neared the church, he sealed the resolve in his heart as the plan of attack was etched in his mind.

The engine of Maxwell's car simmered down to a taunting purr when it rolled into the parking lot. He couldn't resist parking next to the space labeled BISHOP ELLIS JONES. The letters on the sign were big and bold, proclaiming the presiding bishop's reign. Maxwell gripped the steering wheel hard enough to feel his pulse throbbing in his fingertips. Releasing his clutch, he leaned back on the seat while his gaze scaled the massive edifice in front of him. Stained glass windows showcased the etched imagery of angels, the Virgin Mary, and Christ being crucified on the cross. The steeple on top of the church housed a bell tower that sounded off. Maxwell counted the last three explosive bongs: ten, eleven, twelve. He could feel the impact of each striking blow that dispersed sound waves rippling through him and draining his enthusiasm.

He remembered going to Sunday school all those years ago. His mother would pick up the pace as they approached the former church building determined not to be late. Deacon Montgomery always left home early to get the church opened up for those who were sure to pour in and fill the pews. Maxwell shook his head tossing out the shadows of more woes that tied him and his family to Jones.

The church's parking lot didn't provide an automatic comfort zone. Climbing the steps, Maxwell turned and pointed his keys at his car to engage the alarm. At the top of the steps, he pulled at one of the double doors and went inside. Once through the foyer, the church secretary greeted him warmly as he approached the office door.

"Praise God, how can I help you?"

"Maxwell Montgomery to see Bishop Jones." His pulse wanted to surge. Instead, he gave the secretary a weak simper and drew on his ability to conceal true emotion.

"Have a seat, Mr. Montgomery. He's in a meeting, but I'll let him know you're here," she said picking up the phone.

Maxwell took a seat and set his attention on the closed door leading into Jones's office. Though he had dropped by without an appointment, waiting for this man to grant him any kind of permission annoyed Maxwell. The secretary's ringing phone drew Maxwell's burning gaze from the door that kept Jones's meeting private.

Abruptly a gentleman emerged from the office seeming to avoid eye contact. Maxwell recognized Councilman Chambers, a local politician who stayed in the headlines. His presence had Maxwell intrigued. What business did the councilman have with the church?

"I'll talk to you later, Bishop," the councilman said and fled. Maxwell turned and got a glimpse of him scuttling away.

"You can go in now, Mr. Montgomery." The secretary walked ahead of Maxwell, allowing him entrance.

Maxwell went inside the office and his interest in Chambers immediately dissipated. Jones stepped from behind his desk just as Maxwell extended his hand. He was hesitant feeling like the seventeen-year-old he once was when he'd last stood this close to the bishop.

"I apologize for interrupting your meeting," he told the bishop standing face-to-face with him, still apprehensive.

"I've been expecting you for some time now, ever since I saw you at the mayor's meeting."

"Really?"

Jones cleared his throat. "Excuse my voice. I've had several speaking engagements this week, not to mention my sermons." The bishop approached Maxwell with a glare and generic grin, crowding him, forcing Maxwell to take a step backward. Jones said, "What took you so long to get here?"

Geez, Maxwell thought. He was hoping to avoid this moment when the bishop recognized him as the son of Paul Sr., his former treasurer at the old church in Chester. This round of direct hand-to-hand combat was over. The sneak attack had to be aborted. He'd leave without incident and find another way to expose Jones.

"Maxwell Montgomery, have a seat," he offered motioning his hand toward the chair in front of his desk. "The powerful attorney with two first names," he told Maxwell as he sat behind his desk. "Come to think of it, I knew a Gayle Montgomery years ago in high school. Any chance you're related?"

"No," Maxwell firmly replied.

"Well, it's a common name," Jones replied. The phone on the desk rang and Jones held up his index finger, saying, "Just a minute."

Maxwell was relieved. Though he was glad Jones didn't recognize him, Maxwell was agitated that the name Montgomery hadn't set off an alarm. Jones had destroyed so many that one family must have been as forgettable to him as the next. Evidently Ethel and Paul were absolutely nobody, not worthy of so much as an empty reference during small talk. The prison time they'd served because of the bishop rendered no gratitude or asterisk in his memory. His parents were merely weeds trampled under Jones's feet. Maxwell was erupting inside. To think that his parents chose this man over stability threatened to set off his own alarm.

Watching Jones on the phone caused his level of agitation to escalate. Maxwell spread his fingers and pressed his fingertips against each other determined to hold it together until Jones ended his call. A struggle was mounting the more he remembered how much Jones had forgotten. A resolve washed over him, content that one day Jones's memory would be forcibly restored.

Chapter 13

Jones wrapped up the call and turned to face Maxwell. "Now, Mr. Montgomery, what can I do for you?"

Maxwell pressed his palm into his thigh and slid it forward over his right knee before he began speaking. "I'm here to put some money and some muscle behind the lofty ideas discussed at the mayor's meeting. I was thinking we might be able to work together and make this a reality. I know the task won't be easy, but I believe it's doable." Maxwell tried taking the edge off and softening his facial expressions. Yet he couldn't harness his restlessness and kept adjusting his position in the chair. "I also get the impression that you are an influential man with your hands in a lot of things around the city."

"I have a few connections," Bishop Jones said pinching his fingers together.

"Working together, we can bring this thing to fruition," Maxwell responded locking his gaze on Jones, no longer feeling like the naive child he'd once been in the church. That child was gone, forever, thanks to the bishop. Maxwell's words were saturated with purpose and married to his goal of getting close to Jones.

"Well, praise God! Your confidence definitely hasn't been misplaced. I've got a lot of ideas, resources, and people at my disposal," the bishop said.

Maxwell listened to what seemed like incessant babbling. He strummed his fingers across the heel of his right hand struggling to stay engaged. The visit was a means to an end that would soon become clearer, but watching Jones's round belly jiggle and his heavy voice rumble with every monopolizing word irked Maxwell deep in his soul. The stench of arrogance tumbling across the bishop's lips incited Maxwell to shut him up, but this wasn't the right situation. He had to grin and bear his infuriation.

Fifteen minutes of grandstanding ensued.

"I have a few ideas of my own," Maxwell interrupted, snatching the spotlight. Jones creased his brow, stared, and began stabbing his pen against the desk. Maybe he was annoyed that Maxwell wasn't begging and groveling for help from His Majesty. Maxwell wasn't sure and didn't care. He set his feet firmly on the floor. His apprehension had evaporated and been replaced with sheer guts. The bishop wasn't dealing with Paul Montgomery, junior or senior.

Jones invited Maxwell to move over to the conference table where they could crank out a plan. Maxwell stood while Jones clutched the arms of his chair, heaving himself up. The conference table was big enough to seat eight. Maxwell guessed that Jones needed more room for his plump body than the space behind his desk offered.

"Excuse me for just a minute," Jones said as Maxwell sat. "I have to step out. This water pill the doctor has me on keeps me on my toes. I'll be right back."

"Take your time," Maxwell graciously said.

When Jones stepped out of the office, Maxwell was thrilled. Now was his chance. A few solitary minutes to discover any hint that would lead him in the right direction. There was dirt. He just had to find it. Quickly he explored the bookshelf near him and awards on the wall for anything in plain sight that might be of use. He panned his search around the office. A series of family photos lining the bishop's desk caused Maxwell to pause. Envisioning the man as a caring father was inconceivable.

He cringed thinking about the bishop's children growing up with a privileged life as Maxwell's family paid the price. Time was short. So, he harnessed his emotions and set them aside for the moment. They would get nurtured in due season, but right now he couldn't squander this opportunity. After taking in a panoramic view, Maxwell's visual sweep ended at the conference table. There on the other end, beyond arm's reach, was a folder and some loose papers. Maxwell took a split second to listen for heavy footsteps that were sure to announce Jones's return. No movement or no noise was heard which dared him to go for it. Maxwell stood and slid down to the end of the table. He opened the folder and found a thick stack of deeds and what appeared to be mortgage forms. He riffled through the papers and made a hasty withdrawal back to his seat when he heard the rumbling voice approach. No time to rejoice over his find. Jones appeared in the doorway.

"Sorry to keep you waiting; let's get down to business," the bishop said reclaiming his seat. "Let me tell you, I've thought long and hard about what needs to be done." Maxwell struggled to listen. He'd gotten plenty from the visit but wasn't quite ready to go. "We need to teach these kids what it means to put in a hard day's work; to learn how to earn what they get."

"You mean build character?" Maxwell stated.

"Exactly, let them put in the work that we had to do to get where we are. Too many handouts have made our community soft. They're a bunch of cripples waiting for 'the' man to give them what already belongs to them. I don't believe in waiting for what I want. I take it."

"So, I've heard."

The bishop lifted his gaze and drilled into Maxwell. With sharpness to his words, he said, "Can't believe everything you hear, can you?"

"Depends on who's doing the talking."

The bishop maintained his lock on Maxwell. Neither blinked. Both men held their ground, like two lions dueling for the upper hand.

"If I were a man who cared about gossip, you and I wouldn't be sitting here having this conversation," Jones said wrapping his left hand over his right fist. "Come on; your reputation precedes you, my friend. According to the press, you're on direct payroll from the devil."

"That's what they say, huh."

"That's what I've heard based on how hard you go after churches."

"Does that bother you?" Maxwell asked.

"Why should it? I don't have anything to hide." The men stared for a few seconds longer, with the bishop being the first to look away. "Come on," Jones said extending his hand to shake. "We are here to figure out how to help this community. Let's set the other nonsense aside, deal?"

Maxwell had no intention of cutting any deal with the bishop, but he was willing to extend the farce as long as necessary to get what he needed. He extended his hand followed by a nod.

Chapter 14

Jones led the rest of the meeting, laying out his ideas for a mentorship program. Maxwell let him talk, interjecting when he felt too bored to continue. "I'd like for the young men to get their hands dirty by cleaning up a slew of abandoned and foreclosed properties. Hard labor will do them good."

After nearly twenty minutes, the bishop finally said something worth acknowledging, but Maxwell wanted more done sooner. Kids like his nephew, Tyree, were depending on him to step up. "I like your idea, but let's get at the core of this problem. We need to target the failing students, the ones truly at risk. If we don't help them, they'll end up needing a lawyer instead of becoming one," Maxwell said.

"That sounds good but there's so many. How would we go about something like that?" Jones asked.

Passion rose in Maxwell, enabling him to almost forget the true reason he'd come to Greater Metropolitan. "We'd have to get the school board, principals, and teachers involved. There's no other way." Maxwell's head was bursting with ideas. He'd set his contempt aside several minutes ago. For a short period, he didn't see the bishop as his adversary. At this precise moment, he was a respectable ally.

"Hmm, maybe you have something," the bishop said. "We could combine it with my program. I have a lot of property." Jones twirled a pen on his desk and lifted his gaze to meet Maxwell. "I should say the church owns the property, but you know how that goes, right," he said grinning.

Maxwell nodded and grinned too as his euphoria came to a crashing halt. He was instantly reminded of who the man was sitting before him, a refreshing fact, and one that enabled Maxwell to press forward mercilessly.

The shrill of Jones's cell phone interrupted his civil sermon. Jones apologized and promised the call would only take a couple of minutes. Maxwell turned in his chair, taking in the aquarium of exotic fish. He attempted to give Jones some semblance of privacy, but Maxwell could hear every word.

"Did you forget anything?" Jones asked his caller. "Oh I see. Okay, well that's going to create a problem. We need to talk, but I have Attorney Maxwell Montgomery in my office." There was a brief pause as Jones looked away. "Right, right, exactly. Hold on," he said. "Look here, Maxwell. Can I call you Maxwell?"

"Sure."

"I have an emergency brewing," he said muffling the phone. "I hate to cut our meeting short, but I really have to take this call. I have a deal that's going sour and well, you understand."

"Absolutely," Maxwell said standing.

"I'd like to finish our chat soon. There are a couple of people in the ministry I'd like you to meet. They'll be a big help to us in getting this effort off the ground."

"Not a problem," was what Maxwell said. "I'll have my secretary give you a call." Honestly, he wasn't accustomed to being dismissed, but it wasn't appropriate at this juncture to assert his presence. His relationship with the bishop would be a long courtship; no need to prematurely taint the rapport. "I appreciate you making time to talk with me. This has been very enlightening."

"I'll see you soon," the bishop replied.

"No doubt," Maxwell said, realizing the bishop was unaware of just how soon. He nodded with his chin raised.

Jones reciprocated and turned his back. "Now, Councilman, we had a deal with that property. What the heck are you . . ." was the most Maxwell heard before closing the door.

Maxwell's thoughts were wrapped around the stack of real estate documents he'd seen and the comment he'd just overheard. What about the councilman's hasty exit? There had to be something there. He wasn't sure what picture the pieces were painting, but Maxwell was certain Garrett could make sense of it with more digging. He could feel the heat of success pouring over him. He was charged and very pleased with the visit. He had even calmed down about Jones not recognizing him. Actually, he was glad. Maxwell took satisfaction in believing the bishop's lack of attention to detail was going to cost him dearly in the long run.

Maxwell slid into the seat of his car and slammed his fist against the steering wheel, releasing exuberance. The meeting had rendered more than Maxwell expected. He hastily called Garrett. "Can you meet me at my office?"

"When?"

"Right now, if you can?"

"I'm on my way."

Maxwell started his engine then allowed it to settle down to a teasing hum. Turning his head slightly to the left, his gaze couldn't help but to be drawn to the church steeple. Childhood memories, disappointment, and anger swelled up inside, pushing out the excitement that owned him earlier. He yanked the gear shift into reverse heading out the parking lot. In the rearview mirror, he could see the towering steeple that pursued him. Maxwell pressed his foot down hard onto the accelerator to put distance between him, Jones, and the church. He'd be back. That was certain.

Chapter 15

Bishop Jones asked the councilman to hold on while he spoke to his secretary. He stepped from his office for a brief moment. "Get in touch with Maxwell Montgomery's secretary and get us a follow-up meeting."

"How soon?" his secretary asked.

"Right away; getting this program off the ground for our young men is very important to me. Move my appointments around if you need to; make it happen." He thanked her, retreated into his office, and pulled his seat close to the desk. "Now where were we?"

"Like I said, Bishop, I can't get that house for you. You can have the entire block, with the exception of the corner lot."

"Councilman, your word should count for something. We had a deal."

"I know, and I'm sorry, but there's nothing I can do. The seller has changed his mind. We can't force him out without jeopardizing the entire operation."

Bishop Ellis lifted the photo closest to him, the one with his grandchildren sprawled around him and his wife. Church, business, and family each had their share of him, probably equally, but there were situations when one had to win out. His grandson was in trouble and needed a safe place to land once he got out of the detention center in six months. The corner property was an ideal location for a full-service development center, complete with medical care, college training, a fitness program, and housing.

He wanted his grandchild close to the church and sur-
rounded by people who could help him get right. There
was no compromising. He had the other nine properties
on the block, but it wasn't complete without the corner.

"Come on, help me out here. The architectural plans
are drawn up. We've already identified clinicians, a
program director, and even a janitor. This is in motion
based on your promise. I need you to come through," he
said holding the photo.

"It's not going to happen, at least not with my help,
especially not with that attorney hanging around. He's
bad news. We both know it," the councilman protested.

"Ah, don't worry about him. He's interested in putting
together a youth program that the mayor is sponsoring.
That's the extent of our business."

"Are you sure?" the councilman said in an almost
accusatory tone.

"Yes, I'm sure. Why do you say it like that?"

"Because his only interest in churches is to shut them
down; that's a fact. And there's a long list of defunct and/
or bankrupt churches in Philadelphia to prove he's very
good at what he does."

"I'm not worried," Bishop Jones said. Separating business from church was his gift, one that he did very well.
His philosophy had successfully gotten him to where he
was. No sharp-dressing, fast-talking attorney was going
to have him walking in fear. As a boy, he hadn't been
frightened by attacks and was too old to start now.

"Fine for you, but I'm coming up on an election year
and can't take the chance. I need to pull back from
our dealings until you and Maxwell Montgomery have
concluded your business."

"Humph, I don't see that happening. You are my
broker. We have a deal, and I expect you to deliver,
period," the bishop replied. "If you want to run scared

because this young man is dropping by my office, be my guest, but don't waver in your professionalism. And most definitely don't default on your commitments to me. That would be a mistake and reelection would be the least of your problems."

"Are you threatening me?"

Bishop Jones roared with a bolstering chuckle. "Oh come on, Councilman. I'm a man of the cloth; now what would I look like threatening you?" His laughter continued resonating from deep in his gut. Abruptly, he stopped laughing and said, "Unlike you, you can take me at my word. Get the property like we agreed. Now, have a good day." The bishop pressed down hard on the end call button on his cell without giving the councilman a chance to respond.

Bishop Jones held the family photo for a short while longer before carefully placing it back in the rightful spot reserved on his desk. He let his forehead rest in the palm of his hand. Councilman Chambers was right in raising a flag about Maxwell Montgomery, but Bishop Jones was not about to show his concerns. That was a sign of weakness, a sensation he hadn't experienced personally. That was reserved for others. Bishop Jones wasn't stupid. He planned to keep watch over Maxwell Montgomery. Their rapport was going to be short and effective. Bishop Jones would make sure of it.

Chapter 16

By the time Maxwell reached his office, ideas had pounded his brain to the point where he needed Sonya to jot down notes before he exploded. Initially he'd become fueled with animosity sitting in Jones's office, but Maxwell's style wasn't to lash out in an emotional tirade. Only inept fools acted that way. He removed his suit coat. Maxwell preferred waging war on the battlefield where he was most familiar with the terrain—the courtroom. That's where he was going to duel with Jones. Best part about it was that Jones was so arrogant, he didn't suspect the attack which was about to be unleashed. Inspired, Maxwell hustled to his paralegal's desk. He had to get comfortable; the day would be long.

"Sonya," he said standing in front of her desk with his electronic pad neatly tucked under one arm. "How late can you stay tonight?"

"As long as you need."

"Good, because it's going to be a late one," he told her practically oozing enthusiasm.

"What happened with you?"

"What do you mean?" he asked pressing one knuckle into her desk and grinning.

"That look on your face? You seem, oh I don't know, really happy."

"It's a good day. I had a very productive meeting with Bishop Jones from Greater Metropolitan."

"Really?"

"Yup, it went very well. That's all I can say," he told her. "Look, I need you to take a few more notes for me and then let me know when Garrett arrives. Clear my schedule this afternoon. I'll be tied up for a while."

"Don't forget your deposition with Ms. Carmichael on the sexual harassment case."

"That's right," he said pushing his forefinger into his temple and thinking for a minute. It was important but Greater Metropolitan was more important. He'd been chomping for a break, anything to let him get the door cracked wide enough to find dirt and build a case. His instinct said there was more going on with the property deeds. He was too charged to deviate for the deposition. "Call the opposing counsel and get a new date."

"But what do I tell them?"

"Whatever you want, so long as they reschedule and get me freed up this afternoon."

"Okay, I'll call and tell them you had an emergency and can't make it."

"Great, that's why you're on my team. You know what to do without asking me," he said sailing into his office. "Call Ms. Carmichael too and then come on in to take these notes," he told her.

Sonya had seen the gleam in his eye a countless number of times in the past. Seven years of working closely with Maxwell Montgomery as an assistant and paralegal had enabled her to read the signs. Whatever happened in the meeting this morning wasn't good for Bishop Jones. She knew that much without having a single detail about the actual conversation. She'd seen Maxwell's jovial reaction on numerous occasions but never quite this giddy. Her flesh wanted to discount the obvious. But, common sense said to get prepared. As a member of Greater Metropolitan, she better find another church. No question about it, if Greater Metropolitan was on Maxwell Montgomery's list, they were going down and she wanted off the *Titanic* as soon as possible. She made the calls and headed to her boss's office saddened by the pending news that her pastor and church would soon be in big trouble. She wasn't aware of the proposed infractions but it had to be huge for Maxwell to be this pleased.

"Are we all set with the deposition?" he asked as she entered his office.

"Yes, sir, I have you rescheduled for tomorrow afternoon."

"Yikes, I should have told you to push it back to next week."

"Your calendar had a few free spots, so I took it."

"I know, don't worry about it. It's fine. I'll go tomorrow. I'm sure I'll be tied up for the rest of this week, but it's okay. We'll get it done. Now," he said motioning for her to join him at the conference table. "I need you to jot down a few notes for me."

"I'm ready." She pushed the lid on her laptop open.

"Knock, knock," Garrett said appearing at the office door, which was slightly open.

"Come on in," Maxwell said, beckoning him toward the table. "Sonya, do you mind? I need to speak with Garrett."

"What about the notes you wanted me to take?"

"Ah, don't worry about those. I'll catch up with you later."

"As you wish," she said packing up her laptop.

"And hold all my calls. I don't care who it is. I don't want to be disturbed."

Sonya closed the door behind her.

"Have a seat," Maxwell told Garrett.

"So, what's up? I rushed right over. You must be on to something big. What is it?"

"Bishop Jones and Greater Metropolitan," he belted slapping his hand on the table.

"What?"

"We may have a nugget," Maxwell said barely able to contain his glee.

Garrett sat up in his seat. "You got my attention, shoot."

"I went to see the bishop this morning. While I was there, I happened to see a stack of property deeds and a few other real estate documents."

"Hmm, that's odd seeing that they're not a holding company. What would they need with deeds?"

"Exactly what I was thinking," Maxwell said rearing back in his seat with his fingers locked behind his head. "What would a church do with property deeds unless they are expanding or maybe supplying housing for the congregation? A few deeds wouldn't have caught my attention, but I'm talking about a thick stack." Maxwell raised his hand eleven or twelve inches above the table. "Do they have that kind of money?"

"Seems odd," Garrett said.

"Oh, I forgot the key detail. Councilman Chambers was weaseling from the bishop's office when I arrived. He seemed awfully cagey."

"Well, he's a cagey man," Garrett said sparking humor between the two.

"True but there's more to it. Before I left, I overheard the bishop having a heated conversation with the councilman about a deal that had gone bad."

"What kind of deal?"

"That I didn't hear, but if it's with Chambers, we can suspect there's fraudulent activity involved. As a matter of fact, I'm counting on him to stay true to his reputation." Maxwell rubbed his palms together.

"There are a lot of rumors and accusations floating around out there about the councilman."

"Too much for a squeaky-clean ministry to be cutting deals with," Maxwell stated.

"To my knowledge he's never been charged with an actual crime. He's been able to weasel out of each situation he's found himself in," Garrett echoed.

"Huh, the councilman might not have been charged with a crime, but we both know it doesn't mean he's innocent. Oh, he's guilty," Maxwell said tapping his fingers on the table. "We just have to find out what he's guilty of."

"You've definitely piqued my curiosity; wonder what's going on," Garrett said.

"That's what we have to find out. That's why you're here. If there are skeletons lurking in the bishop's real estate closet, I have no doubt you will find them."

"I'll see what I can do."

Maxwell peered at Garrett. "I'm counting on you to get what I need."

"There's another case I'm working on, but it's wrapping up soon."

"Whatever you're working on, cancel it. Make this your top priority. You know I'm good for the money; double your rate if you'd like. I don't care. I just don't want to lose our momentum. We're on to something and I can tell it's going to be big, real big. Can I count on you?"

Garrett gave a thumbs-up gesture. "I'm on it."

"Just what I want to hear," Maxwell said and relaxed in his seat. Finally, he would get the retribution he and his family deserved. The sweet taste of justice lingered on his lips long after Garrett was gone.

Sonya didn't rush into her boss's office, but the suspense was unbearable and equally alarming. She could ignore the inevitable, write out her check for tithes and offering, go to church on Sunday like usual and pretend that her Greater Metropolitan world was the same last week as this one. The bishop along with the rest of the congregation believed so, but she knew better. Even if she wanted to pretend, the reality wouldn't allow her. Maxwell Montgomery never wasted his time. She had to find another home. Five churches in seven years should have soured her on religion, but it hadn't. God was at one of the ministries in Philadelphia. She just had to find Him.

Maxwell came out of his office.

"Are you ready for me to take those notes now?"

"Oh, don't worry about it," he told her. "I was able to take my own in the meeting with Garrett."

"So, you're working on a big case."

"Probably the biggest I've ever done. That's what I'm hoping."

Sonya wanted to push for a little more information to confirm her fear. "Is it with Greater Metropolitan?"

"Why? How much do you know about them?" he asked.

She clammed up, unwilling to let him know her affiliation with the ministry. She needed her job and wasn't about to get on his attack list. "It's the biggest mega church in the area. Everybody in Philadelphia knows about Greater Metropolitan."

"Right," Maxwell said letting his gaze wander.

She could only imagine what was on his mind. "Did the bishop do something illegal?"

"Let's say I've acquired a special affinity to the church," he said too smug for her to feel comfortable.

"Well, let me know if I can help with the case."

"It's not a case yet," he stated with an eerie tone of seriousness. "We are only investigating a hunch, no more, no less." He prepared to return to his office, then turned to her and said, "Sonya, remember you have a confidentiality agreement."

"I remember," she answered wondering why he felt the need to remind her. He hadn't done that in the past.

Worry swooped in causing her to fidget and stumble over her words. "I never talk about the work I do for you with anyone."

"Good. I knew that, but as an attorney I had to point it out."

"If you want, I can sign another confidentiality agreement. I don't mind at all."

"No, your loyalty is a good enough contract for me."

When Sonya was alone, she contemplated Maxwell's comment. She didn't have to sign another agreement but might as well have. The fact that he emphasized how important secrecy was going to be with Greater Metropolitan had her terrified. She couldn't end her membership fast enough. Going to church on Sunday to turn in her letter of departure and to say her good-byes wasn't going to work. She couldn't take the risk of running into her boss at the church during his investigation. She needed another plan. Perhaps she'd mail the letter. On second thought, she wasn't mailing, calling, or contacting the church in any way. God would just have to forgive her for church hopping, but until certain ministries got their acts together, she had to stay a step ahead of her boss.

Feeling a sense of hope now that she had a plan, Sonya typed in Faith Temple on the laptop searching for an address. Pastor Harris's church had a good reputation. She'd go there Sunday and start a new quest for a church home now that Greater Metropolitan was in front of the firing squad. She felt a twinge of sadness. Death of the ministry was closer than they realized.

Chapter 17

Bishop yawned unable to resist the exhaustion over-taking him. This was a shame, he thought, having to come in at midnight. He couldn't wait to get the neighborhood expansion project constructed, paid in full, and off his mind. Helping his grandson get straightened out and others like him kept the bishop going. However, the financial burden was more than he expected, and it began chipping away at his sanity. Where was the rest of the money coming from? Help definitely wasn't coming from the church's budget. Those were separate funds. The constant worry kept him stressed. Bishop had to figure something out.

He trotted down the hallway leading to his office, wanting to get in, take care of business, and get home. He envisioned laying his head on the soft pillow, next to his wife of thirty-eight years. He'd hustle, grab the recent real estate papers, and be gone in less than fifteen minutes. He yawned again, reinforcing his determination to cut the trip as short as possible. Halfway down the hallway, the bishop stopped in mid-step. He heard a faint noise coming from the education wing. He stayed frozen listening for the noise again. Who could be breaking into God's house? Wisdom said get out of the building, call 911, and wait in the car. *No,* he decided. As head of the church and a man of God, he was fully prepared to stare evil down. His steps quickened the closer he got to the voices. Fear had fallen away about ten steps ago. He was ready for combat with the villains. He could hear voices strengthening as he got closer to the classrooms.

"Do your part and don't worry about the rest. That's my business," he heard a woman say.

"Speaking of business, let's finish ours. It's late and I need to get home. Tax season has been over for months, so I can't keep telling my wife the lie that I'm getting the church books in order," he heard coming from a male voice.

"Women are a lot smarter than you think. She knows what's going on," Bishop heard a woman say.

"How can you be so sure?"

"I just know what women know, okay?"

"Well, she better not find out, and she definitely better not hear anything from you. Give me the package so I can get out of here," the man said, that time sounding very familiar.

The voices were completely clear. By the time Bishop made his trek down the hallway, his fear had completely transformed into authority. Whoever was in the church without permission was going to get chastised.

Finally reaching the doorway, he leaned one hand against the frame and caught a breath. At sixty-five, walks weren't as easy as they'd been in his twenties. Much had transpired in the past four decades; age taking over had been one. Bishop poked his head into the nursery and his back stiffened. He cleared his throat, very loudly, making it impossible not to hear him.

"Oh, uh, excuse me, Bishop," Simmons said, stumbling over both his words and shoes. A bunch of pills spilled from a bag the woman was holding. There were different shapes: some large, others small, yellow, white, blue. There appeared to be every other color in the crayon box represented.

"Minister Simmons, what in tarnation are you doing in here?" he asked as the woman scrambled gathering the pills. She snatched up a jumbo freezer-sized bag full of pills and shoved them into her large purse. Bishop didn't recognize her. She could have been a member but with over 5,000 people in any given service, admittedly he didn't know everyone personally.

"Bishop, I can explain."

"I'm sure you can and you will." He turned to the young lady. "Excuse me, miss, do you mind leaving us alone?"

She grabbed her sweater and purse, and quickly said, "I'm out of here."

"It's late; do you want one of us to walk you to your car?" Bishop asked.

"I don't have a car," she said moving toward the door. He didn't have to beg her to get out. She was practically gone before he could say anything.

"We can't let you walk out of here in the middle of the night without an escort."

"Ah, she'll be okay," Simmons uttered.

"You're right, yes, I will," she agreed clutching the purse tightly.

"I don't feel right and Minister Simmons, you shouldn't either." Before Bishop could say another word, the woman burst out the doorway, ran down the hallway, and out the door. Bishop's sense of decency wanted to run after her but his tired body wasn't remotely considering the possibility.

With the woman gone and anger gripping him, Bishop reverted to his new associate pastor. "What were you doing in here?"

Minister Simmons didn't readily speak up which instantly upset Bishop. "I know you hear me; speak up."

The minister took a seat and stared at his feet, unwilling or unable to look up. "Her name is Jill Smith. She's a friend of mine."

"Am I supposed to believe you?" Bishop hesitated before responding. He'd worked tirelessly for decades building a leading mega church. Reflecting on past years, sacrifices had been great and challenges too numerous to count. He was on the downside of his days as a pastor and every day counted. He was so close to realizing his dream of building up Greater Metropolitan and solidifying his legacy. No sideshows were going to derail his plans. "What was she doing with so much medicine? And don't lie to me in the Lord's house." Minister Simmons didn't answer immediately causing Bishop to get agitated. "Did you hear me, Minister? What was she doing with that big bag of pills? What was she doing here, period, at midnight with a married leader in my church? And, Minister, before you say anything, it had better be a good answer, one that will keep you on staff at this church."

Minister Simmons rubbed his hands together refusing to make eye contact. That was okay with Bishop so long as Simmons started talking in the next few seconds and could explain his actions. The mere notion of a leader defiling his church was crazy, not possible. Simmons couldn't be that stupid. Mistakes were permitted by his staff, but marriage had to be honored and indiscretions were off-limits. He totally respected the institution and everyone in his circle had better do the same.

The silence was finally broken. "Jill and I have a special friendship."

"Are you involved with that woman?" Simmons looked away. "Man, don't make me have to ask you again."

"No, not really," the minister stammered.

"Oh come on, Minister, do you think I'm a fool?"

"Okay, I admit that we slipped once but never in the church. It was somewhere else."

"And that makes all the difference I suppose?"

"To me it does."

Bishop chuckled to cool his scorching disdain. "What was she doing here?"

"Just talking."

Bishop glanced at his watch. "It's twelve forty-five in the morning. Don't play games with me, Minister. What are you trying to say? Because I need to get home. What was Ms. Smith doing with the bag of pills?"

"Those are mine."

Bishop wasn't prepared for his answer. By the size of his bag, Minister Simmons must have been suffering a mountain of ailments. "I didn't know you were sick."

"I'm not."

Bishop was admittedly confused and annoyed. "Then what are you doing with the medicine, and if it's yours, why did Jill run off with it?"

Simmons stopped prolonging the inquisition. He came straight out with more than Bishop was equipped to hear. "She sells the prescription drugs for me."

"What! I know you aren't selling drugs in the church? Are you crazy? If you get caught, this ministry will be shut down. Do you understand you're putting the entire ministry in jeopardy? And for what, so you can make a few dollars? Shame on you," Bishop said, leaning against the door for support.

"It's a lot more than a few, more like three thousand."

"Money can't buy your soul the peace it craves."

"Maybe not," Simmons said with his head lifted up and squint locked into Bishop's. "But, the money certainly helps."

It was difficult for Bishop Jones to listen to Minister Simmons and remain calm. He hadn't labored for decades to watch his ministry be crushed by a greedy, misguided soul. A single snake brought down the Garden of Eden, but the bishop and Greater Metropolitan weren't going to be deceived. "I could have given you an extra three thousand dollars at the end of the year if it will help you out."

"I meant three thousand a week."

Bishop Jones gulped quickly doing the math in his head. "That's over a hundred and fifty thousand for the year. Is that what you're telling me?"

"Yep, tax free, and that's with me keeping this on a small scale."

"Where do you get these pills? Are you robbing pharmacies, too?"

"Oh heavens no," Simmons responded emphatically. "I have a friend who's a warehouse distribution manager at a pharmaceutical company in Jersey. I get the pills from him and pass them to Jill. She takes them to my five buyers, or as I prefer to call them, traveling pharmacists."

Surprisingly, it didn't sound complicated to Bishop. He was intrigued. "How long has this been going on?"

"Five months."

"That's what, fifty or sixty thousand dollars?"

"About that much," Simmons replied shaking his head up and down. "I'll have you know that I did right by the church. I paid my tithes and offering on every dime I've earned."

"And so what?" Bishop Jones asked hunching his shoulders. "That makes it right?"

Simmons let his gaze drop to the floor. "Not saying it's one hundred percent right, but I'm doing the best I can. I'm not ashamed to admit my finances were drowning. I was close to bankruptcy. I needed this money to dig my way out and to take care of my family. Fault me if you want, but I needed a miracle and there it was."

The bishop was thinking heavily. How could he ignore the financial help being shoved in his face? He needed a miracle too. Perhaps he'd been too aggressive with the expansion project. Perhaps the project was in order, and it was his faith in question. Perhaps this, perhaps that. Reality was that the expansion project was struggling financially, but he couldn't dare tell the deacons. He'd always led the congregation to bigger and better accomplishments. He couldn't dare fail them now, not after forty years in the ministry. Maybe this money was a solution to his problems. There was no need to ask God for money again. Why ask a question if the person already knew the answer and didn't want to hear it? God had never given him confirmation about doing the project from the beginning. Bishop had been on his own all along, which meant he had to make it happen without God's anointing. Hadn't been simple, but he was staying afloat. How could he ignore this lifeline? Desperation gripped him.

"Father, oh, Father," he wailed as Minister Simmons went silent. Bishop Jones felt a surge of energy gush through his weary body being fueled by both his anger with Simmons and curiosity about the drugs. He turned his back to the minister and shoved his hands down into his pants pockets. Moving slowly toward the door, he appraised the room. Flat-screen computers, a smart board for lecturing on each wall, fiberglass desks, towering bookshelves filled to capacity, and plush carpet which swallowed up his shoes with each step. The church had started and finished great things. The expansion project would be no different. It too would be completed.

The bishop pivoted his body half facing Minister Simmons. "Follow me."

"Where are we going?" Simmons questioned.

"To my office. We're going to talk more about this drug thing."

"Bishop, I'm tired. I should probably get home to my wife."

The bishop jerked his hands from his pockets and turned fully facing Minister Simmons. "You should have thought about your wife sooner. It's too late now, because we're talking this thing out tonight."

Simmons lifted both hands with his palms facing up. He surrendered to the bishop's demand and followed him in silence.

Chapter 18

Bishop Jones unlocked his office door, turned on the light, and planted himself in the chair behind his desk. Minister Simmons stopped a few feet in front of the bishop's desk.

"I've told you how the drug process works. I don't know what else you want me to tell you." Simmons hunched his shoulders up and down.

Bishop struggled to find balance between reprimanding with a heavy hand versus mentoring a young minister who was clearly misguided. Compassion compelled him to see beyond the flesh. If someone had helped Bishop in his early years, many mistakes could have been avoided. "Look, I don't condone what you've been doing, but I want to understand your situation. It's too bad you took this route to solve your problem."

"It's not what you think," Simmons replied glancing down at his watch.

"Really, well let me be the judge."

Simmons paced the floor and began spilling out a story layered with a tone of irritation. "The supplier is a guy I knew from college. He told me about the venture, and I got involved."

Sound of the minister's voice faded for Bishop Jones as the pangs of his money woes grew. He was committed to completing the multimillion dollar church expansion project. They'd secured most of the property but that was only one phase. $2 million was required to break ground.

Bishop had been sleeping with that number for months. Campaigns and various fundraisers had produced most of the funds, except $200,000.

"The money just rolls in," Simmons uttered.

Bishop Jones tussled with the notion. His spirit told him not to entertain the thought but his flesh and desperation spoke equally as loud, telling him not to pass up this one-time opportunity. His internal war raged as justification took center stage in his conscience.

Money coming into the church from Simmons's drug setup definitely wouldn't be a God-given miracle. But, perhaps, a manmade miracle could suffice. Bishop Jones shook his head, rebuking the temptation. Casting down the seed of temptation was his best and only option if he was going to triumph this round.

"That's how it happened. I'm not proud to say it, but my bills and needs were long and my money was short, real short. I was in trouble financially, and this was my opportunity to make some quick money. I'm doing it on a small scale. If need be, I could kick it up a notch and there would be more money to go around," Simmons said staring directly at Bishop Jones.

Bishop Jones swiveled his chair to the left and peered from the window, quickly breaking their visual connection for a few seconds. "Sit down, Simmons. You've paced the floor enough. You're making me dizzy."

Simmons shifted the watch on his wrist and stepped closer to the bishop's desk. "I really need to go."

The bishop slammed his heavy hand onto the top of his desk and jumped up. "I said sit down," he bellowed. Silence flooded the office. Simmons claimed a seat as Bishop Jones rose and pressed both knuckles against the desk. Simmons sat up with his spine straight and eyelids widened. Resolve rose in Bishop as he spoke, unencumbered. "I don't see how you can justify your behavior in this church," he shouted. His sharp stare threatened to slice Simmons in half.

"Fifty or sixty thousand dollars in just a few months is a lot of money. Like I said, I'm not proud of this but a man has to take care of home any way he can. I guess necessity is a powerful incentive."

Bishop Jones recognized the cry of necessity. It was a loud and constantly compelling voice which was crying out this second in the secret places of his mind. Could this be the financial breakthrough he'd been seeking? No didn't leap to the forefront. Bishop couldn't bask in self-righteousness knowing he was so close to falling into the same hole Simmons was wading in. Quick, interest-free, and steady money?

"Can I go?" Simmons said with a noticeable edge.

"Shhh, I'm thinking," Bishop fired at him.

Simmons interrupted Bishop again. "As for Jill, well, I made a mistake. Trust me when I tell you that. I love my—" His chirping cell phone cut him off. "Excuse me, Bishop. This is my wife." Simmons moved toward the door with his back to Bishop, and answered his phone.

Bishop stared at the back of Simmons's head for a few seconds then plopped into his seat. Moonlight lit up the blanket of darkness claiming the sky, summoning him to the window near his desk. He massaged his temples with the fingertips of both hands, desiring to pluck faithless images from his mind. Necessity continued warring with righteousness, but Bishop's spirit wasn't giving in.

He sighed and drew in a deep breath.

Escaping the torment pursuing him, he turned his whole body quickly from the window. His gaze fell squarely on the family photos lining his desk. He snatched up the picture frame displaying his grandson for the knockout blow. This expansion project had to work. His gaze lingered on his wife. She spoke to his heart like no other person could.

Bishop pounded his forehead with the heel of his hand thrice to silence his confusion. He set the frame down then planted both palms flat on top of the desk as he leaned in. "Let's wrap this up."

Minister Simmons whirled his body around facing the bishop. His eyeballs were bulging with one hand flailing in the air, pleading for Bishop to stop talking. "Honey, I've got to go. I promise; I'll be on my way home in just a few minutes."

Bishop's tenacity gurgled up out of his soul, plowing through boulders of worry labeled debt and insufficient capital. "Minister Simmons, this business of yours ends tonight. You need money and the church needs money. Still, it is never right to do the wrong thing even if it's for what appears to be a good reason. If money is an issue for you, we'll just have to deal with it."

Simmons took four brisk steps toward the bishop's desk. "But, money doesn't have to be an issue for either of us or the church," he said shrugging his shoulders.

Bishop thrust his body forward pointing his finger toward Simmons. "Stop. Stop, right now. Not another word." The bishop stepped from behind his desk.

"Okay, okay, I'll stop. But, I don't know that I can just cut it off like that," Simmons argued, snapping his fingers in the bishop's face. "I've got an awful lot of product to get rid of."

In two seconds, Bishop Jones was toe-to-toe with Simmons. He could see the twitching in the young minister's eye. "Get rid of it. I don't care how you do it. Flush the crap down the toilet; toss it in the Delaware River; give it back to your friend; or bury it in your backyard. Just get rid of it if you want to remain on staff here, and I'm not playing around," he scolded. "We are men of God." Simmons took a step back, creating a small amount of space between him and Bishop. "Act like it." Bishop drew in a loud breath that inflated his chest. He exhaled slowly speaking more deliberately. "Get a second job and streamline your expenses," he suggested. Absolutely exhausted, Bishop Jones retreated to his desk and dropped down into his chair. "I can bump up your salary an extra few thousand dollars. However, you have to figure out what it will take to live within your means."

"What about Jill? She's involved in this thing too," Simmons replied.

"You just do what it takes to terminate your end. I'll take care of her. And from now on keep your eyes and heart where it's supposed to be. If I find out about any more issues, you will be removed from the ministerial team." Simmons let his gaze slump. "We can't lead God's people if we are not allowing God to lead us. Do you understand, Minister?"

Simmons plucked his keys from his jacket pocket. "Yes, Bishop, I hear you."

"I need to hear you say the words."

"I'll put an end to the prescription med thing."

"Tonight, Minister Simmons."

"Tonight, Bishop; I'll do it tonight."

"Go home to your wife."

Simmons didn't respond. Bishop watched him take hurried steps to get out, glancing back with a blank stare.

Squeezing his eyelids tightly, Bishop Jones prayed aloud as the door closed shut, hoping Simmons was to be trusted with disbanding the drug operation. If not, Bishop wasn't worried. It was on God to handle the wayward young leader. He'd done his part by admonishing the minister. Bishop would have to rely on faith for the rest, just like he'd do with the expansion project. "Heavenly Father, give me the strength needed to continue resisting the devil's temptation. Help me to stand steadfast, my feet immovable from what I know to be right. Your Word and promise, I know to be true. If this expansion project is your will, then I am confident you will provide the necessary resources. Amen."

Bishop Jones lifted the picture frame from his desk again. Slowly, his thumb traced the curvature of his wife's face. God, his family, and his commitment to both would remain intact. He put the frame back in its rightful place next to his Bible. His cell phoned chimed as he turned out the light and locked his office door. "Sorry, I'm so late, sweetie. I'm on my way home," he told his wife and left. His body was worn out but his spirit was energized and leaping for joy.

Chapter 19

Just as Maxwell backed out his driveway, his cell phone rang. Who could possibly be calling him at daybreak on a Saturday morning? Garrett's name flashed across the screen. Maxwell answered eagerly. "Garrett, what's up, man? It must be something good if you're calling this early on the weekend. Talk to me."

"I thought twice about calling you before eight, but I knew you wouldn't want me to sit on some serious information."

"You know it. What's going on?"

"This is going to make your head spin. I know it's early but can you meet me at your office?"

"Yes," Maxwell exclaimed, pushing the heel of his hand into the steering wheel. "I'm already in the car. See you in twenty minutes." A warm sensation washed over Maxwell. It felt like satisfaction. His curiosity soared wondering what secrets Garrett had unearthed. Maxwell relaxed in his seat and leaned onto the armrest acknowledging that his short ride would most likely account for the only free minutes he'd get today. He decided to check his personal voicemails, which his tight schedule had forced him to completely ignore the day before. He fast-forwarded and deleted several messages, stopping when he heard Nicole's voice. He listened to half the content before deleting and making a mental note to call her later. He continued with the routine of fast-forwarding and deleting. None of the messages were pressing, until he got to the last one and it made him sit up straight.

"Uncle Max, my birthday is tomorrow. I'm having cake and ice cream and a party, too. You have to come, Uncle Max. You have to come." His nephew's voice melted away his staunch disposition.

The call continued. "Hey, Maxwell, this is Christine. Tyree wouldn't take no for an answer. He just had to call you. Does his determination remind you of anyone? His party is at six tomorrow, here at the house. I left you a message and we sent an invitation to your office since we don't have any other address for you. How crazy is that? I don't even know where my own brother lives because you are determined to keep us at a distance. Anyway, I haven't heard from you. I thought I would make one last attempt. Hope to see you. Take care."

He'd heard the messages from his sister but had ignored them. Over the years, that had grown fairly easy to do, but Tyree's voice sliced past the secure façade and went straight to Maxwell's heart.

Traffic whizzed by as Maxwell reflected on the last time he'd seen Tyree. It had been awhile and it was one of his few regrets. But he didn't want to get caught up with the expectations of regular visits and phone calls. Tyree was too young to understand but his mother knew very well what the issues were. The remainder of his ride to work was consumed by an internal struggle. He didn't want to disappoint his nephew, but what was he supposed to do? Irritation and compassion wrestled within him. He was confident that whatever news Garrett had was big and would most likely demand his undivided attention. That meant another long day and breaking up the momentum with a party didn't factor into Maxwell's agenda. He tried settling on that reason, but it didn't stick. Truth had a way of surfacing, regardless of how deep it had been buried.

Reality was that he didn't want to deal with his family, especially his father. Maxwell shook his head and pressed down on the accelerator. He watched his speedometer climb. Maybe he was trying to outrun his demons, yet they dogged him at every turn. The closer he got to the office, his domain, the more he was able to crush his spurts of emotional weakness.

Maxwell pulled into the parking lot next to Garrett's car. Minutes later they were upstairs in Maxwell's office behind closed doors. "Okay, what did you find out?" Maxwell asked sitting at his desk.

"Well, you were right. There are definitely some dirty dealings going on between Bishop Jones and Councilman Chambers. There have been over fifty property deeds filed in the name of Greater Metropolitan over the last eleven months alone and another thirteen last year. The properties were all sold way below market value." Garrett pressed his index finger down hard onto the desk as he repeated the words, "Way below."

Maxwell leaned forward planting his elbows into the desk. "I know he's tied up into something crooked. I can feel it," he said slapping his hand across the desk. "Snakes don't change; they just shed their worthless skin, and slither on toward their next victim," Maxwell said fixated on a paperclip he was twisting.

"I'm not following you," Garrett muttered.

Understandably so since Maxwell was speaking of the bishop's past sins, ones he'd never shared with Garrett and never would.

"Oh, excuse me. I'm basically thinking out loud and obviously making no sense. Let's get back to business," he said putting down the paperclip. "What else did you find out, because we'll need more," Maxwell told Garrett with narrowed eyes and a pinched brow.

"Not a problem. Most of the property was bought from small local business owners in the neighborhood like barber shops, hair salons, little food joints, and even a few small churches. I also found out Chambers told some of the business owners that the zoning laws were going to change and their leases would not be renewed. Instead of closing their businesses and selling their inventory at a loss, they opted to take the buyout offered. I've got to poke around a little more because I hear that Chambers is also involved with several more zoning violations." Garrett rubbed his hands together back and forth then announced, "Here's the best part." He paused, dangling the information carrot in front of Maxwell.

"What is it? Tell me."

"The title company that was used to broker all the deals is owned by Chambers' nephew." Garrett leaned back in his chair, pushed his fist into the palm of his left hand, pointed both forefingers at Maxwell and said, "There's the smoking gun."

Maxwell jumped up from his chair, walked around his desk and gave Garrett a high five. "I knew Chambers would live up to his reputation and that's going to work in our favor. You are worth every penny I'm paying you. How in the world did you get that information?" Maxwell began flailing his hands rapidly. "No, no, don't tell me. I don't need to know." Maxwell started pacing his office floor, talking aloud and rattling off the next few things he felt needed to happen. He snatched up a pad from his desk and created a list. He wrote almost as fast as he was talking. "We've got to get the names of those business owners and start interviewing them to find out just what the details were behind those shady deals." He stopped pacing for a moment. "Garrett, do you smell that?"

"What?"

"The stench of extortion, fraud, larceny, racketeering, coercion, and the list of possibilities is endless." Maxwell resumed pacing with increased energy. "You got to love the bishop. He's making this so easy for us. The beauty is that we don't have to trump up charges. There is a plethora waiting for us," Maxwell said, releasing a loud chuckle. "Garrett, all we need is a list of owners to get this show on the road."

Garrett stood up, reached inside his jacket pocket, and pulled out a white envelope, which he tossed onto the desk. "Relax, I've already got it." He reached over his left shoulder to pat himself on the back. "I guess I am worth the big bucks, huh?"

Maxwell grabbed the envelope, pulled out the paper and scoured every name from top to bottom. The excitement of what he was holding in his hands sent a rush of adrenaline through his body. He looked up at Garrett, snapped his fingers, and told him, "This is what I'm talking about. Man, you've just earned yourself a bonus." With unquenchable vigor, ideas flowed and inspired Maxwell to get moving. He shook Garrett's hand firmly. He walked Garrett to the elevator praising him for his investigative skills. "For the record, you can call me at six o'clock in the morning any day of the week, including Saturday, if you've got the goods like you had today."

"We'll see about that," Garrett uttered igniting humor in both of them before departing.

Chapter 20

"Thanks for coming in, Mr. Branson. I will be in touch with you if I need anything else." Maxwell stood up from his desk. He shook the man's hand and helped him with his overcoat.

"Mr. Montgomery, I worked a lot of years to build up my business. I poured my life into that barber shop. My dad handed it down to me, just like his dad handed it down to him. The day I put the OUT OF BUSINESS sign in the window and took down Branson and Son's Barber Shop, a part of my soul died." He pulled a handkerchief from his pants pocket and wiped at his eyes. "It just ain't right to take away a man's dreams and his way to make a living for his family. It ain't right I tell you."

"I understand," Maxwell said handing Mr. Branson his top hat, which was lying on the table. "It's hard to watch something be taken away from you that you don't want to let go of. But I can't stop this."

Walking toward the door, Mr. Branson turned and looked at Maxwell. "I wasn't the only one, you know. A lot of business owners had to sell and not because they wanted to. The city, Councilman Chambers, and I guess progress is what we have to blame." When he reached the office door, he turned again and stared at Maxwell. His face, etched with lines of despair, spoke the defeat. "I don't know why you're asking questions about a business deal that's already done. Still, I hope what I told you will help in some way. Maybe what's wrong can be made right."

"Sooner or later it generally is. I appreciate your coming in today. Take care of yourself." Maxwell watched him walk to the elevator. His stature, broad shoulders, strong voice, and the fact that he had been taken advantage of reminded him of his father. The thought of Paul Sr. flew right out of Maxwell's mind with the sharp ding the elevator made when the door opened.

Maxwell stepped out of his office doorway and called for Sonya. No answer. Further investigation deemed her nowhere in sight. From her desk, he buzzed his receptionist; she hadn't seen her either. Just as he was about to check the conference room, Sonya came rushing out front with two thick law books and a stack of documents in her arms.

"Yes, Mr. Montgomery. Did you need something?" she asked, setting the books and documents down onto her desk.

"When is my next appointment?"

Sonya spun the day planner on her desk around to face her. "Let's see. Mr. Branson was the fourth person on the list you gave me. Ms. Fricks is next and she will be in at one-thirty. You've got just enough of a break to eat a quick bite. Would you like me to order you some lunch?"

"I'll pass. I'm going downstairs to get a cup of coffee. I'll be right back." Maxwell took the stairs. He didn't have time to wait for the elevator. Standing in the line at the coffee shop, he was forced to inhale the sweet perfume of the woman standing in front of him. She ordered a Frappuccino, paid the cashier, and swiftly made her exit. Her thick hair bounced on her shoulders as she walked away. He glossed over the implications having no room for carnal attractions. Besides, Nicole's ultimatum was more than enough to handle.

As Maxwell waited for his coffee, a familiar voice hooked him, forcing him to turn around and face the flat-screen TV in the corner. Maxwell listened while watching Bishop Jones's lips form his words in front of a small group of onlookers.

"We as a community have to do something to provide a safe haven for our youth. Once they've made a mistake, been to prison, a detention center or wherever, we have to welcome them into the fold with open arms and options. I am working on a project right now which will provide support, direction, and training for our youth. This will get them what they need and put them on the right track. I am committed to doing whatever it takes to get this project off the ground."

Maxwell watched the crowd erupt with cheers and applauses.

"Sir," the cashier repeated until Maxwell acknowledged him. "Your coffee is ready."

Maxwell shook off the paralyzing hold Jones's words had cast over him. He paid for his coffee and headed upstairs. His meetings with Garrett's list of people were going well. Maxwell was anxious to hear what the next person had to say. He took the stairs and extended his break since it wasn't quite one-thirty. When he reached the waiting area, the sweet-smelling woman from the coffee shop was sitting in one of the leather chairs. Trying not to wear his surprise so prominently, he stopped at Sonya's desk to ask if there were any calls.

"No, Mr. Montgomery, but your one-thirty appointment is a little early." Sonya stood up and waved her hand in the direction of the woman. "That's Ms. Fricks."

Maxwell approached her and extended his hand. "Ms. Fricks, thank you for coming in today. If you will give me just a few minutes, I will be right with you."

"Not a problem, Mr. Montgomery. Take your time," she responded.

***

Maxwell shuffled through the mail Sonya handed him and gave her instructions regarding a package he was expecting. Then he invited Ms. Fricks inside his office and closed the door after she entered. "Have a seat, Ms. Fricks. I'll get right to the point. I'm working on some zoning issues in the business district and could use your help."

"I'll help if I can," she replied.

"I understand you used to own a beauty shop that was sold earlier this year." She nodded in affirmation. "Would you mind telling me about your business and why you decided to sell?" Maxwell wanted to stay as close to the truth as he could without giving away too much information about his motive.

"How much time do you have?"

"Excuse me?" Maxwell said.

"I can tell you exactly why I ended up selling my business. And, it didn't have anything to do with my wanting to sell it. That sneaky, low-down Councilman Chambers is the reason. When I found out how much I could have gotten for my property, it makes me sick." She pushed out a windy sigh, closed her eyes, counted to three, and started talking again. "I was told the zoning laws were changing for my business, and I would no longer be in the right area to do hair. He also told me the city was working on a major reconstruction project that could take the land my business was sitting on whether I agreed or not."

"Did he say how?"

"He was going on and on about eminent germain."

"You mean domain," Maxwell said.

"What?"

"Eminent domain, the government's ability to take your land if it's deemed necessary for the commonwealth," he clarified.

"You sound like you know what you're talking about, throwing all those big words around. I guess it could have been domain. Germain, domain, doesn't make a difference to me. Either way, my land is gone."

"Is that right?"

"Yes indeed," she retorted, clearly agitated. "You don't think I'm lying do you?" she bellowed.

"No, of course not," Maxwell replied even more intrigued.

"Humph, I get mad just thinking about the whole business. Councilman Chambers said he was doing me a favor by giving me a heads-up on what the city was planning. I don't know, maybe it was all on the up and up. But I do know that I should have gotten more money for my property."

Maxwell listened intently while drawing a red line through her name on the list. He leaned on the arm of his chair and rested his right ankle on top of his left knee. He soaked in every single word that she so willingly hurled out.

Chapter 21

Garrett had done just what Maxwell asked of him. He'd made the investigation of Bishop Jones his highest priority. He was thorough, which was why Garrett was sitting in the parking lot of Greater Metropolitan on a Sunday morning. He'd already attended a couple social events and a Bible class at the church. His assessment would not be complete without attending a Sunday morning service.

He sat in his car watching the mass of people flow into the huge parking lot. Men in orange jackets waving flashlights directed the heavy traffic. Fancy suits, pricey cars, flashy pocket books, and oversized church hats paraded past him. Garrett reached for the Bible lying on his car seat, the one he'd gotten from a thrift store for fifty cents yesterday. He couldn't remember when he'd last opened one, but he thought it would help him appear to fit in. He got out of his car and walked toward the church, allowing himself to blend in with the group of people walking in front of him.

Once inside, he was greeted warmly by the usher at the door. "Praise God, and good morning," she offered cheerfully, handing him a program of the day's service. "Step right in and one of the young folks inside will seat you. Enjoy the service. We're glad to have you with us."

Garrett lifted his hand and walked right past the person who tried directing him inside. He strategically chose his own seat in the rear of the church opting for an unobstructed view of the crowd. Garrett subtly gazed around taking in the high ceiling, stained glass windows, and the overflowing choir stand, complete with an organ, piano, and a small orchestra. A soft, melodious, unfamiliar sound beckoned for his attention. In the far right corner, a harp and flute came to life with a duet that silenced the whispers and chatter. It wasn't long before every seat was full and the church exploded with the choir singing several songs highlighted with a solo performance.

Bishop Jones entered from the side door and went to the platform. Jones hadn't been seated twenty minutes before three people had whispered in his ear. A fourth person handed him an envelope. Garrett turned to the young lady sitting next to him. "Excuse me, how long have you been a member here? You are a member, right?"

"Absolutely; I've been a member here about nine years."

"I hear that Bishop Jones is a good man." Garrett turned his head in her direction awaiting a response.

"He is. I mean, I haven't had any up close and personal time with him, because the church is so big. But, he's a good pastor," she said.

Garrett wanted to check out the church a little bit while people were engrossed in the service. "Would you mind saving my seat for me, please? I need to step out just for a few minutes."

"Sure, no problem," the young lady said without turning her head to look at him.

A silver-haired woman walked up to the end of the aisle they were sitting in. Her white-gloved hands flopping at the wrist captured both the young lady's and Garrett's attention. She pressed her index finger against her lips and thrust a thick shhh at them both.

Garrett felt duly admonished. Not having been to church in years, he'd forgotten it was a cardinal sin to talk in church. He lifted his hand in front of his mouth and motioned that he was locking his lips and throwing away the key. He waited a couple of minutes after the usher walked away then got up and made his way from the sanctuary.

Bishop Jones was about to start his sermon, and by the glare Garrett received from the usher when he stepped out the sanctuary, he figured out that movement wasn't appreciated while the pastor was preaching. Garrett asked for directions to the men's room. He didn't think snooping around would raise alarms. Garrett went inside, washed his hands, and stopped by the water fountain a few feet away. The lobby was empty. Surprisingly, he must have been the only one roaming aimlessly. Everyone else must have known better. Around the corner, however, he heard two male voices, one fused with anger.

"I'm not a magician. I can't get it done. I've tried. I don't know what else to do. I'm out of options."

"Well, you better dig down deeper into your little bag of tricks. The bishop is not going to be happy if you can't deliver. You can bet that if you can't make it happen, Minister Simmons will be the next person up to bat. He's not going to let the bishop down under any circumstances. You need to make it happen. I've got to get back to the service. I'll talk to you later."

Garrett moved briskly, careful not to make a sound. He entered the men's room and closed the door gently. He waited a few seconds then walked out the bathroom hoping to see the man whose voice he'd heard. No luck; he must have gone a different way. Garrett peeked around the corner where he'd heard the voices. The hallway was quiet and empty. He returned to the sanctuary and reclaimed his seat, nodding at the young lady who'd safeguarded it for him. Garrett sat quietly, giving Bishop Jones's sermon only half his attention while his eyes roamed the room.

Forty minutes and a countless number of amens later, Bishop Jones asked the congregation to stand as he gave the benediction. The still quiet that had washed over the sanctuary was rinsed away by voices and people filing out the moment Bishop Jones said, "Amen."

Garrett watched Bishop Jones close his Bible and tuck it under his arm. Another usher handed the bishop a glass of water and a fresh handkerchief. A bright-skinned man with a stocky build walked up to the bishop, dismissed the usher, and then leaned in close. Garrett wondered what was being whispered as he handed Bishop an envelope. The crowd was moving slowly. Garrett was just about to reach the end of the row and step out into the aisle when he lightly touched the elbow of the young lady who had sat next to him.

"Who is that man talking to Bishop Jones?" he asked glancing toward the platform.

"Oh, that's Minister Simmons, one of our newer leaders."

"I see." Garrett's eyes were glued to Minister Simmons as he made a mental note to check him out.

"Thanks for holding my seat," Garrett chimed shuffling along behind the young lady.

"You're lucky," she whispered. "I was holding the seat for my friend, Sonya. Guess she slept in today," the young lady said peering into the crowd. "Her boss keeps her shackled to her desk. She's probably at the law firm downtown working right now."

"I know a Sonya," Garrett stated.

"Sonya Gaithers?"

"No, I guess there is more than one Sonya in Philly." Garrett released the lie into the air. He clutched the edge of the pew as he walked past the stragglers, determined not to bolt through the thick crowd of people to share his discovery.

Chapter 22

Nicole turned onto Maxwell's street. His house sat at the end of the block, and it was clearly in her view. She took her foot off the gas pedal allowing her car to crawl along. She rolled into the long driveway and pushed the gear shift into park. Peering into the lighted mirror over her visor, Nicole brushed the front of her hair with her fingertips and pushed the longer strands behind her ear. She touched up her lipstick and folded the visor back into place. Five minutes passed and Nicole kept sitting in her car contemplating how to best broach the relationship conversation again. She didn't want to seem pushy or come across as a needy woman. Though, she did need something more from Maxwell than he had given in the past. Sitting in her car was ridiculous. There was only one way to deal with Maxwell and that was directly. She got out.

When the doorbell rang, Maxwell pressed down hard onto the top of the ink pen in his hand leaving an imprint on his thumb. He sat quietly and didn't move. He knew it was Nicole. She'd called earlier. The doorbell rang a second time, and he released the ink pen letting it drop onto his stack of papers. It was getting late, and he really wasn't at a good stopping point. She had been adamant about seeing him tonight. There was no cordial way to abruptly send Nicole on her way. He had to see what she wanted. Perhaps then he could return to his business undisturbed.

Maxwell emerged from his home office and ambled through the house as the buzzer rang repeatedly. With no hint of urgency, he eventually reached the front door and opened it to find Nicole standing there holding a shopping bag, lovely as ever. His disposition relaxed seeing her after nearly a month apart. "Well, hello, stranger," he greeted as he gave her tall frame an attentive once-over.

Nicole walked up close, leaving no distance between them and folded her arms around his neck. She held him tightly without confessing a word. "Took you long enough to open the door."

"I know, and I'm sorry. I was tied up with work." He reciprocated with a tight hug and then planted a kiss on her lips. "Come on inside," he told her reaching for the shopping bag she had in her hand.

"That's something I picked up for you when I was in Italy. Open it," Nicole insisted as she slid her jacket off.

"I didn't realize you'd gone out of the country, especially after that crazy flight a few weeks ago."

"I've spent most of my career on planes. I can't let one bad experience keep me bound in fear," she said touching his shoulder. Nicole sat on the edge of the sofa, next to Maxwell as he peeled away the wrapping paper. "It's not fragile. Just rip off the paper." She bit her bottom lip while strumming her fingers on the sofa cushion as Maxwell finally opened the box's lid exposing the engraved briefcase. She'd spent an entire afternoon looking for just the right one made from the best leather Italy had to offer. "I hope you like it."

"It's nice," he told her rubbing his hand over the name plate with the initials M. M. prominently displayed. "Thank you. I really do like it."

"I'm glad you're pleased," she said sliding her fingers over the supple black leather. She pried the briefcase from his hand and pulled his arm around her waist.

She'd missed him more over the last few weeks than she ever had before. The nagging tug inside had become commonplace.

"Maxwell, we need to talk," she whispered in his ear as though she didn't want anyone else to hear. She pinched her eyelids shut tightly, kissed Maxwell on the cheek, and then relinquished her hold on him. She stared into his gaze. "I don't like the way we left things a few weeks ago." She'd laced her fingers into his.

"We're fine. The airplane ordeal had you a little edgy that night. Don't worry about it."

"It was more than that. My priorities have changed. I want something more than just a great career. I'm tired of my constant companion being the work I take home every night." Nicole glanced away from Maxwell, swallowed the sharp bite in her voice and modestly asked, "Can we finish the conversation we started at the restaurant? We just left things up in the air. I have to know where our relationship is headed." She nestled into the corner of the sofa, not sure what to expect.

"Things between us have always been smooth. No bumps. We haven't pushed or pulled each other. Things have gone along fine. We've both been comfortable with what we have. I still don't see the need to redefine who we are to each other," he told her and slid away.

"The truth is we've both been complacent," Nicole retorted. "But that's over. I'm simply not satisfied with what we have. That's not hard to understand. It's not like we just started dating last year. Relationships progress; they go to the next level," Nicole stated firmly with her eyelids widened and both palms turned up toward the ceiling.

"Nicole, I can't tell the future any more than you can. What I know right now is that I'm working on a case that consumes me. That's not going to change anytime soon.

I've invested, what feels like, a lifetime getting to the brink of something this big. I can't risk being distracted. I have got to stay on track." He rested his arm across the back of the sofa allowing his fingertips to brush over Nicole's hand. "You've always understood my business."

"A distraction? That's what I am to you, a distraction?" she shouted, standing up and walking over to the stone-framed fireplace. She picked up a crystal scale Maxwell received from the Mid-Atlantic Legal Association. The scale was balanced to the right side of justice. He was focused; the award said so. He'd been nothing but focused since she'd met him. Didn't he want more than work? Didn't every sane person at some point? Nicole swung her body around like a spinning top to face him.

"I'm sorry; I didn't mean to call you a distraction. I just meant we're both really busy." Maxwell went to Nicole as she returned the award to its spot on the mantle. "You know I care for you, right?" He lifted her chin with his fingertip forcing their gazes to connect.

"What I know for sure is that I want a relationship with a future. I want to know we're working toward a commitment." She wanted her words to be firm and not soggy with emotion. Yet, her feelings were pouring over each word with frustration and sentiment starting to prick at her tear ducts, but not for long. Nicole was intent on staying poised. "Maxwell, if this relationship isn't going anywhere, maybe we need to end it. There's no sense in wasting time. God knows we're both too busy for that, right?"

Maxwell drew Nicole into his arms. "Let's take a breath to think about this before we make any heavy decisions."

The antique grandfather clock chimed eleven times signaling the end of this round. It was another draw, with no winner declared. Nicole didn't have any idea what was next for her and Maxwell. She retreated to a neutral position, breaking his hold on her. Nicole walked past the arm of the sofa and swooped up her jacket with no pause in her stride. Without looking back, she hurled two empty words at Maxwell: "Good night."

Chapter 23

It was the middle of the week and Maxwell was working from home. He was hard at work though his day had gotten off to a slow start. He hadn't gone for his morning jog yet which had him slightly out of sorts. Many of his great legal strategies had been birthed on the jogging path. On his way to the kitchen for a second cup of coffee, his cell phone rang drawing Maxwell back to his office. Two more rings and he grabbed the phone from his desk without looking at the caller ID. "Maxwell speaking."

"Hey, it's Garrett. Can you meet me?"

"Sure, what's going on? You sound anxious."

"We need to talk. Things are heating up. What time should I swing by the office?" Garrett asked.

"I'm at home today."

"Maxwell Montgomery, taking a day off. That's a shocker."

"It's not a day off, believe me. I woke up with a headache that just subsided a couple hours ago. I'm trying to get some work done now, but give me an idea of what's going on."

"Let's just say secrets are crawling out of their hiding places."

"Wow, how soon can you be here?"

"I'm on my way."

Maxwell pressed down on the end button hard and walked to the window in his office. He squinted at the bright sunlight that poured into the room as he opened the blinds. His gaze stretched past the patio, across the lawn, landing on his pool. It wasn't used much, but Maxwell enjoyed the clear water dancing with colors painted by the sun. As the water fought against the sides of the pool, Maxwell felt a legal storm brewing. He stared out the window another few minutes then hurried upstairs and took a quick shower.

Just as Maxwell fastened the last button on his collared shirt, the doorbell rang. He slipped on his brown leather loafers and went downstairs to answer the door. "Come in, Garrett. You weren't kidding when you said you were on your way."

"Time is money. Isn't that what you always tell me?"

"I guess I do. It's something I used to hear my father say often." Maxwell briefly caught himself thinking about the past, about his father, and pulled himself out of the cloud called yesterday. "Let's go into the kitchen. Would you like some coffee?"

"Sure, coffee will definitely work." On their way to the kitchen Garrett pointed at a painting hanging over the fireplace. "Is this new?"

"Man, you don't miss anything."

"That's my job," Garrett replied while chuckling.

"It's a John Holyfield original. Let's just say it was a trophy for winning the case against Reverend Morgan."

"Sweet."

"Have a seat." Maxwell poured Garrett a cup of coffee and placed it on a coaster in front of him. "Now, what's going on? What secrets were you referring to earlier?"

"Actually, I'd like to hear how your meetings with the folks on the list have been going. Then what I have to tell you will be even sweeter."

Maxwell rubbed his index finger underneath his chin. "Really, okay, okay, I'll go along for the ride. This must really be good," he said taking a sip of his coffee. "Okay, well, I met with the last person on the list yesterday. My hunch was right. There is no doubt that the expansion of Greater Metropolitan has come at the expense of landowners who were swindled out of fair market value." Maxwell became restless. He got up and paced the floor as he told Garrett the details. "The first former landowner used to live right next to the church. He lost his lot and adjoining restaurant due to an alleged rezoning project. Everyone I spoke with had basically the same story. They were forced out. Rezoning swallowed up all the small businesses."

"What's your gut telling you about this project?" Garrett took a gulp of his coffee.

Maxwell slapped his palms together. "Councilman Chambers is behind this. I know it, but where's the paper trail leading to him or the bishop?" Maxwell poured another cup of coffee and leaned against the breakfast bar, crossing his ankles. "We've officially got grounds for a legal battle, but we've got to establish a strategy." He set his cup down after taking a sip.

"Let's do it," Garrett interjected.

"I'll start by recruiting the landowners and pitch them on a class action lawsuit."

"There is strength in numbers," Garrett stated.

"True, but the more people we get involved the more things can go wrong."

"Looks like it's a risk you'll have to take on this one."

"Looks like it." Maxwell took another sip of coffee, cautiously tasting victory on the horizon. "Okay, so tell me what you have?" Maxwell asked as he regained a seat at the kitchen table across from Garrett.

"The information is hot; fire and brimstone, man, fire and brimstone." Maxwell could barely contain himself, like a starving dog waiting to be fed. Garrett continued. "You know I spent some time over the last few weeks checking out Greater Metropolitan and some of the bishop's staff. I attended a few church events including Sunday morning worship." Garrett flipped open a leather portfolio. "One of the ministers, Simmons, is definitely someone we want to know more about. I found out one of the six positions on the pastoral staff will be vacant soon. He wants to be promoted to assistant pastor. Simmons definitely has his eyes on the prize." Garrett stabbed the notepad with his ink pen. "From what I can tell, he's willing to do anything to get it. I overheard two men talking at the church about the bishop needing something done. If they weren't able to make it happen, they said Simmons would get it done."

"Simmons, huh? I haven't heard much about him," Maxwell stated.

"Well, there's plenty you need to know." Garrett pulled a five-by-seven photo of Simmons from his portfolio and pushed it across the table to Maxwell. "He's been spending a lot of time with this single mother named Jill. From what I can tell, she has two young boys. She's on disability for some type of back injury and started attending Greater Metropolitan about six months ago. That's all I have right now, but you can believe I will get more very soon."

Maxwell slapped his palms together hard, making a loud noise. "I can see it all coming together," Maxwell exclaimed.

"There's one more thing I discovered that you should know." Maxwell perked up listening closely. "I think you might want to take a closer look at the folks you have on staff."

"What are you talking about?" Garrett closed his portfolio and leaned forward on the table with his arms folded. "Spit it out, man. What are you trying to tell me?" Maxwell demanded.

Garrett slumped hard in the chair and released the revelation. "Your paralegal is a member of Greater Metropolitan Church."

Chapter 24

Maxwell surveyed the row of brick buildings as he parked in front of one. He pulled his sleeve up to see his watch. It wasn't quite four o'clock yet. Garrett was usually early. Maxwell leaned his head against the headrest and closed his eyes. His body was weary as his thoughts continued running a marathon in his mind. What was the next move? Had he missed anything in drafting the documents that would be the cornerstone of his case against the bishop? Was there someone else he should talk with who he didn't yet know about? His thoughts began overtaking him. He couldn't become overwhelmed and overlook key details. Not a single fact could be dropped on this case. Every drop of information had to be recorded. Maxwell took both hands and pulled them slowly down his face, tossing out the concern that plagued him.

The sound of a car door slamming behind Maxwell drew his gaze toward the rearview mirror. He got out of his car and walked toward Garrett while loosening his tie slightly.

"Glad you could meet me on such short notice," Garrett said.

"This is too important not to make myself available. You say the word day or night, and I'm there," Maxwell affirmed. "So, what do you have for me?"

Garrett stepped onto the curb. "Remember those dilapidated buildings you found out Bishop Jones and

Chambers were so concerned about? Well, here they are."
Garrett pointed at a row of buildings. "That multilevel
one, the second one from the corner is going to be a
low-income housing unit." Garrett stretched out his arm
and pointed his index finger at the building garnering
Maxwell's attention. "The other brick building on the
corner is earmarked as a safe haven for children on the
street."

"That's all good, but there has to be something strange
going on here," Maxwell commented.

"What do you mean?" Garrett asked.

"I can see one or two buildings but the whole block?
Look at the buildings in this area, not a decent one in the
bunch. Jones will have to throw a boatload of cash at this
to get these buildings renovated."

"Funny you should say that. Word on the street is
that he is totally committed to this project. Apparently,
he wants to restore the community around his church.
Maybe his intentions aren't all bad," Garrett suggested
pushing his hands down into his pants pockets.

"You can't be serious. The only thing Jones is sincerely
concerned with is how quickly he can get his mega
ministry vision completed, and how deep he can line his
pockets in the process."

"Whatever the driving force is for him, he's pressing
his way forward. He's doing whatever it takes to make it
happen. He's already filed the necessary paperwork with
the city to classify the units as low-income housing and a
safe haven for troubled youth on the street. Both are key
buzzwords for this community. He's bound to get funding
and get this project off the ground. Of course, the zoning
for both has to be approved. Somehow, I doubt that will
present a problem for the bishop," Garrett told Maxwell
staring at the properties again.

"He definitely knows somebody, and I doubt if it's God." Maxwell walked across the street with Garrett following. He walked up the front steps of the building that would be the low-income housing unit. He turned the doorknob and pushed, but the locked door wouldn't allow him entrance. Maxwell yanked the tie from around his neck. He unbuttoned the top of his shirt and turned to Garrett. "I refuse to believe there is any goodwill or genuine civic duty driving this project. I need you to dig deeper. There has got to be deeper reason for his trumped-up interest in this housing concept and a safe haven or safe house, whatever it is he wants to call it. I want to know what that reason is. I want to know everything about Bishop Ellis Jones." Maxwell pressed two fingers together, keeping them just a fraction of an inch apart. "As a matter of fact, I want you to be so explicit with the details surrounding Jones that you can tell me what he had for breakfast yesterday and the last words he said to his wife before they went to bed last night."

"Okay, I got you, man. I got you," Garrett said surrendering and lifting both palms into the air.

"Maybe Bishop Jones is getting government subsidies for the buildings. Federal funds and government fraud means automatic prosecution." Excitement clung to Maxwell's words and hung in the air. His gaze widened as he nodded up and down.

"That's a great angle to check out," Garrett stated.

"I wouldn't put that past the good bishop at all. Do what you do, my friend. Do what you do best. I'm counting on you." Maxwell patted Garrett on the shoulder as they walked down the steps and toward their cars. He looked back at the buildings envisioning when the walls would come tumbling down around Bishop Jones. Maxwell would be right there, up close to witness the reaction.

Maxwell drove to his office and picked up some files he'd forgotten. The workday was probably over for most folks in his building, but not for him. He would go home, kick off his shoes, and keep working on the case. Just as he was locking the door, a voice from behind paralyzed him.

"Hi, Mr. Montgomery," Sonya greeted him as she walked closer.

Maxwell squeezed the keys in his hand so hard, they left ridged imprints in the palm of his hand. He turned responding, "What are you doing here?"

"I'm feeling much better now. That bout with the stomach flu almost had me out. I wanted to come in this evening and get a jump on my work, since I'm sure there's plenty to catch up on."

"No, you won't." His voice was cold. His words were firm. "Let's step into the office for a minute. We need to talk, and it won't take long." Maxwell didn't wait for her response. He unlocked the door without turning on the lights and walked straight to his office. Only the security auxiliary lights and fading daylight lit the pathway.

Sonya followed Maxwell quietly. He placed his briefcase and keys on top of his desk. "Have a seat," he told Sonya firmly, gesturing toward the chair in front of his desk. Maxwell traipsed the window and stared at people and traffic moving below. He wanted to calm himself before starting the conversation that had been simmering for days. He wondered if she would lie about her membership at Greater Metropolitan. Had she been a spy for Jones all along and just playing him in the process? He had to know.

Maxwell approached Sonya. He stopped at the corner of his desk and stood behind it singeing her with his piercing stare. "I don't believe in beating around the bush. I'm sure you know that much about me." She nodded in affirmation. "So, how long have you been a member of Bishop Jones's church?" Maxwell kept his gaze locked, daring her to look away.

Sonya's feet appeared to be pressed hard against the floor. Her hands dropped from the arm of the chair into her lap. He watched as she laced her fingers together, digging her nails into the back of each hand. "Mr. Montgomery, I've only been a member there for a little over a year. I wanted to tell—"

Maxwell cut her words off with the firm down stroke of his hand to the desk. "Do you think I'm a fool? You work in my firm, which gives you privileged access to information. You know I'm mounting a case against the pastor, and you've never said anything to me about your affiliation there. You didn't think your membership at Greater Metropolitan would be of interest to me?" Maxwell placed both hands on the desk. Supporting his weight with his fingertips, he leaned closer to Sonya. "Just recently, I even reminded you of our confidentiality agreement. What have you told Jones? And you better not even try to lie."

Sonya's bottom lip quivered with her futile attempt to respond. A confession erupted. "I didn't know in the beginning. Honestly, I didn't. By the time you told me you would be investigating Greater Metropolitan, I was afraid to tell you about my membership." She sniffed hard and wiped at both eyes with the heels of her hands. "Somehow, I felt like my job would be in jeopardy if I told you. So, I just started looking for another church. I was going to tell Greater Metropolitan that I'd be moving my membership. Then I decided the best thing to do was just leave quickly and quietly."

Her explanation sounded plausible. He gained composure. "Sonya, you still should have told me. I rely on honesty and full disclosure from the people who work for me. It's not acceptable for you to keep something this important from me," Maxwell chided. He felt the veins in his temples pulsating.

She stood up and her words were hard to decipher through the tears and emotion stuck in her throat. "Please, Mr. Montgomery, don't fire me. I've left many churches since I started working for you. Every time I join a church, and start to feel like I can get comfortable there, you start investigating them."

Maxwell felt sorry for her, because he suspected she'd be looking indefinitely for a good church, if there was such a beast.

"I grew up in the church. It's an important part of me. I just keep choosing the wrong one. I've never even had a conversation with Bishop Jones about anything. His membership is so big. Most members never interact with him personally. Please believe me; I would never ever betray you in any way. I need this job. My nephew is ill, and I want to help my sister financially. Please, please don't fire me." She wiped the tears from her now-puffy eyes only to have them followed by another stream of salty water.

He was touched. Maxwell reached across his desk and handed her the box of tissue. The knowledge of her ill nephew pricked at his heart. He thought about Tyree. He also thought about the impact that his pursuit of corrupt churches had on Sonya without realizing it. But in essence, he had done her a favor. Maxwell was about to do her one more favor.

"Stop crying, Sonya."

"I can't help it. I really don't want you to think that I'm disloyal. I don't know what I'll do if I lose this job." She pressed her fingers against the corners of her eyes preventing the forming tears from falling. Sonya then pulled two tissues from the box and blew her nose.

"Relax; I'm not going to fire you. But, understand me, and understand me good. I will not accept anything remotely resembling disloyalty, conflict of interest, half-truths or nondisclosure in the future. Let's be clear, you will be terminated immediately. Look, I'm not trying to give you a hard time. I just have to be sure there is no cause to doubt you."

"No cause," she echoed and hugged him quickly. "Thank you, thank you so much. I won't let you down. Oh, yes, I'm considering checking out Pastor Renaldo Harris's church, Faith Temple. He's not on your hit list is he?" Sonya giggled. "I'm sorry. I mean he's not on your list to be investigated is he?"

Maxwell let out a light snicker. "No, he's not yet but join at your own risk." He was pretty sure Sonya was being honest and hadn't been planted in his office by Bishop Jones. Besides, Garrett had already checked her out thoroughly once he found out she was a member of Jones's church. Although nothing detrimental was discovered, Maxwell felt justified in confronting her. She had to know how much value he placed on loyalty and trust. He was certain she'd gotten the message.

Chapter 25

Maxwell's drive home was quick since it was late and the evening rush hour traffic had long died off. Once inside the house, he tossed his briefcase, keys, and suit jacket onto the leather chaise in the corner of the living room. He sank into the oversized sofa and folded his hands behind his head. Tranquility was elusive. Maxwell was very anxious about having so much mounting evidence against the bishop, but he hadn't come up with a real headlining theme yet. He tossed and turned on the sofa. Every piece of evidence, every clue that led to another investigative opportunity, and every conversation with each landowner flashed through Maxwell's mind like a slide show. He couldn't decide whether to make the civil case surrounding the land scheme or press the prosecutor for criminal charges.

For a few minutes, he thought about what his father went through years ago. An innocent man behind bars, his livelihood, family, and reputation all ripped away. Maxwell swung his fist hard into the air. He had enough to build both a civil and criminal case. The more he pondered, the more agitated he became. Why did he have to choose? He'd go after it all. Bishop Jones would have to pay for his sins. His reputation would have to be destroyed just like Maxwell's father's had been. He wanted revenge. Lying there, he imagined the rage in the bishop's eyes. Maxwell could see the humiliation painted on the bishop's face as the criminal courtroom echoed "Guilty" and the civil case resulted in "We find in favor of the plaintiff". Jubilations washed over Maxwell's body. The wrinkles on his forehead faded, and he stopped clenching his teeth. His breathing slowed down as he fell asleep.

The third ring of the doorbell summoned Maxwell from his peaceful nap. His eyelids popped open, and he peered at his watch. He'd been asleep for about thirty-five minutes. The doorbell rang again with Maxwell panning around the room a little groggy. He rubbed his eyes and released a wide-mouthed yawn. He peeked through the long side panel of beveled glass next to the door. Nicole stood there with her cell phone out. Maxwell opened the door.

"I was just about to call you. I've been ringing your doorbell for over five minutes. Are you okay?" Nicole gently touched his face allowing her fingertips to slide down along the frame of his jaw and then over the curve of his bottom lip. She stepped into his space and planted a soft peck onto his lips.

"Hey, yeah, I'm okay; I just fell asleep for a minute on the sofa. Come on in; sorry I kept you standing outside."

Nicole took hold of Maxwell's hand, squeezed it, and led him over to the sofa where they both sat. "How have you been?" she asked.

"Fine, just busy; you know how it goes." Maxwell wasn't fully alert. With the strain between him and Nicole, he didn't know what to say even if he had been fully alert. He'd have to stumble along. "You look nice. Were you out of town?"

"Yes, I was actually. I stopped by here before going home. I was hoping we could talk again. We haven't spoken since my last visit."

"I guess so."

Her eyes fell away from his as she caressed the backside of his hand. "Well, you know, we both needed space to think." Her eyes darted back to his while a few moments of silence made the short distance between them feel like a valley to Nicole.

"I haven't really been able to think about much of anything other than work."

"Come on, Maxwell, that's exactly what I'm talking about. You can't live your life with work being your only interest. There are some rewards that can never be attained through a career, no matter how much you invest. That is just not the way life is designed." Nicole traced the edge of his hairline with her finger and kissed his cheek. "I've learned that myself over the last few weeks. I want my life's legacy to be more than a six- or seven-figure salary and a slew of awards." She glanced at his award sitting on the mantle.

Maxwell got up and pulled a large brown folder out of his briefcase. "I really can't do this right now. I'm tied up on a big case and that's not going to change anytime soon. I should be working right now." Saved by his ringing cell phone, Maxwell held up his index finger and said, "Give me just a few minutes. I need to take this call. I'm sorry." He walked down the hall and into his office.

Nicole's eyes scanned the room, taking in the assortment of beautiful things. She especially admired the cathedral ceilings and the glossy black piano, which was showcased in the open space just above the living room in the loft area. Each piece of art, sculpture, and painting represented something or made some type of statement. The fact that Nicole didn't see one single family photo in Maxwell's home or his office also made a statement. She was forced to wonder why he was so empty inside. Was he incapable of feeling or wanting anything on a personal level? What stripped away the tenderness from his heart? There had to be something that prevented him from thirsting for anything other than the next win in the courtroom.

Maxwell returned. "I'm really sorry about the interruption. It was business, and I just couldn't put it off."

She took one more look at the award sitting on the mantle then stood up and went to Maxwell. "I guess work is the only thing you are willing to be fully committed to. The only real thing you can give all of yourself to and not hold back on any level." Maxwell looked away. "I know I can't change that about you. And, I guess I don't really want to. It's who you are and unfortunately I have to accept that." She stepped closer to him, as close as she could possibly get. Nicole wrapped her arms around his neck and nestled her face against his cheek. She inhaled, slowly, drawing in one last whiff of him, not wanting to let go. "We're not traveling the same path. We don't want the same things." Her eyes burned, so she squeezed her lids together tightly. "That makes me sad, but it is what it is." She blew out an elongated exhaled. "I wish you well. I hope one day there will be someone truly special in your life." She released her hold on him. "You deserve more than a stack of folders to spend your evenings with." Nicole pressed her lips against his briefly. She walked away from him without another word and without waiting for any response he had to offer.

Maxwell followed her to the door in silence. Dignity ushered Nicole to the door and she left without resistance. He closed the door pressing his hand against the frame as the other was holding on to the knob. Maxwell thought about the day he'd met Nicole. They'd simultaneously pulled up to a corner parking space. Neither was willing to give into the other. He knew then she was headstrong and would offer him a challenge. Despite their recent conflict, he had plenty of fond memories. Their relationship may have been unconventional, but he enjoyed having her in his space. Maxwell knew he was going to miss her, but there wasn't an option. The boundary lines were drawn. He absolutely couldn't allow anything or anyone to mean more to him than his mission to annihilate Bishop Jones. Sacrifices were his and had been his faithful companion for nearly a lifetime.

Chapter 26

Bishop waited patiently in his office. As the night rushed in, silence hummed throughout the office. Church events had concluded an hour ago. His secretary had been gone for hours, and the janitor had just left. Bishop Jones was alone, as it should be for his upcoming meeting. He'd gotten Jill Smith's contact information from Simmons. When Bishop Jones called to make the appointment with her, he was careful not to fully reveal his intent. Hopefully Simmons hadn't clued her in. He wasn't sure and couldn't worry about unknowns. About ten-fifteen, the phone rang.

"Bishop Jones, I'm at the side door."

"I'll be right there," he said rushing out to let her in.

They didn't speak much on the way to his office. It was awkward but necessary. Once they reached his office, he offered her a seat and closed the door.

"Why did you want to see me?" she asked seeming to squirm in the seat.

Bishop sat in a seat next to her. "Can I call you Jill?"

"Sure, that's fine, but can you tell me why you wanted to meet with me so late or do I already know the answer?" she stated.

"Whoa, sister," Bishop said drawing away. "I'm not Minister Simmons."

The worry in her face didn't vanish. "Then what do you want?"

"For you to stop your dealings with Minister Simmons. He has a family, and there's no place for you in that picture."

Fear appeared to sweep over Jill. She became visibly restless. "I will," she mumbled until Bishop interrupted.

"I'm not here to judge you, but I do plan to get my message across."

She began crying. "I didn't want to do any of this, but I had no choice."

"We always have choices."

"Not me. Without the minister's help how am I going to get my medicine?" she screamed out.

The outburst shocked Bishop and he was initially unprepared to respond. Careful not to cross the line, he refused to touch her even in a comforting way. She was vulnerable and he wasn't getting caught in that age-old trap. He'd seen too many colleagues get crushed in those situations. The best he could do was hand her a tissue. "What's this business about your medicine?"

"I have chronic back pain and my doctor won't give me what I need anymore."

"Why not?"

"He says I'm already on too many other medications and the one that works for me is too addictive. So, he won't prescribe it. Minister Simmons lets me have a supply every month and it helps a lot. I wouldn't be able to function without it. I couldn't take care of my kids without the relief I get from the medicine," she replied becoming overly emotional again.

"I wasn't aware of your situation." Her explanation caused him to pause. Maybe she wasn't just a wayward woman looking for a quick fix and wad of cash. He had children. It wasn't difficult to have compassion for her, but he had to set his personal feelings aside. One thing about him, he knew how to separate emotion from achieving goals. There had been countless instances in his ministry when he'd felt sorry about having to make moves that were unpleasant for others. "Maybe I can help you?"

"How?" she asked, sniffling. Reluctantly she said, "I'll do whatever I have to do." She leaned toward him and he stood to move farther away.

"Well, I want you to do what's pleasing before God," he said gripping the chair's arm. "Let's think about how the church and I can help you."

"My medicine; I need to keep getting my medicine. Can you help me with that? That's all I want. That's all I need," she said, much calmer.

"Then you'll get your medicine. However, it will be done legally and under a doctor's supervision. The church will help you find a doctor who will assess your medical needs."

Jill wiped at her eyes with the back of both hands and cleared her thoughts. "I can't pay for it."

"I know, and that's what the church is for, to help those who can't help themselves. We'll cover the cost," he said walking to his desk. The notion snipped at his heart thinking about his grandson's situation.

"Really, thank you. Thank you so much," Jill responded after blowing her nose.

"Ms. Smith, I have to be very clear. You are to stop seeing Minister Simmons. The pills and whatever else you're doing together has to stop right now," Bishop Jones stated firmly as he stood stabbing his forefinger down into the top of his desk. "I've spoken with Minister Simmons, and I've told him the same thing. Do we understand each other?"

"I hear you, Bishop, loud and clear."

"Good, I'm glad we have an understanding. I'll have one of the church mothers call you about setting up the doctor's appointment."

"No, Bishop, I don't want anyone else to know about me and this pill thing."

"Don't worry. Everything will be done in the strictest of confidence. The church doesn't want to judge or punish you. We just want to help you."

Chapter 27

It was midmorning and Maxwell had been shut up in his office for several hours scouring city records, statements from the landowners, Garrett's copious notes, and several law books. His meticulous consideration of every aspect of the case against Bishop Jones was an absolute necessity. Normally, Maxwell relied on Sonya to provide most of the research, legal precedents, and statutes used to build a case. Not this round. He didn't trust anyone to be as thorough on this one as him. He stopped writing his brief to review what he'd come up with so far. His finger moved down the paper, guiding his eyes carefully over every word. He turned the page with so much force it made a popping noise. He read the sixth page, planted his elbows on the desk, and lowered his forehead into the palm of his hands.

Minutes of taunting quietness passed as Maxwell thought about what this case meant to him, how much he had invested and how much he had lost along the way. He slowly dragged his hands over his head. He massaged the back of his neck squeezing hard at the ball of tension resting there. He started to pick up the pencil again. Instead, he picked up the cup of coffee sitting on his desk and hurled it across the room into the wall.

Sonya knocked on the door rapidly and then yelled out. "Mr. Montgomery, are you okay?" Maxwell didn't respond. Just as he wiped at his forehead with a handkerchief, Sonya opened his door. "I'm sorry for barging in, but I heard a loud noise, and you didn't answer. Is everything okay?"

"My coffee cup had an accident."

Sonya followed Maxwell's gaze to the wall behind the door. "Oh, my goodness, I'll get some paper towels and clean it up," she offered, letting her gaze shift from the mess on the floor to Maxwell and then to the mess again.

"That can wait. Come on in and close the door, please."

Sonya walked closer and stopped in the middle of the floor. "Yes, Mr. Montgomery."

"Have a seat. I want to ask you something." Maxwell nodded his head toward the chair in front of his desk.

"I haven't been back to Greater Metropolitan. I promise," she announced. "I have not."

"Relax, Sonya. You're not in trouble. I'm curious about something else. Why did you start attending Bishop Jones's church in the first place?"

Sonya looked down briefly, rubbed her palms together and told Maxwell the truth. "I used to attend Rising Star. When I realized you were investigating the pastor, I started asking around about a good church that was involved in the community and really cared about its members. I kept hearing about this wonderful ministry and dynamic pastor. Greater Metropolitan is big and very well known in the community. It has lots of young adults and a decent singles' ministry. Believe me, those are hard to find," she said feeling livelier. "They have a rocking choir, too," she added. "A close family friend invited me to visit. I went one Sunday and three months later I became a member." Sonya quickly let the enthusiasm in her voice and the gleam in her eyes fade away when she noticed the frown plastered on Maxwell's face. "Joining seemed like a good idea."

"Was there anything you liked about Bishop Jones, specifically, as a pastor?"

"I like his messages, and he was always down to earth." Sonya wasn't sure why Maxwell was questioning her. She'd left the church. Wasn't that enough? She crossed her legs, rested her elbow on the arm of the chair and hoped her answer hadn't antagonized her boss. His silence suggested more explanation was warranted. "I also liked how fondly he spoke about his family, especially his wife."

"So, you think they have a decent marriage?"

"From what I can tell, they've been together a lot of years." Sonya stared at her boss. "Mr. Montgomery, the truth is I don't know what you have on him, but Bishop Jones seems like a good man and a great preacher."

"People aren't always who they appear to be. We can't just overlook the wrong he's done."

Sonya maintained visual contact as she spoke in a low voice, "May I ask you a question?"

"Sure, what is it?" Maxwell swung his chair side-to-side a couple of times, tapping two fingers on the desk and glaring right into Sonya's eyes.

"Why are you so determined to bring down Bishop Jones? What has he done that's so terrible?"

Maxwell looked away from Sonya briefly. "He's done terrible things to a lot of people. You obviously don't know much about his background."

"No, I guess I don't, but I know we all make mistakes and if God can forgive us, why can't we forgive each other?"

The word "forgive" pulled Maxwell right up out of his seat. He walked toward the windows and turned the handle opening one of the glass panels. He stood there for a few seconds allowing the cool breeze of early summer to rush in and wash over him before responding. Glaring out the window, Maxwell had something to say. "He's not only hurt individuals; Bishop Jones has also destroyed

many families without caring two hoots about them."
Maxwell moved over to his desk, sat on the corner of it
and picked up a stress ball, which he hadn't held in quite
a while.

"I don't know anything about that, but he's human.
Humans make mistakes."

"I'm not buying it. Church leaders have to be held to a
higher level of accountability and integrity. And, in order
for someone to be forgiven, they would have to acknowledge their indiscretion and then ask for forgiveness." He
tossed the ball into the air and snatched it down, quickly
smashing it as flat as possible between both hands.

"I'm not used to this coming from you. This case seems
so personal for you. You're always so matter-of-fact about
things." Sonya shifted in her chair.

"Let's just say you know one man, and I know another,"
he said slamming his fist on the desk.

"I don't understand, and I'm not trying to pry. It's just
that your attachment to this case seems more intense
than normal."

"For the record, Bishop Jones had a very direct impact
on a family I once knew very well. He was Pastor Jones
back then. The family was totally committed to him and
the church. They trusted him. You know how he repaid
their trust?"

"No."

"Well, Jones took their hard-earned money and squan-
dered it away in an investment scheme. The church
treasurer invested his children's college fund; even put
his house up for collateral to help finance the venture.
When it failed some people lost everything they had. The
treasurer took the rap and ended up losing his house,
self-respect, and he even his freedom. He spent five years
in prison for fraud and his wife did six months."

"That's awful."

"Jones didn't serve a single day in jail even though it was his program."

Sonya didn't respond. The imprint of Maxwell's finger-nails covered the stress ball. "The man's children suffered the most. And, I know for a fact they are still feeling the devastation today. So, yes, I have a personal interest in this case."

There was a knock on the office door.

Maxwell and Sonya stood as he invited the person in. Sonya walked toward the door, but the visitor came in before she got there. "It's just me, Garrett. Hope I'm not interrupting anything."

"No, not at all. Sonya and I were just discussing Bishop Jones and his redeeming qualities."

Garrett nodded hello at Sonya and responded to Maxwell, "I didn't think you considered Bishop Jones to have any redeeming qualities."

"Sonya was just trying to reform my thinking about Jones. She certainly seems to think he has some good in him somewhere." Maxwell stifled a laugh by coughing into his fist as he held his head down and peered up at both Sonya and Garrett.

"Well, I'm not a fan of Bishop Jones, but he has gotten something done in the community that other folks couldn't seem to make happen," Garrett said. "I hear he's serious about getting young people off the street. We all know that's desperately needed." Garrett raised his hands into the air, with palms up, scrunched his face and said, "I can't say for sure, but maybe he does care a tiny bit about the community. He has definitely sponsored projects for the youth. That's a fact. Now his funding methods may be questionable but you have to admit, he's done some work."

Sonya turned her head toward Maxwell. He saw her and intently restrained his comments.

"On that note, I'll leave you gentlemen to hash that one out alone."

"Ugh," Maxwell moaned while shaking his clutched fists in the air. "I've heard quite enough about the admirable Bishop Jones and his good deeds." Maxwell brushed his hand through the air making a sweeping motion to dismiss the dialogue.

Sonya pointed to her wrist. "Don't forget, you have a client coming in at one-thirty."

"Oh, shoot, thanks for reminding me." Sonya closed the door behind her and it wasn't too soon for Maxwell. He'd heard enough about Jones to gag. The bishop might fool Sonya and maybe even Garrett, but Maxwell knew better. He mellowed believing the truth would soon come out and Jones would be history.

Chapter 28

Maxwell and Garrett sat at the conference table and jumped into the business at hand. "I need you to work your magic and get me some information on Bishop Jones's tax returns. If his hands are messy dealing with the church's money, I'll bet he's just as dirty with his personal finances."

Garrett frowned. "Sure you want to go there?"

"Without a doubt; I don't want to miss anything that will speak to the bishop's true character." Maxwell slapped his hand down hard onto his thigh.

"Not a problem, I'll get right on it. Give me a few days, and I'll get back to you."

Maxwell pulled a white envelope from his desk with Garrett's name written across the front. He handed the letter-sized envelope to Garrett. "I appreciate your hard work and your discretion. You've never let me down," he told Garrett patting him on the back.

"It's not always easy work, but it pays well." Garrett chuckled, tucking the envelope inside jacket pocket. "I'll give you a call next week."

He watched Garrett depart. Maxwell knew that somehow the information he'd asked for would soon be in his hands. He sat down to finish the legal draft that had been started earlier. After rereading the last page of the document, he began writing. Maxwell couldn't help but to dwell on his history with Bishop Jones and Sonya's statement. She was right; the case was personal. He wrote Bishop Ellis Jones's name, pressing down with so much force the pencil lead broke. He pressed on the top of the pencil with his thumb, demanding it produce new lead. He began writing again sensing the end was near. Maxwell stared at the words while memories tried holding him captive.

The sharp pitch of his ringing cell phone caused Maxwell's body to jerk as it broke the heavy shackles. He grabbed up the phone silencing the ringer as he read the name across his screen. It was Christine. He wondered why she was calling. His work was pleading for progress. He could let the call go to voicemail, but his heart said maybe she needed something for his nephew. Maybe his father had gotten worse? There were many questions dancing around. He was torn about what to do. Family was a liability requiring too much risky emotional collateral, but he decided this was a call he had to take.

"Maxwell here," he said, intentionally not sounding enthusiastic or familiar with her call.

"Well, miracles never cease. You answered the phone."

Maxwell ignored her sarcasm while the corners of his mouth turned up. "What's up?"

"Actually, things are pretty good. Dad is feeling better, and you know their fiftieth wedding anniversary is in two weeks. I'm giving them a surprise party." Christine waited for a bit before continuing. "I'd like for you to come. It would mean so much to them if you were there. Please say yes." More waiting ensued. Finally she added, "It's been much too long since our family has been in the same room together. The party is Saturday, the twenty-fourth, at five o'clock. Please say you'll come."

Maxwell folded in his bottom lip and gritted his teeth. "Christine, no, I can't make it. I'm under a tight deadline and there is no getting past it. I can't make any commitments. I might even be out of town that week."

"No is such an easy word for you to say when it comes to your family. You are the most stubborn person I know. Actually, I take that back. You and Dad are the two most stubborn. Sometimes I think you deserve one another. You're so much like him and it drives me crazy. Ahh, I just want to scream at the two of you. For heaven's sake, when are you going to let the past go?"

"What makes you think that it's me?" Maxwell closed his eyelids and let her ranting continue. There wasn't anything else he wanted to say.

"Because, I know it's you and him too. You're mad at him for what he did a long time ago. He's mad at how you're acting now. This is silly. Mom and I are caught in the middle. Come on. Who's going to step up and be the man in this situation? We have to work this out as a family, before it's too late. So, stop being a butt, Maxwell. Put your pride aside and do something."

"Me, do something? You're the one with the answers. You act like I'm the bad guy and that this is my doing."

"I didn't blame you, but you certainly have a share."

"Christine, look, I don't have time for this. I have more important issues."

"Maxwell, when are you going to stop pretending that you don't think about our parents? You act like you are totally removed from your family. That can't be how you truly feel." There was no point in answering. He just let her talk. "I know that you've been paying Dad's medical bills. Mom and Dad know it too. It's okay for you to care about us and for you to love our parents. You don't have to pretend to be so coldhearted when I know you're not."

Maxwell sat straight up in his chair, reached for the pencil and legal pad. "Hey, I've got to get back to work. I'll send a nice gift to your house before the party. How is Tyree?"

Tension echoed loudly on the phone briefly before Christine answered him. "He's good. He's growing up, getting bigger every day. You're missing out on that, too." Another few moments of hush haunted the phone line. "You know Tyree was really disappointed when you didn't make it to his birthday party."

Maxwell refused to open that emotional door and ignored her statement. "Did he like the new PlayStation and his games?"

"Of course, he did; way too much, actually. I had to restrict his playing time with a schedule. All he wants to do is play that game. Seriously, Maxwell please try to come to the anniversary party. You can't shut us out forever."

"I'll make sure the gift gets to you before the party. I've got to go. Say hello to Tyree for me." He made a quick escape from the call by not waiting to hear her say good-bye. He pressed the end button on his cell phone and dived back into his document. Maxwell looked at the last few words he had written, ripped the entire sheet of paper from his legal pad, balled it up with both hands, and tossed it into the trashcan by his desk. Just as he regrouped and began typing directly into his laptop, Sonya buzzed the intercom on his desk. "Yes, Sonya."

"I almost forgot. I need to come in and clean up the broken cup on your floor. Is now a good time?"

"Sure," he answered. Maxwell looked across the room at the broken pieces of the cup and wondered if the other areas of his life would ever come together. He wasn't ready for a wife, kids, family vacations, or a dog. He pulled his glance away from the broken pieces and shook his head, tossing the foreign notions out of his mind. If he was to reconcile with his former family or begin a new one, it would be somewhere far down the road and over the rainbow. There was no room for anything in his scope right now except the case he was determined to win.

Chapter 29

Cars whisked by as Jill stayed close to the building and as far from the street as she could. She didn't want to take a chance on anyone seeing her go into the church at ten-thirty at night. Images raced around, zooming, with no sign of slowing. What did the bishop want with her this late? He'd already told her what he didn't want and it had been fine with her. If only Minister Simmons had tried to help her in a different way, perhaps her circumstances would be better now. When she came to the church six months ago, he'd found out that she was struggling with chronic back pain. Her steps slowed as she drew closer to the rear door of the church. Standing there, Jill reflected on how she'd gotten to her spot of darkness. She had already stood in disgust and wasn't interested in staying in that predicament any longer. Just as her hand was about to touch the handle, something said, *run, run, get out of here*. It wasn't too late, not yet. She hadn't crossed the line. There was a chance to walk away. She was turning to leave, maybe not running but definitely in a brisk walk. The door opened, stunning her for a second.

"Ms. Smith, right on time," Bishop Jones said standing in the doorway in a dark blue suit and striped tie. She froze wanting to leave but her legs wouldn't budge. They were heavy as logs, just like her heart.

Something about this second meeting with the senior pastor didn't feel right, even if she was on the pain meds and muscle relaxers. Her body might have been somewhat relaxed but not enough to feel comfortable doing wrong in the church. God was watching. She eagerly wanted to meet and get out of there as fast as possible.

"I see you got my message. Thanks for meeting with me again," he said standing to the side so she could enter the building. "I hope this isn't too late for you."

Not too late to bolt and save herself, she thought.

"Come on in and join me in my office." She hesitated. Bishop must have picked up on her discomfort because he said, "I'm not going to bite you, for goodness' sake."

"Then why am I here?" she asked setting only one foot inside the church. She was afraid of Minister Simmons, cringed near the bishop, but was absolutely terrified of God's wrath if she kept defiling the church. "Nope, Bishop, I'm not coming in there."

"Well, we can't very well stand here and talk, now can we?"

"Yes, I can," she boldly conveyed to him.

"Come on in, please," he offered extending his hand.

She didn't reciprocate. "Nope, right here works for me."

"Okay, then that's the way it is," he said leaning against the door to keep it propped open. "We'll talk here if this is what you want."

Her speeding thoughts slowed as the anxiety that had overtaken her minutes ago began subsiding. "I can only stay a few minutes anyway." Her children were staying with a neighbor she didn't totally trust. In a pinch, like this one, her children could stay but only for a brief period.

"I understand; I'll ask a few questions, and you can be on your way." Jill nodded determined to watch the time. "After we met last week, I couldn't help but to think about our discussion. How exactly did you get into this situation, you know, with the medication?"

"Why do you ask?"

"Besides getting you another doctor, maybe I can help if I understand the root of your problem."

Bugs were buzzing around the light hanging overhead. Some were flying in the open door, and some were nipping at her skin. Yet, she wasn't bothered enough to go inside. "Do you really want to know?"

"Yes, I do," he said crossing his arms still leaning against the door. "You can trust me."

She knew too well what that meant. Words she'd heard over and over: once from her father, then her children's father, and now the church father. "It's something that just happened."

Bishop shook his head in disagreement. "That's not true and you know it. Tell me your story and let me help you."

Her guard almost came down in that quick second where it seemed like someone cared. She was certain he didn't but the only way for her to get home as quickly as possible was to answer the bishop's questions and get out of there. "When I came to this church, Minister Simmons led one of the counseling sessions. I told him about my chronic back pain. I was hoping to be healed because the doctor wouldn't give me any more pills for my back."

"And, did you get healed?"

"No," she said not really expecting to get healed anymore. "Instead of begging the doctor to help me, I confessed to Minister Simmons that I'd been buying undercover drugs."

Bishop looked startled but not a lot. "What did Simmons say when you told him?"

"Nothing that night, but about a month later he offered me a lump sum of cash in exchange for introducing him to the person selling me my medication. He said he had a friend who could help us make a lot of money by supplying him with much more meds than we'd ever seen."

"I see."

She felt drenched with guilt and judgment. "I needed the money." There was no way Bishop Jones could possibly feel her pain. He had a fancy car, nice clothes, and probably a mansion on the Main Line. He couldn't relate to her as a single mother unable to work but still having to feed two growing boys.

"I understand. You have a family and needed the money."

"Honestly, money was the least of it for me."

"What other reason could there be?" he asked. "Do you mind if I pull up a chair?" She didn't mind, so he did and set it directly in front of the door to keep it open.

"I was promised a monthly supply of my pain meds in return for my services," she said as the shame dragged her gaze to the filthy ground. In the beginning that's all he gave me, my meds and cash. A few months ago, Minister Simmons added other requirements." It was clear to see that the bishop appeared uneasy addressing the subject, but Minister Simmons was his problem, not hers.

"Why did you go to him?"

She hunched her shoulders and then said, "Because, I was desperate, and he helped me. I resisted his advances for weeks, as long as I could." Depression hounded Jill standing on the church's doorway but her reality came forward. She was a mother and providing for her crew allowed her to nudge away some of the guilt. "I'm ashamed," she said as her voice cracked.

"I'm sure you did what you felt you had to do."

"I did."

"You do know there are other ways, better ways, to have your needs met."

"How?"

"By trusting in God."

"I've tried that and trusting people in the church, too. It hasn't worked for me so far."

"I'm sorry your past experiences have made you skepti-cal. I'm not making excuses for anyone, please understand me. But, the church is made up of men and women who mostly want to please God and serve the people. They're not perfect. When a person in leadership falls short, they have to step down, and let God work on their flesh. What happened to you was the result of a minister's weakness to sin. I'm sorry, but trust me; it is being addressed and always will be in this church."

"After what I've been through, I can't trust anyone."

"You're wrong. You absolutely can trust God, and you can trust me." Bishop pushed a white envelope into Jill's hand.

She turned the sealed envelope over, examining both sides of it then asked, "What's this?"

"It's the contact number for a physician who will help you manage your pain just like I promised. Just call and make an appointment. You'll never see a bill."

Jill glanced back and forth between the envelope and the bishop twice. "Why? What is this going to cost me?"

"Nothing, I told you. The church will take care of the doctor's bill and the prescriptions."

"I heard you say that. But every gift ain't free," Jill protested placing her hand on her hip.

"Ms. Smith, you don't have to do anything but let the church help you. God loves you and wants to meet your needs."

"Bishop, I don't really have time for a sermon," Jill interrupted as she took two steps backward. "I have to get home to my children. My crazy neighbor is keeping them for me, and she can't last more than an hour. I'd better go," She said hesitantly, feeling like she needed his approval to leave but was unwilling to wait for it. She dashed from the doorway as fast as her legs could go. She'd breathe once the road got closer and the church farther away.

Bishop Jones was left with a heavy heart weighed down by his concern for Jill and the ugly situation Simmons had brought to the church's doorstep. Yet, he could empathize with Simmons. That was him many years ago. There was a time when an opportunity to make quick cash for the church drove him, especially when he didn't have to follow any rules of right and wrong. Those days were long gone and far behind him. He'd grown in God and his Christian character was stronger.

He looked out into the dark after Jill left knowing she could not run away from her problem. The bishop knew he couldn't run away from his problems either. He was accountable to God to get this mess straightened out with Simmons and the drugs. He had to make the wrong right.

Chapter 30

Jill's legs just wouldn't cooperate. In her mind, she was sprinting. In reality she had barely cleared the back side of the church. She had to speed up. As she cut around the corner, bam, Jill ran right into an older-looking short guy. "Oh, I'm sorry," she stammered, avoiding eye contact and trying to push around him.

"Wait a minute, miss," he said stepping in front of her. She shifted to the left and he matched her step. She moved back to the right determined to get past him. He shifted in the same direction, as if they were dancing.

"Excuse me, but I have to get by you," she said very agitated.

"Who are you and what are you doing behind the church?"

Her nerves were screaming, the adrenaline flowing. "Nothing," she said kind of loud. Fear was speaking, and she didn't seem to have control.

"Listen, young lady, you better start talking or I'm calling the police," he demanded pulling a cell phone from his pocket.

"No, wait," she yelled reaching for the phone as he pulled back. Visions of her children's welfare overtook her. She couldn't get locked up. She just couldn't. What would happen to them?

"Were you breaking into the church?"

"No," she said. "I was meeting with Bishop Jones. He asked me to come to the church and I did. That's why I'm here."

"This late and you expect me to believe that story?" he said practically laughing in her face.

"You don't have to believe me. Go in the church and check for yourself. He has on a dark blue suit with a blue and white striped tie and a baby blue shirt." Jill's nerves settled. She wasn't afraid to tell the truth. Neither Bishop nor Minister Simmons was worth sacrificing her children. She'd give up their names and anyone else's if necessary.

Jill could tell the guy wasn't quite sure if she was lying but he seemed more interested in what she had to say the more they spoke.

"Why would you be meeting with the bishop this late in the rear of the church?"

His accusatory tone didn't bother her. She was sticking with the truth and leaving it at that. "Why do you want to know? Who are you?"

The little man pushed his chest out and said, "I'm Deacon Burton."

"Deacon Burton, I'm telling you the truth."

"Then why are you in such a rush to get away? Why don't you go with me and we can see Bishop Jones together. Maybe he can tell me why you're here."

"I wouldn't mind doing that but not tonight," she said staring at her watch. "I have to get home to my children. My babysitter isn't going to keep them much longer."

"I'm no dummy, young lady. I'm not going to let you steal from the church and get away with it. Either you come in with me or I'm calling the police," he said reaching for the phone again.

Anxiety rising she blurted out, "I wasn't stealing. If you want to find out what's going on, talk to Bishop Jones or, better yet, ask Minister Simmons about Jill. He's the real thief here."

"What are you talking about?"

Her world was spinning. Acts she'd committed with Minister Simmons meshed with embarrassment and desperation. It was too much. At that precise moment she just didn't desire to keep the secret anymore. Maybe it was the excruciating pain roaring around her spine or the weight of humiliation pushing her words out. "He's the reason I'm here. He's the one who made me sell the drugs."

"What drugs? Who made you sell them? What are you talking about?"

"Minister Simmons made me help him sell prescription meds."

"Do you mean drugs or medication?"

"Meds, drugs, it's all the same." He seemed confused but sincere. She had no reason to trust him or anyone from Greater Metropolitan. Intuition told Jill he was different. She was tired and had to believe someone could help her. Maybe Deacon Burton was the man.

"Does Bishop know about this?"

"Yes."

He dropped his gaze and clapped his hands together. "It's very late, and there's no need to keep standing out here. You can go on your way."

"Does this mean you believe me?"

"Shoot, that's a tough story to believe, and I sure hope you're lying. It would be much simpler if you were a common thief trying to cover up your crime, but I don't know."

"So, what are you going to do?"

"Go and talk with Bishop Jones and get to the bottom of this, that's what I'm going to do."

Jill glanced at her watch once again. She had five minutes to walk a distance that would normally take fifteen. She snatched a crumbled piece of paper from her purse and scribbled her phone number. "Here," she said shoving the paper into his hand. "I'm Jill. Go ahead and ask him about me. When you find out I'm telling the truth, please call me if you can help me out of this situation. I'm tired and I need somebody's help. Somebody in this big old church has to be genuine. Maybe it's you. I don't know, but I'm out of options."

Reluctantly he took the paper, glanced over the writing, and shoved it into his pocket. Jill breathed a sigh of relief, glad he hadn't tossed the paper away. Hey, maybe there was a chance he'd help. Her hope meter rose, then reality set in. He probably wasn't going to help but she was encouraged if for only a few minutes.

Chapter 31

That woman must be crazy. That's what Deacon Burton wanted to believe, but there was an inkling which didn't sit right. His mama used to call it "following his first mind," which basically equated to going with the feeling in his gut that told him what was right. He meandered toward the rear door of the church, meditating on the woman's words. It would have been nice to discount her. After all, there were plenty of trifling characters in the neighborhood who were out to get whatever they could. Robbing a church wasn't out of the question, but there was something about how she said what she said that rang true. He didn't want to believe her, but it was his responsibility as a man of God to find out.

He reached for the door handle and went to pull on it as Bishop Jones was pushing it open simultaneously.

"Deacon, oh my, you scared me, man, coming in this late," Bishop Jones said, letting out a deep sigh and then straightening his blue striped tie.

"I could say the same thing. You sure scared me too. I didn't expect to find anybody here this late," he said. "It's after eleven o'clock."

The bishop looked off to the side. "Yes, I had some business to handle."

Deacon Burton looked squarely at Bishop Jones. "I didn't know there were any business meetings at church tonight. I must have missed this one," the deacon said, not ready to hastily draw any conclusions. There was a good reason for Bishop to be at the church, and he'd give his spiritual father enough respect to explain.

"You didn't miss anything," Bishop said patting Deacon across his shoulder. "It was a small meeting."

"With the woman that I met outside?"

Bishop jerked his neck around. "What woman?"

"Uh, Jill, I believe it was." Deacon reached for the paper in his pocket, the one with her name and number, and at the last minute decided not to pull it out. "I ran into her as she was leaving, and I was coming in."

"Jill huh, well yes," the bishop answered straightening his tie again even though it didn't appear out of place. The bishop's voice dropped as he continued. "Ms. Smith was here for counseling."

"This late and with you by yourself?" The bishop nodded in affirmation. "That's not so good, Bishop. It can be dangerous around here at night. Why couldn't she come during the day?"

"She said something about her kids and a sitter. She was reluctant to talk about her challenges. The two of us meeting one-on-one was best. All I know is that she needs help, and I'm going to make sure she gets it."

"Meet with you, humph. She says you wanted to meet with her."

"Jill is clearly going through a tough situation and needs help. Hopefully I can counsel her through this. I really do want to help her."

"Don't you worry about it, Bishop. I'll get her signed up with one of the church mothers tomorrow. She will get as much counseling and prayers she can handle."

"No," the bishop called out.

Deacon Burton was surprised to see Bishop Jones react so negatively to such a basic suggestion. New members coming into the church with heavy problems were always assigned to the mothers and deacons of the church. This

Jill lady might not be new, but he'd never seen her before and assumed she was. Deacon Burton refused to believe what she had told him, but Bishop Jones had to come up with a better story soon; otherwise truth was bound to lean her way. "I don't mean any disrespect, Bishop, but why are you so wound up over this woman?" He hated to ask but had no choice. "You aren't into anything with her that would create a problem for the church, are you?"

Bishop Jones's eyelids squinted as he reared back on his heels. "Absolutely not, Deacon Burton. I'm disappointed you even felt the need to ask me. You know me better, Deacon, at least I thought you did." Bishop fell into a chair situated not too far from the door.

"Look, I'm sorry, but I don't know what to think. You're here so late and alone, and a strange woman comes running out of the church, practically in the middle of the night, claiming she was with you."

Bishop closed his eyelids briefly. "You can't believe everything you hear or see for that matter. It's not what you think, trust me. It's not what you think."

He hoped not, but admittedly Deacon Burton wasn't convinced. The woman had proven her case better than his senior pastor had.

Bishop Jones stood. "I have to get home. It's terribly late and my wife will be worried." He plucked a set of keys from his pocket. "After thirty-eight years, she won't go to sleep unless I'm at her side. For my wife's sake, I'm gone," he said pushing the door open and holding it for a few seconds. "Are you going to be okay here by yourself?"

"I think so."

"By the way, why are you here so late?" Bishop Jones inquired holding his keys in one hand and patting Deacon Burton on the shoulder with the other.

"I couldn't sleep. Thought I'd get a head start on some of the financial reports for next month's business meeting."

"Okay then, I'll see you Sunday."

Bishop told Deacon good night and left not only the building, but also a list of questions. Deacon's gut was talking and it wasn't telling a good story. He walked toward the offices. Each step was laced with an unpleasant feeling gnawing at him. He was loaded with doubt, which generated more questions, especially about why the woman was there so late. Bishop Jones's answer didn't make sense. Deacon knew it and he suspected his bishop did too.

The church was empty. Bishop was gone. The woman, Jill, was gone. That could have been the end of it, but instead, Deacon Burton decided to check out a few things before doing anything. He picked up his pace more determined to get to the office.

A week passed and then another and another. Deacon Burton was buried in preparing the church's financial documents for the bank loan. He didn't believe in the church taking on such large amounts of debt but there wasn't much he could do. Bishop Jones and the board approved it, and he wasn't going to complain. There was too much to do in the church and in the community to spend energy bickering over decisions that had already been made. So long as he kept his hand in God's, Deacon Burton was absolutely confident everything would work out.

He popped the latches on his briefcase open and paused. Jill Smith's name scribbled on the paper screamed out to him. It was as if she wouldn't let him get any farther into the stack of papers unless he addressed her first. *Nonsense,* he thought shoving the card to the side and continuing his pursuit of last year's income statement. He paused again, scratched at his beard, and then got up. Ignoring his curiosity hadn't made it go away in nearly a month. There was only one way to rid his mind of Jill's accusations, and it wasn't getting answers from Bishop Jones. He'd already tried that route and failed miserably.

"Can you get me logged into the contributions database?" he asked the church's financial recorder. Only four people had the access code for the church's contribution records: the recorder, auditor, Minister of Finance, and Bishop Jones. Asking either of them might have led to more questions, ones he preferred avoiding.

"Sure," she said having no clue about what he was getting ready to do. The recorder should have told him no but thank goodness she didn't.

Once she got him set up, Deacon Burton went straight to the list of tithes, offerings, and other donations paid over the past months. He typed in Simmons, which brought up twenty-five names. He scrolled through the list until the cursor reached Otis. Deacon Burton placed his finger on the screen and traced across the line, month by month. He reached for his reading glasses to be sure he was reading the amounts correctly.

"Wow, you look so serious," the recorder commented walking past the deacon.

"I'm just checking a few numbers," he said, not drawing attention to exactly what he was doing. Nobody needed to know, not now and hopefully not ever. After reviewing three months of donations, his fear was growing. $1,200 in January, $1,600 in February, $1,500 more in March, and that was enough for Deacon Burton to sit up and take his glasses off. He fingered through his beard attempting to put a positive spin on what he was seeing. No reasonable explanation came forward. "Thanks for your help," he told the church recorder. "You can log me out."

"Did you find what you were looking for?" she asked.

"More than I was looking for," he said without letting his somber feeling show. He schlepped back to his office and got his briefcase.

He couldn't stop wondering where in the world Simmons got so much money. From what he remembered, the junior minister worked a modest job as a security guard for a housing development in the city. Deacon Burton didn't know the exact amount of Simmons's salary. At the rate of ten percent for tithing, Simmons would have to make about $12,000 a month to justify his level of giving. Deacon Burton was pretty sure the city wasn't paying Simmons nearly that kind of money.

The deacon buried his forehead in the palm of his hand. The inkling had converted to facts and facts to a major concern. He pulled the piece of crumpled paper from the briefcase and pressed it out flat on the desk. Jill may have been telling the truth. His flesh said ignore what he'd found, go home, and have dinner with his wife and two sons. Leave the church business to the church folks. The rationale could have worked, except he was the church. Not just as a member of Greater Metropolitan, but as the larger body of Christ. He was appointed to handle the church finances and to operate with integrity. If there was a suspicion of wrongdoing, he had to point it out, no matter who got exposed from the bishop on down. He slammed the briefcase shut and tucked the paper into his pants pocket, not sure what to do next. He had to act, acknowledging that his first allegiance was to God and the church. He had to do something but what?

Chapter 32

A muggy, warm breeze blew across the church parking lot and deposited dust into Deacon Burton's face. He fiercely rubbed his eyes. Once his vision was clear again, he saw Minister Simmons getting out of his car down a ways and walking toward the church with a Bible in hand. Deacon Burton had been at the church for over an hour unlocking doors, checking bathrooms, and preparing the building for Bible Study. He'd also been in the sanctuary down on his knees in prayer. He'd stepped outside to get some fresh air and free his mind as the meeting he planned to have with Minister Simmons weighed heavily on his heart.

Boldness blossomed and he decided talking with Simmons was an absolute must. There was no better place to confront evil than in the house of God. Deacon Burton closed his eyelids and prayed silently for guidance. A honking horn ended his prayer abruptly as his eyelids popped open.

"Hey, Deacon Burton, good to see you," a woman shouted.

He waved at her but didn't offer the wide, bright smile he was known to have. He stroked the hairs of his beard twice, glanced up at the bell tower sitting on top of the church, and headed inside as Bishop Jones pulled into his parking space.

Bible class was lively and very interactive. The small pockets of chatter, which had formed after class, were breaking up and people were leaving. Deacon Burton maneuvered through the maze of members filing from the building as he looked for Minister Simmons. He found him walking down the hallway toward a side exit. "Minister Simmons, can I speak with you. Can we go into one of the conference rooms?"

"Deacon, I'm sort of in a hurry. Can we talk tomorrow?"

"Actually, no, I really need to speak with you tonight."

"Okay, how can I help you?" Minister Simmons responded and twisted the conference room door's handle to be sure it was unlocked.

"I think we're going to want to have this discussion behind closed doors. Let's go in," Deacon Burton said, nodding his head toward the door.

"Deacon, I'm really pressed for time. Why don't you walk with me to my car, and we can talk on the way."

"You don't understand. The topic is sensitive. I want to talk about Jill and the prescription drugs."

Minister Simmons flung his head from left to right ensuring no one was within hearing distance. "Deacon, what in the world are you talking about?" he asked while thrusting the door open and quickly stepping into the conference room. He tossed his briefcase and Bible onto the chair by the door. Once Deacon Burton was safely inside, Minister Simmons shut the door and pressed the palm of his hand against it hard then turned to the deacon. "Now, what's going on?"

Deacon Burton jumped right into the matter. "A few weeks back, I saw a young lady named Jill coming from behind the church. I stopped her. It was late, and she was nervous. I figured she was stealing."

"She probably was. What does that have to do with me?"

"When I questioned her, she had a lot to say."

Before the deacon could open his mouth to form the next word, Minister Simmons demanded with a strong tone, "What exactly did she say?"

The deacon stood in front of the wall-to-wall bookshelves and ran his fingers down the spine of a book. He inhaled his courage and turned to face Minister Simmons. "Well, she said you've been forcing her to help you sell prescription medication."

"She told you what? You've got to be kidding, right?" Minister Simmons's light brown complexion was immediately changed to a fiery red color, which crawled through his face and lit up his bulging eyes.

"I wish I were kidding. This is a serious matter and it's why I'm coming to you."

"You can't possibly believe her."

"What if I do?"

"Then you'd be making a mistake. I'm being falsely accused and slandered. I see what this is. There is no truth to her vile, ugly lies." Minister Simmons took a few steps closer to the deacon. "How can you bring such a ridiculous accusation to me?"

"Doesn't the Bible say go to your brother? Well, here I am, Minister Simmons. We both have a responsibility to God first and then to this church second. This is not something that I could ignore."

"Come on, Deacon." The volume in his voice stepped up a notch. "This is an insult. You can't go around falsely accusing God's servant of wrongdoing." He walked away from Deacon Burton. He shook his head in disbelief and tossed his keys onto the table, causing papers to scatter.

"Minister Simmons, I couldn't act as if nothing happened after speaking to the woman. I'm accountable for what I know. So, I am simply asking you if there is anything, anything at all to what she said. Before you answer, I have to tell you, she was quite adamant about the drugs and your involvement." Deacon Burton stood in front of Simmons and leaned his weight on the table. "Look, if there is something going on, something that's not right, something that could hurt this church, tell me now. Let me help you. It's never too late to do the right thing."

Minister Simmons stood up straight like puppet strings were directing him. "I've been coming here long enough for you to take my word over hers. There is not a blemish of truth to what this Jill woman told you." He jabbed his index finger into his right cheek and twisted it into his skin like a drill. "My actions and diligent labor in the church should speak for me. If I weren't a minister, I'd be angry at such a bald-faced accusation." He stepped to the deacon, allowing minimal barrier between them. "Actually, I am angry."

"I imagine you are, but surely you understand why I had to address such a serious accusation. The validity of something like this would not only be damaging for you but for the church, too. We're both defenders of the gospel, and we must protect the house of God. I had to bring this to you."

The two men stared at each other. A vein on the side of Minister Simmons's neck was throbbing against his skin like the beat of a drum. Small beads of sweat attacked the tip of his nose. "For some reason this woman wants to discredit me, assassinate my Christian character, but I won't be defeated." He walked away from the deacon, snatched up his briefcase, and lifted his Bible into the air. Minister Simmons walked out with his words reaching for the deacon. "Don't waste your efforts on a liar."

Chapter 33

Deacon Burton plucked the thick ring of keys from his pants pocket and locked the door on his way out. Rambling down the hallway, the revelation nagged loudly. Minister Simmons's defensive tone and the edge in his voice seemed haunted by fear. Deacon wasn't discouraged. He had to see Bishop Jones again. Heading upstairs to the bishop's office, Deacon Burton took the steps one-by-one, sensing his confidence rising.

Standing in front of the bishop's door, the deacon folded his fingers into a ball before actually knocking. A thick, weary voice spoke from behind the heavy door separating them. "Who is it?"

"Bishop Jones, it's me, Deacon Burton."

"Come in. How are you tonight?" Bishop waved him into the office. "You had some great feedback in class tonight." The bishop stopped writing, silently read over a couple of lines, and laid the ink pen he was holding on top of his notepad. "Did you need something?"

"Yes, sir, Bishop Jones, I do."

"That scowl on your face tells me something is troubling you."

"You're right. I am troubled."

"Okay, have a seat. What's the problem?" Bishop Jones pushed the papers on his desk to the side.

Deacon Burton leaned forward with both elbows planted into his knees wringing his hands together. "Bishop, that Jill woman said you and Minister Simmons are involved with these so-called prescription drugs. I just spoke with Simmons about it."

"And, what did he say?" Bishop Jones asked, taking off his reading glasses.

"He said it wasn't true."

"Did he now? Well, I think you're putting too much energy into this. It's like I said before, you can't assume everything you see or hear is accurate." Bishop Jones picked up the thick Bible on his desk with both hands. "Deacon, it takes God's Word, our patience and prayers, to help folks through their spiritual issues and challenges. I told you Jill is a very troubled young woman. I can't share with you right now the things she discussed with me. Just know I'm on top of it, and I'll do all I can to help her. As for Minister Simmons, we have some decisions to make regarding his leadership failures. You should know I won't allow anything to tear down what the Lord has allowed us to build."

"Bishop, there's something I think you need to know." Deacon Burton stood, pulled out a handkerchief and brushed it across his forehead. He stared directly at the bishop without saying a word.

"What is it, Deacon? What is it you think I need to know?"

Large raindrops began crashing into the window. With no warning, the clear night's sky had erupted into a torrential downpour. The deacon's resolve was swept off topic for a brief second. "If there's some shady business going on here, God's wrath could be upon us."

"You are right, Deacon. It's a message I've been preaching for months. I'm glad it has resonated with you." Bishop Jones said.

"No, I'm trying to tell you we have to be sure we're clean and that the church is clean. The offering coming into the church also needs to be clean. And I'm concerned about the large amounts of tithing Minister Simmons is paying to the church." Deacon wiped at his forehead again and pushed the handkerchief into his pocket.

"Minister Simmons pays his tithes faithfully. That is what I expect from each minister on my staff."

"Yes, but I've checked the contribution database. He definitely pays his tithes faithfully. It's the amount of money that I question. He's tithing between a thousand and sixteen hundred a month. Unless something drastically changed with his job, there is no way, he's making over ten thousand a month. His money has to be coming from somewhere else. Jill swears Minister Simmons is caught up in some type of drug business. That would account for the kind of money he's giving to the church."

"I wouldn't rush to judgment. We don't know what's going on in his household. Only God knows the whole truth. Have you considered Minister Simmons may have gotten a raise? Maybe his wife got a raise. I don't know, maybe they came into an inheritance or one of them is working a second job. What I do know is that I'm thankful Minister Simmons is faithful in his stewardship. You know as well as I do that we have some members who are yet growing." The bishop cleared his throat, took a sip of water from the glass sitting on his desk then gazed over his shoulder and out the window. The rain continued to fall hard.

"Bishop, aren't you concerned?"

Bishop Jones moved his hand slowly back and forth over the top of the Bible that was within arm's reach on his desk. "I'm concerned about a lot of things, Deacon. I'm concerned about the community projects the church is involved with. I'm concerned about getting our youth off the street and into a safe haven. Every one of those initiatives takes money. I'm concerned with doing the right thing and helping souls find their way to Christ.

We've got plenty to be concerned with and someone paying their tithes is just not at the top of the list."

Deacon Burton lifted his hands up in front of his chest and pressed them together tightly. "Well, I've done what I'm supposed to do. I've given you the information. Thank you for hearing me out."

The bishop pushed his chair back from the desk. He walked up close to the deacon, squeezed his forearm with one hand and patted his shoulder with the other. "You're a good man, Deacon. Now, you go on home and don't let this worry you any further. I'll lock up the church tonight." Bishop Jones guided the deacon right on out his office with a firm hand on his back and words rumbling in his ear. "Everything is under control."

Bishop closed his office door and leaned his forehead against it while holding on to the doorknob. The deacon had left the room but his questioning and convicting presence remained. Bishop hurried to the window. Through the thick raindrops attempting to cloud his view, he could see Deacon Burton hurrying to his car. The deacon made no attempt to shelter himself from the downpour of rain crashing on top of his head and over his body.

"We have to be sure we're clean, that the church is clean. The offering coming into the church also needs to be clean." The deacon's words continued haunting the bishop as he sat at his desk working on Sunday's sermon. Bishop paused to rub his eyes. He let his head fall onto the thick, cushioned headrest. He knew the deacon was right. Everything had to be clean and would be. Admittedly, Satan had tempted Bishop with quick money in a moment of desperate financial need. Thank God for strength and grace. He'd clung to every ounce in resisting the drug deal. He'd offered Simmons more salary as an incentive to stop his involvement, but he couldn't tell Deacon Burton. He couldn't tell anyone.

He meditated, wanting the tension with Deacon Burton and the scowl on his face to fade away into the darkness. Awhile later he could still see Deacon Burton's face and the concern on his countenance. Bishop grabbed the pad of paper in front of him and picked up the calculator. He did a quick tally of what he intended to pay Simmons. The church salary coupled with, what he guessed to be, Simmons's regular wages would hopefully generate the tithing amount Burton had mentioned. After pushing a few buttons, the numbers didn't add up. Bishop wanted very much to help Simmons get on the right track, but the numbers didn't lie. Unless the church could come up with another couple of thousand a month, they weren't close to matching what had been Simmons's illegal part-time income.

Bishop hunkered down on his sermon. He jotted a few lines before the deacon's words played heavily in his head. He wasn't able to escape the admonishment. His integrity was on the line. What good was leaving a legacy for the community if his own reputation was destroyed? Bishop was confused. Sound of the raindrops beckoned him to the window. Standing there, he equated the hundreds of raindrops hitting the glass with each church member. Bishop watched one raindrop slide down the window and splatter on the windowsill. Shepherds protected their flock from harm. He had put a stop to the selling of drugs and any other accompanying improprieties. Bishop would talk with the minister again to be sure. He couldn't let Simmons slide into a comfortable place of spiritual compromise. Watching him fail didn't benefit the church. Bishop had to forgive and then help the young minister become a strong man of God worthy of honor. If that meant not telling Deacon Burton the whole truth, then so be it. He was the spiritual head of Greater Metropolitan and that meant he was accountable for his flock even to the point of his reputation being smudged if his sheep were saved.

Chapter 34

Bishop Jones drove home from the church in a blinding downpour of rain. Bishop considered the modest beginning of his ministerial service which began so many years ago. Times had changed. His car glided onto a private winding road lit by small silver lanterns ushering him to a circular drive. The light coming from the stone water fountain situated in front of the house guided the bishop's steps until he passed a set of mahogany double doors. He pulled into the garage around back and entered the house through the rear.

Seconds after he entered the house, he'd punched his security code into the alarm panel, and was meandering toward the front of his house with his heels clicking along the marble walkway. He was quickly greeted by his wife who was at the top of the staircase. "Ellis, I was worried about you in this rain. When I left church, you said you would be home in an hour. That was almost two hours ago."

"I know, I'm sorry," he offered hanging up his trench coat and hat in the hall closet. "I had an unexpected meeting, and time got away from me." Bishop Jones trekked up the stairs, disrobed, and took a quick shower. He hoped the hot water would warm his bones and relax him enough to let go of his run in with Deacon Burton hoping he'd done enough to rectify the situation. He'd agreed to a pay raise. He'd spoken to Jill and Simmons, admonishing them both. Bishop had reaffirmed the vows of matrimony with Simmons, although there was no guarantee he was going to adhere. Bishop was exhausted.

Half an hour later and Bishop Jones was snoring overcome by a deep sleep and the comfort of his wife cuddled up next to him.

The quiet of the dark bedroom was interrupted with a whispering wind sailing past their open window and someone calling his name. Bishop Jones's eyelids popped open; he turned to look at his sleeping wife then spanned the dark room for movement. There wasn't anyone or anything present. Bishop figured it was the wind. He rolled over facing the window and the bishop fell fast asleep. This time a brisk wind whisked through the window rattling the blinds and he heard the voice again. Jones sat straight up in bed, turned on the bedside lamp and searched the room with his bulging, wide eyes. With nothing and no one in sight, he shook his wife. "Did you hear that?

"Hear what?" she moaned.

"I can't believe you didn't hear the voice calling my name."

"Ellis, I can't hear anything but your snoring. Go back to sleep, dear. It was probably just a dream."

Bishop Jones panned the room again. The bedroom door was shut and so was the door to their master bath. His wallet was lying on the dresser and his wife's jewelry box didn't look disturbed. With both index fingers pressed in his ears, he jiggled his fingers back and forth attempting to clear up his hearing. Maybe it was a bad dream; although he rarely had those. When he did, it was only after eating something spicy before bed. He turned off the light, kissed his wife on the cheek, and laid down in the dark waiting to hear his name called again. The piercing red numbers of the clock located on the bedside table sliced through the darkness displaying two-fifteen in the morning. He'd heard no voice and had no sleep for the last twenty minutes. Weariness took over and sleep once again cradled him.

A stirring deep within wouldn't give him rest. Anxiety was rising, building. Jones tossed off the covers, swung his legs over the side of the bed and rushed to the window. Twirling the arm of the window crank, he watched the glass slide snuggly into the windowpane. He yanked down the latch locking it into place. His wife rolled over in bed sleeping comfortably. Jones crossed the wide space of the room shoving open the bathroom door and the two walk-in closets. Each was empty and void of sound. Out the bedroom and into the hallway, he leaned over the staircase railing stretching his vision in the dark and straining his ears only to hear the silence that clutched the air.

He didn't know if it was the Lord's prodding he was experiencing or his conscience gnawing away at him. Either way the message was clear. The bishop needed to have another session with Simmons and this time the young minister had better get the message. Bishop Jones headed up to his office on the third level. He shut the door behind him and knelt down in front of the leather sofa accepting that prayer was his only way to silence the voice denying him both sleep and peace.

Chapter 35

After having slept on his conversation with Bishop Jones, Deacon Burton remained confused. He couldn't think straight. There was something fishy going on between the bishop, Jill, and Minister Simmons. He could smell it but nobody was talking except for Jill, an admitted drug abuser. He stood in his driveway wondering what to do. He could accept Bishop's half-baked explanation and forget about Minister Simmons's cash contribution and walk away. No one in the church would have to know. Besides, what exactly did he know? He fumbled with his keys the same way he was fumbling with the truth. He leaned against the car and stared at the ground. Sometimes ignorance was a blessing, he admitted. So long as he didn't know anything, he didn't have to do anything. Once he had knowledge, he was accountable. There was no way around his position. The ringing sound of righteousness cried out from the depths of his spirit. It was too loud to ignore. So, he didn't try.

"Lord, show me what to do," he prayed softly and got into the car. He decided to set his troubles aside, go see his niece, and let the Lord work out the mess. There should have been a sigh of relief laying this on the Lord, but honestly he didn't feel much better. He knew there were some people who could pray and release everything to God. That wasn't him. He started the engine and pulled off.

Fifteen minutes later he was in West Philadelphia pulling up to a soul food diner. He took his time getting out since his niece wasn't expected for another twenty minutes. He wandered inside, carrying a load of worry. He found a seat and a menu but no peace. After a short while, he saw his niece approaching the table. At least that's what he'd called her since the day she was born to his childhood friend thirty-two years ago. She wasn't blood, but his niece was definitely family.

"Hey, Uncle Steve," Sonya said giving him a peck on the cheek and pulling up a chair across the table from him. "Am I late?" she asked opening the menu.

"No, not really," he responded unable to season his words with any resemblance of warmth or enthusiasm. His favorite niece usually got a better reception, but today he didn't have any to spare.

Both perused the menu saying nothing.

"What are you getting, Uncle?" Sonya questioned closing her menu. "Remember this is my treat."

"Then I better get the sweet potato pie and the cobbler, because I don't know when this day will happen again." He grinned but couldn't muster a full heap of laughter.

Finally the two placed their orders. One got smothered turkey wings and the other fried catfish. "I started to get the potato salad, but I decided to stick with greens, yams, and a side of mac and cheese. The same as we get every time." Deacon Burton heard his niece chattering but didn't process a thing. "Did you hear me, Uncle?"

"No, what?" he said kind of embarrassed.

"Never mind; how's Auntie and the boys?"

"Oh, they're fine. Junior is growing fast and Mark is a good kid."

"I need to come by and see them," she said. Deacon stirred the straw in his glass and let Sonya's words hit the floor. She immediately responded. "Uncle, what is going on with you?"

"What?" he asked startled.

"You're barely talking," she said as the waiter placed their food on the table. Sonya seemed to pause long enough to get all the dishes situated.

Every inch of the table was crammed with a dish. The smell of fried catfish usually had him mesmerized to the point where he had to take a bite in order to calm his craving. This afternoon, he poked his fork at the fish.

"Okay, now I know for sure something is wrong."

"Why do you say that?"

"Because no one plays over a plate of greens and fried catfish, especially nobody in our family. Are you sick?" she asked appearing concerned.

If he'd answered yes, there would have been an element of truth in his response. He was sick to his stomach about the church. The nagging ache of accountability wasn't going to let him walk away in blissful ignorance. His spirit continued crying out, louder and louder. No attempts at quieting it had worked.

"Don't tell me nothing because clearly it's something."

"I'm all right."

"No, you're not. What's going on?"

He squirmed in the seat. She was very perceptive; always had been, even as a child. Law was the right field for her, and he was proud of her job any day except this one. She wasn't going to back off. He'd visit, package up his meal, and get out of there before she figured out too much.

Before he could speak, she admitted, "I'm the one who should be downtrodden."

"Why?"

Sonya set her fork down and wiped her mouth with the napkin. "Well, you know my boss, Maxwell Montgomery?" Deacon Burton didn't know the attorney personally, but between Sonya and the local news, he knew of him. Who didn't in the Philadelphia area? "He almost fired me."

"You're out of a job?" he said sitting up.

"No, I was able to keep my job, but it was a close call." She gathered a fork full of greens. "Much closer than I ever want to experience again."

"What happened?"

She bit into the leafy greens, as he waited for her to speak. "He found out I was a member of Greater Metropolitan."

"Wait a minute, how does going to church get you fired?" he asked totally confused. Sonya chewed more food and wiped her mouth again. She paused and chewed some more. "Sonya, what does the church have to do with your job?"

"Huh," she exclaimed. "I might as well tell you."

"Tell me what?" Deacon Burton said becoming increasingly anxious.

"He's investigating the church," she replied burying her gaze into the yams.

"What kind of investigation? And don't hold back. Tell me what's going on."

"Okay," she barked. "He believes Bishop Jones is in the center of illegal dealings, and that's all I'm going to say."

She offered very little. He had to find out more. If he had to, he would drag the details out of his niece. "What kind of dealings?"

"Honestly, I don't know. He hasn't told me. He's been very hush-hush."

"Really," Deacon Burton said, assuming the investigation involved the prescription drugs. His zeal smashed to the floor, but he couldn't let Sonya see the extent of his dismay. To believe Bishop Jones and Minister Simmons actually had some mess going on in the church was almost too much to digest. They'd both lied to his face, too. He felt sick to his stomach and pushed the plate of food away.

Sonya continued. "He was going to fire me because I was a member of the church, and he thought I was working as a snitch."

"That's crazy."

"I know, right. I was surprised he'd believe something like that about me. I've been nothing but loyal to him. It just goes to show how intense he is about this case. You can trust that if he's putting this much effort into the investigation, somebody at Greater Metropolitan is headed for a brutal defeat in court. You can be guaranteed, it won't be Maxwell Montgomery. That much I know for sure."

Deacon Burton grew more vexed with each sentence. By the sound of Sonya, Bishop Jones and Minister Simmons were going down, but he didn't think it was right for the church to go with them. He had to step up and do something to save the congregation and distance the church and its reputation from the callous acts of two greedy men.

"When is he going to make this public?"

"Not sure," she said wiping her fingers on a napkin. "I'm pretty sure he hasn't gotten all the information he needs, otherwise the church would have heard from him by now," she said scraping the remaining mac and cheese from the small bowl.

"Maybe I can help him."

Sonya flashed her gaze in the direction of her uncle and said, "How?"

"By telling him what I know."

Her disposition spoke volumes. She drew in closer to him, placing the crumbled napkin onto her mostly eaten plate of food. "Please tell me you're not a part of any craziness at the church," she said wearing the shroud of fear.

"I'm not involved, but I know who is."

"Are you serious?" she asked as her eyelids widened. He nodded too ashamed to acknowledge verbally. "So, you want to tell Mr. Montgomery what you know?"

"I think so," he said figuring this was the answer to his prayer. He'd asked for guidance before meeting his niece and now he had it. Walking by faith, he knew there were no coincidences. He was supposed to meet with Sonya at this precise hour. She was supposed to share her news about the attorney's investigation. He was convinced there was divine order associated with him reaching out to the attorney. There was a quick gut check, but he shunned it off. Truth had to reign or he would be no better than the perpetrators. It was decided "I'm sure I want to meet with him. Can you arrange it?"

"Absolutely, if you're sure this is what you want to do."

"It is," he said without thinking. It was best that way. Too much thinking was bound to lead him away from where he had to go.

"On second thought, you better call him directly. I don't want him to think I'm involved. I really would lose my job. I'll give you his number. Call him, but don't mention my name."

"All right."

Sonya hesitated and then said, "You realize this will put Bishop Jones in big financial trouble, because Maxwell Montgomery doesn't bother going to court unless he's asking for millions. The church will probably end up paying the settlement for the bishop, and it won't be cheap."

"I can't worry about what-ifs. I have to do the right thing before God. Write his number down for me. I will call him when I get out to my car. I want to meet with him as soon as possible," Deacon Burton said, pulling the fruit cobbler toward him and taking a large spoonful. His appetite was returning. The catfish was cold and the greens, too, but the sweet taste swirling in his soul was sufficiently satisfying. Peace was entering the restaurant and approaching their table. He sighed relishing the soon-coming relief.

Chapter 36

Deacon Burton turned around catching glimpses of the folks sitting behind him as he patiently waited for Sonya's boss. He paid close attention to the color, make, and model of every car pulling into the parking lot. Fortunately no familiar faces or cars had transported anyone to his discreet spot situated outside the city limits. He'd set up a meeting with someone he hoped would be able to help him sort out the truth about Minister Simmons and Bishop Jones. Yet, he needed to be discreet because he didn't have sufficient facts.

The waitress poured Deacon Burton's third cup of coffee. He stirred in the cream and sugar for over two minutes before realizing it. A male voice behind him drew his attention to the parking lot once again.

"That's a nice-looking Porsche," another patron said. "That must be a custom paint job. Look at how that baby shines."

Deacon Burton watched the man get out of the Porsche, tug at the lapel on his suit jacket, and take what appeared to be confident strides toward the building. Burton began stirring his coffee again, wondering if he'd made a mistake calling Maxwell Montgomery. Reaching out to the attorney seemed like the right decision, but that was several days ago. This was now. He didn't fully understand everything and maybe what he thought he was sure about wasn't right at all. He felt a nervous poking at his gut telling him something was terribly wrong. Anyway, it was too late. He'd arranged the meeting.

Maxwell was standing in the doorway of the restaurant looking around. Deacon Burton stood up, holding a spoon in his hand. "Mr. Montgomery, I'm over here, sir."

Maxwell came to the booth and offered him a firm handshake along with a greeting.

"Thanks for meeting with me, Mr. Montgomery." Deacon Burton sat and finally placed the spoon onto the saucer.

"Call me Maxwell."

"Okay then, Maxwell it is."

"Since we're getting introductions out the way, what made you call me?"

Deacon Burton believed in truth but wouldn't let Maxwell know Sonya was his niece. She'd already told him how mad Maxwell had been with her about Greater Metropolitan. Deacon Burton wasn't going to take a chance and jeopardize his niece's job. For that reason he decided to withhold the truth. He wasn't outright lying or that's what he told his soul to keep it quiet. His spirit knew better.

"First, let me say, I came to you because I didn't want to go directly to the police and cause any scandal for the church. Your reputation is very well known in the church community. Since I don't condone illegal activity in the church any more than you, I felt you could help me figure out what to do."

"I can appreciate that. What do you have to tell me?" Maxwell shifted in his seat and maintained eye contact as the deacon continued.

"A few weeks ago, I ran into a young woman outside the church late one night." Deacon Burton started there and told Maxwell about Jill's accusations and his conversations with Minister Simmons and Bishop Jones. When he'd finished painting a very vivid picture for Maxwell, he sat tall in his seat and pushed out a heavy sigh, causing his shoulders to hunch.

"It's extremely hard for me to tell you these things. I feel disloyal to Minister Simmons and certainly to Bishop Jones. I've served with the bishop for years. I've prayed with both of them and labored side-by-side to win souls for the Lord. And now, I'm coming to you, an outsider, accusing them of something so ugly and wrong." The deacon glanced at his cup of coffee and pushed it to the side.

A waitress stopped at the table and before she could say anything, Maxwell dismissed her with a wave of his hand. "Mr. Burton, if what you're telling me is actually happening, you've done the right thing by coming to me. Maybe this will set your mind at ease. I was already investigating your church and your bishop. With what you've told me, and the information that I've already confirmed, the case against Bishop Jones will be a strong one."

"I can't help but feel badly about how this will impact Greater Metropolitan." Deacon Burton looked across the parking lot at the shimmering specs of light dancing on the hood of Maxwell's car. "One thing is clear, my commitment to God has to come before any loyalty to man."

"Are you involved in this in any way, Mr. Burton?"

"Of course I'm not. If I were, would I have called you?" The deacon slid his right hand from the back of his neck, forward, over the top of his bald head. "My hands are clean. I'm not involved."

"Perhaps you are and you don't realize it. If what you're saying is true, then there is a potentially long list of charges that could be brought against the bishop and other leaders at the church, such as money laundering, illegally dispensing pharmaceutical drugs without a license, sexual harassment, and possibly several others."

"Wait, I never said that Bishop had any personal dealings with the woman," Deacon Burton lashed out not wanting to embellish a single factor or unsubstantiated speculation. The church was already in enough trouble without the devil throwing extra punches.

Maxwell must have sensed the restlessness, because he said, "That's fair. I won't put words in your mouth. Let's stick with what you know, the illegal money filtering through the treasury. Being a deacon, I imagine you have a tremendous amount of responsibility and have to support the ministry in a variety of ways."

"I would agree," the deacon said.

"Did you sign any documents? Did you validate any of the church's financial statements?"

Deacon Burton placed both hands flat on the table, lowered his head and mumbled, "What a mess."

"What did you say?" Maxwell questioned.

Deacon Burton's gaze shot up to Maxwell. "Nothing," he uttered waving off the comment. He drew on his faith and spoke. "I'm the chairman of the deacon's board. I've signed a lot of financial paperwork on the church's behalf. I've signed loan documents. I've verified sources of revenue, yearly tithing totals for loan purposes, and countless other things. I've been a deacon at Greater Metropolitan long before we built the new church." Deacon Burton lifted his left hand from the table, twisting his wedding band encrusted with three diamonds. Maxwell watched him twirl the ring in silence. "It sounds like you've probably signed incriminating documents without knowing what the information actually represented."

"I can't go to jail. I have a family, a wife and two children. I'm responsible for them. I need to be able to take care of my family. Mr. Montgomery, I mean, Maxwell, I can't go to jail."

"Unfortunately, ignorance of the law isn't a defense. It does not absolve you of any criminal activity."

Deacon Burton grabbed the spoon sitting idle in front of him. "I can't believe this. This can't be happening to me. I've done nothing wrong."

"I might be able to help you. If you've really done nothing wrong then you shouldn't have any problem working with me to provide information that will help build the civil case against Bishop and Minister Simmons. If you are willing to do that, I can help you walk away with immunity."

Deacon Burton scanned the restaurant once more for familiar faces, glanced to his left and then his right briefly to assess cars in the parking lot. He strummed his fingers on the top of the table. "How can I help?"

Maxwell took copious notes with his pen seeming to sail smoothly across the paper as Deacon Burton answered questions and spoke freely about what he'd found out. He included the large amounts of tithing. The last detail the deacon shared was what he'd learned from his one and only conversation with Jill. Now, Maxwell knew about the selling of prescription drugs, possible sexual harassment, and the bishop's alleged involvement. Deacon Burton didn't leave out what he believed to be Simmons's part in the whole ugly scandal that seemed to be boiling. Fumbling with the slip of paper in his pocket, finally, his decision was made. Deacon inched the slip of paper, covered by his palm, across the table in front of Maxwell. "Call her. Maybe she can help you figure out this puzzle." Maxwell handled the piece of paper with Jill's name and number on it delicately when he'd tucked it inside his suit jacket. He hoped it would lead to more answers and ultimately an ironclad case.

Chapter 37

Maxwell huffed into the phone. "I'm waiting on that revised case law for sexual harassment. I'd like to get it this morning," He continued riffling through papers on his desk without finding what he wanted. He searched files, paperwork, law books, and the notepads coming up empty. He glanced across the room. Maybe he'd left it over there. Canvassing the conference table as if he was digging for gold rewarded him with a small piece of paper. It was the one Deacon Burton had given him with Jill's phone number. He'd already added her name to a list of possible witnesses. But he wanted to hold on to the piece of paper written in her handwriting.

Maxwell sat at his desk and tugged the cuffs on his shirt. Just as he was about to put pen to paper, a knock at his office door interrupted him. "Yes," he said shifting his sight from the paper to his door.

Sonya cracked the door and peeked around the edge of it. "I've got the law book and the information you requested."

"Come on in, you're just in time. I need to get finished with this." Maxwell stabbed the legal pad with the point of his ink pen. Sonya placed the book in front of him, pointed out the specific legal verbiage, and abruptly turned to leave.

"I apologize for snapping at you earlier. I have to get this information in order to finish up what I'm doing."

"Don't worry about it, Mr. Montgomery. I know how you are when you have your teeth dug into something. Let me know if you need anything else."

Maxwell spent the next two hours fine-tuning his strategy. He'd just finished up his list of questions when Sonya informed him that Jill was waiting in the outer office. Maxwell rubbed the palms of his hands together and moved the books, notes, and papers on his desk over to the conference table. Now, he was ready. He stepped into the outer office, introduced himself to Jill, and ushered her into his office. "Have a seat, Ms. Smith."

"Jill is fine." She sat slowly in the chair situated in front of Maxwell's desk.

"Jill it is. Call me Maxwell," he said. "I appreciate you agreeing to speak with me. We can accomplish more in person than we can over the phone."

"I have to tell you, I don't feel comfortable being here," she said wringing her hands.

"Relax, this is informal," he told her.

"I can't relax. I don't know what else I can tell you. I told you everything I know over the phone. I'm pressed for time. I have to get my kids from the babysitter in less than an hour."

"Then we better get moving if you have a time constraint. Shouldn't take long for you to give me the information I need."

"I don't know what else you want from me." Jill leaned forward slightly and massaged the lower part of her back gingerly.

"I want you to pursue sexual harassment in a civil court case against Minister Simmons and Bishop Jones."

"Oh no, Bishop Jones didn't do anything to me."

Maxwell heard what she said and allowed it to fuel his contempt. Decades of deceit and people were willing to squander their freedom to protect this man. He couldn't or wouldn't believe that Jill or Deacon Burton was telling the truth about Bishop Jones's lack of involvement in the shady dealings. They were lying and Maxwell knew it.

"Stop trying to protect a guilty man. Do the right thing. Come forth and tell us about those guys.

"I can't do that. I can't get involved." She turned sideways and leaned her weight onto the arm of the chair.

"You're already involved. You've purchased illegal prescription drugs. You've taken money to broker a relationship between your drug supplier and Minister Simmons."

She appeared stunned and lowered her gaze. "How do you know this?" she stammered.

"I have my ways," he said twirling a pen between his fingers.

"Excuse me, Mr. Montgomery, I have a stabbing pain in my back and it's crawling up my spine. Do you mind if I stand?"

"Not at all," Maxwell answered watching her rise carefully from her seat, wincing. He preferred to think her sudden surge of pain was meant to distract his line of questioning, but his inclination said no. Her pain was real. It seemed to ravage her body with each passing second.

"I haven't forgotten my role in this. You probably think I'm a shiftless nobody addicted to drugs who's willing to do anything to get a hit." She walked around the chair and braced herself by firmly planting both hands on it. Honestly, Maxwell didn't have an opinion about her and resisted responding. "I bet you come from a two-parent household with plenty of money. You probably went to a private school and never had kids tease you because you didn't have decent clean clothes." She grimaced in pain as she struggled to stand straight. "I'm all my children have, and I've done what I absolutely had to do in order to provide for them. We don't have a big, fine house and money in the bank, but my kids are clean, and taken care of. I love them and, most of all, we're together. And that's the way it has to stay. If I testify about the sexual harassment, Minister Simmons is bound to tell about the pills." Jill's voice elevated. "I can't risk it, because the department of children and family services will end up in the picture. I could lose my kids." Maxwell' was distracted by the boulders of tears forming in her eyes.

Maxwell stood and pulled tissue from the dispenser on his desk and handed it to her. "I understand your concern. However, I don't think you've considered the money that could be gained from a civil suit like this one. You could end up not having to worry about money ever again. Taking care of your children financially would no longer be a problem, and then you could afford the best medical care." Maxwell handed her more tissue.

"I grew up without my father. He just walked out on us. My mother died when I was young. I just can't take the risk of my children being caught up with some crazy child protection agency that will split them up. I won't lose my kids. If you try to force me into this, I will deny everything." She wiped her flowing tears and blew her nose. "I won't lie on Bishop Jones. I just won't do it. I won't participate in any way."

Maxwell could hear the tenacity in her voice. Jill's only concern was keeping her children, and that was one area he was not willing to touch. If only his parents had shown such commitment to their children, perhaps the Montgomery's of Chester, PA would have turned out differently. He dwelled on his family and their fractured relationships briefly before casting it aside. He had more pressing matters to handle than poking around old wounds. However, without Jill's participation on the civil angle, the bishop would only have to contend with criminal charges. Building criminal cases wasn't Maxwell's arena, but he'd gladly make an exception for Bishop Jones. Although Maxwell didn't trust any prosecutor with a case this important, he didn't seem to have much choice. He'd just have to package the evidence in such a concise way that no one could fumble the litigation, or so he hoped.

Chapter 38

The sun had long set and the day was slipping away by the second. Maxwell was alert, focused, and alone in his office. When Jill left earlier, she took with her the hope of having a stellar plaintiff. What twelve reasonable people wouldn't have their hearts pricked by a single mother struggling financially to take care of her children and enduring constant pain in the process? She reached out to a minister in the church who, instead of helping, took advantage of her for his own monetary gain and entangled her in an illegal drug business. Maxwell propped his feet up on top of his desk, envisioning the impact those facts and her testimony would have in a courtroom.

Minutes later, Maxwell yanked his feet down and pounded the corner of the desk with his fist. He wasn't going to be able to use Jill. That meant he would have to proceed with the zoning violations and then turn the findings over to the district attorney for criminal prosecution. He wasn't pleased. His trademark had consistently been to cripple the perpetrators where it mattered most—in their wallets. That's why he lived for civil cases. Criminal law was too much work for too little gain. Sitting in some posh jail for a few months or even years didn't constitute sufficient restitution, but bankruptcy cut much deeper for greedy pariahs like Bishop Jones and Minister Simmons.

His anger swelled. He couldn't let Bishop Jones get away with anything less. Maxwell wouldn't accept a partial defeat. He had come too close to a full-fledged victory, and he wasn't about to give up. He paced the floor racking his brain to come up with a way to build a solid case and link the church to the wider-scaled crime. He stopped in the middle of the floor, rolled up his sleeves and loosened his tie. Maxwell pulled four boxes from his closet. He ravished the boxes one-by-one meticulously scrutinizing every piece of paper related to the case. He must have missed something that would give him the concrete victory he yearned. Papers covered his desk and the conference table; he even had a stack as high as the trashcan, sitting on the floor next to his desk.

Four hours into his scavenger hunt, Maxwell grew with excitement. He moved swiftly to his desk, knocking the stack of papers onto the floor. He pushed the documents underneath the bright lamp on his desk. Maxwell's gaze, swollen with anticipation, followed his index finger as he slowly read each word. He pinched his eyelids with his fingertips determined to be sure of what he was reading. With his weary eyes refocused, he read the documents again. Finally, he had linked several zoning violations with questionable real estate transactions that Chambers had brokered for another church. He whizzed to the stack of papers he'd just struck gold in and there it was; the final nail. He had Chambers' signature on a deal with Greater Metropolitan dated before the rezoning transactions began, which meant somehow they influenced the zoning changes. Business owners had been forced out of their places due to underhanded tactics. The shady dealings had apparently been in the works for some time.

Maxwell was giddy with pleasure. His victory at the end of a long journey was in sight. He had to talk to someone. He needed to hear the words out loud. Maxwell didn't let the fact that it was past midnight sway him from calling Garrett. Both men had invested many hours building this case and neither needed a lot of sleep.

Maxwell glided to the window, shoving his cell phone up to his ear. He peered into the dark of the early morning. It may as well have been a day filled with sunlight. He could see the bright path at the end of the road. Maxwell snapped his fingers, and Garrett answered on the second ring.

"Maxwell, what's up?" Garrett sounded slightly groggy, but Maxwell wasn't deterred.

"I've got it. I've got the information we need to help the prosecutor build a solid case against Bishop Jones. I've got him and Greater Metropolitan in the palm of my hand." Maxwell lifted his open palm up into the air and snatched down a clenched fist. "I've got him."

"What about the civil case? Is this Jill woman you were telling me about going to substantiate the sexual harassment and drug charges?" Garrett asked.

"No, that's not going to work out."

"Wow, that's too bad," Garrett uttered. "Without her you don't have a case, unless there's someone else you can use?"

With energy in his voice like he'd had a full night's sleep, Maxwell told Garrett about the documents he'd uncovered tying Chambers and Greater Metropolitan to land deals and possible zoning violations. "The small business owners can bring a civil case against Bishop Jones and Greater Metropolitan."

"Have you spoken to any of them?" Garrett asked.

"Not yet. I figured you could help me out."

"Sure thing, but are you sure this is the route you want to take?"

"Not really. You know I've always avoided class action suits with multiple plaintiffs. The more you have to deal with on one case, the more something is likely to go wrong. People can't agree on a settlement amount or their accounting of the facts. It can be a legal nightmare."

"I know that. That's why I asked."

"Reality is that I have to pursue the class action cases and then rely on the prosecutor's office to seal the deal on the criminal side. It's not my winning strategy, but what choice do I have?"

"You can always walk away."

Maxwell wanted to curse but choked the words back. "Man, you must be kidding. After years of pursuing this church?" he shouted.

"Relentlessly I might add," Garrett interrupted.

Maxwell raised his open palms in the air and emphatically said, "E-x-a-c-t-l-y, which is why running away isn't remotely an option. This might not be playing out as ideally as I would have liked, but at this point, I'll take what I can get in the way of a conviction."

"That's heavy stuff. Sounds like you're finally where you want to be. What about Simmons?"

"Oh, he's too easy. I'll toss his sorry behind to the prosecutor." Maxwell snorted. "His stupid behind left so much evidence exposed that a law clerk fresh out of school could get him convicted for five to ten years." Both men were amused. They continued going back and forth recounting the challenges in the case that had brought them to this point.

Maxwell ended the conversation with Garrett as cheerfully as it had begun. "The civil award in this case should be large enough to significantly impair, if not shut down, Greater Metropolitan. That tower of sin and iniquity is coming down." Maxwell burst into a roar of jubilant laughter as he pressed the end button on his phone. His gusty roar filled the room as he unlocked the bottom drawer of his desk. He pulled out a list with names and numbers of the former small business owners who were robbed of their land. He and Garrett would make calls later this morning to elicit their participation into a class action lawsuit. They had to get it done before the criminal charges surfaced. He wanted the crippling reality of doom to be felt by Bishop Jones and Greater Metropolitan from every angle. Maxwell figured it would probably take a month to file if he worked night and day preparing the complaint. Gleefully, he would be counting the days.

Chapter 39

Unrest swept across the church office. "Simmons, where is Chambers? I called him over an hour ago. He should be here by now." Bishop Jones hastily plucked the phone receiver from its cradle and growled at the church secretary. "Have you heard from Councilman Chambers?"

"No."

"Are you sure? Could you have missed his call?"

"I'm sure, Bishop," his secretary affirmed. "He hasn't called."

"Okay, let me know the minute you hear from him, no matter what I'm doing or where I am in the church." He pushed the receiver down with a loud noise startling Simmons who was placing the fourth call to Chambers on his cell phone.

"We need to finish this deal and get moving." Bishop's grandson was being released from juvenile lockup in about a month. Adequate time for completing the proposed rehab project wasn't on his side. Bishop pointed his finger at Simmons. "I don't know what's happened to the councilman, but it better not be connected to your foolishness," he shouted.

"What?"

"Don't what me. I'm not convinced you've shut down your operation. I truly hope, for your sake, that you didn't take my kindness and compassion for weakness. You best believe that it's not too late for me to kick your

behind so far out of this church that when you look back
you can't see the steeple," the bishop yelled and then
remembered where he was before bringing his tone
down. The walls of his office were thick enough to muffle
his angered volume, but he didn't want to disrespect the
house of God. He gained composure and folded his arms
across his chest. "Maybe the councilman got word of your
foolishness here in the church and is distancing himself
from our real estate dealings. I certainly hope I'm wrong,
very wrong," he said staring Simmons down and letting
the tension hover. Bishop wanted to knock the minister's
head off for putting the church and his staff at risk. Thank
goodness restraint prevailed. Bishop prayed for help.
For Simmons's sake, God had better continue giving him
strength to maintain control. Otherwise, Simmons was
in big trouble, not with the law but at the hands of his
spiritual father.

"I know, Bishop. I know, and I'm sorry," he said with
what appeared to be remorse. Simmons shook his cell
phone vigorously causing his whole body to shake. "I
can't get through to the councilman. When I try his cell
phone, I just get his voicemail. When I call his office,
his secretary keeps telling me he's in a meeting. You
would think we could get him on the telephone based on
the amount of deals we've already done with him," the
minister said.

"I should be hearing from our accountant and attorney
within a half hour," Bishop stated. "One of them should
know something about those last property deals. Sit
down, Simmons, you're making me nervous."

Simmons sat in front of the bishop's desk. They hadn't
been talking longer than ten minutes when police sirens,
slamming car doors, and loud voices pulled the bishop
up from his seat and drew him to the window in his
office. The church parking lot looked like the scene from
a SWAT episode. Simmons rushed to the window as well.

"What in God's name is going on here?" Noise coming from outside the bishop's office sounded like the ground invasion of army troops. On the heels of his question, his office door swung open and a crowd of police officers swarmed into the office led by the secretary.

Bishop was fuming. "What do you mean by bursting into my office? This is a church. I'm Bishop Ellis Jones, and I'm in a private meeting." The bishop challenged the intruders in his office with a stern voice and bulging eyes, which landed on the face of each officer standing before him.

Frantically, his secretary said, "I tried to stop them, Bishop, but I didn't know what to do." She was crying and chaos was rampant.

"Don't worry, you go on home. I'll handle this," Bishop told her, not so sure if he was more anxious or mad about the predicament.

"No, ma'am, we need you to wait out there. We have to ask you some questions."

The same officer stepped up to the Bishop. "We have warrants for your arrest and to search the premises." The policeman shoved both warrants at the bishop.

"Warrants! Arrest! Under arrest for what? What are the charges?" Bishop Jones's words fell out of his mouth and left it hanging open with him waiting for an answer.

"You're under arrest for dispensing pharmaceuticals without a license, racketeering and sexual assault."

"What? Assault, are you kidding? Assault? This is a mistake."

"Bishop Ellis Jones, can you please step forward," an officer said, "and place your hands out front." As he placed the cuffs on Bishop, he said, "You have the right to remain silent."

Bishop was pretty sure the police recited the rest of the Miranda rights but nothing processed. He felt delirious.

This wasn't happening, couldn't be. Although he had allowed this crisis to fester, he instinctively cried out to God. Who else could he call?

Simmons attempted to slide toward the door unnoticed. Two police officers stepped into his path. "Mr. Otis Simmons, you're also under arrest," an officer said, slapping the warrant into the minister's hand. "Read Mr. Simmons his rights, but don't escort them from the building just yet." The same officer turned to the policemen standing in the secretary's office and said, while making a circling motion above his head with his hands, "Bring in the dogs."

"Dogs," Simmons said shifting his gaze toward the bishop.

Time crawled by with the bishop and Simmons seated at the conference table in the office. Beads of sweat burned on Bishop Jones's forehead. He was unable to freely swipe at his brow, hindered by the handcuffs that were causing his wrists to swell. Minister Simmons sat next to him bouncing his leg up and down.

The bishop was used to maintaining composure and attempted to regain some. "I've had enough of this. I want to know what you're looking for. Where is my secretary? I need to call my attorney." No one responded to the bishop. But, it wasn't long before he had more information than he wanted to know.

"Captain, we've got something here," a voice cried out in the crowd of officers.

The fierce chaos got louder as they approached the front office. How many cops were there and what were they hoping to find? The bishop wasn't sure as he leaned forward, hoping to see past the officers standing in front of him. The sea of black uniforms parted and there stood an officer holding a box. Bishop could tell the officer had rank by the number of colorful bars on his jacket.

"What's that?" Bishop asked.

The officer set the open box on the table. Bishop's eyelids widened with disbelief. There were Ziploc bags of colorful pills and stacks of money the length and width of bricks wrapped in cellophane.

Bishop Jones turned slowly to look at Simmons. The bishop's breathing was rapid and deep, and his eyelids had narrowed into slits almost as thin as a dime. Simmons looked at the pills being dangled in the air, then at the money, and dropped his gaze.

Bishop Jones stood up shouting with a forceful wrath in his voice, "Where did you get that? Did you plant it here?"

"Sit down," the officer commanded.

The bishop reluctantly obeyed the order, but he didn't keep quiet. "This is the house of God. I demand to know where you got that." His shoulders shuddered with anger and anxiety.

The officer ignored the bishop's demands. "Bag it and tag it. I want a thorough search of the premises. If there are street drugs on the premise, I want to know that too. Don't leave a single Bible unturned."

More officers, noise, and chaos engulfed the bishop's office. He was powerless witnessing the invasion of his privacy and enraged at the carelessness of Simmons. He turned in the minister's direction and pulled away his seething stare quickly.

Simmons hadn't said a word in the midst of what unfolded in front of him, but his tomato red face and the tear crawling down his cheek spoke loudly. Bishop Jones was far from silent. He rose from his seat steadfast, furious and demanding his rights.

"I want to call my attorney. Right now; I know my rights," he protested lifting his handcuffed wrists out in front of him.

"Not a problem, Bishop Jones. You can call your attorney as soon as you've been booked and fingerprinted," the policeman replied and then gave the order, "Let's get them downtown."

The bishop was led out of his office in handcuffs and in sheer disbelief. As he passed through the outer office, he saw his secretary being questioned by an officer. He held on to her with his gaze, practically willing her to look in his direction. Disappointingly, she didn't read his mind or give him what he needed before he'd asked. He was marched down the hall, past the life-sized painting of Christ hanging on the cross. With two husky officers on each side, the bishop stumbled underneath the large wooden archway with his name on it, proclaiming him Bishop of Greater Metropolitan.

The double doors leading down the front steps of the church were next. The bishop cleared his throat, attempted to walk slower, but the officers escorting him were setting the pace. The two officers leading the way reached the double doors first. They swung them open with force, allowing the sunlight and every willing spectator to catch a clear view. Cameras, news reporters, church members, and more police offered Bishop Jones a bitter greeting. As he descended the steps, flashing cameras and microphones were thrust into his face. Recognition, interest, and scores of people appeared riveted by his presence but not for the reasons he wanted.

Chapter 40

Garrett was glued to his wide-screen TV as he quickly dialed Maxwell's cell phone. His call was eventually answered on the fourth or fifth ring. "It's about time you got the phone, man."

"Why, what's up?"

"Get to a TV and turn to Channel 10 as fast as you can."

"What's going on?" Maxwell asked pulling a remote from his desk drawer.

"Hurry up. Turn it on."

Maxwell stood and aimed the remote at the cherry wood credenza. The double doors parted to reveal a TV. Maxwell pressed the power button and sailed to the channel. His living room illuminated with camera crews, reporters, and scads of people watching Bishop Jones and Minister Simmons being escorted down the steps of Greater Metropolitan church in handcuffs. Maxwell moved closer to his desk and sat on the edge keeping one foot on the floor. He latched on to the bishop's face, intrigued by every expression, while he listened to the news reporter recount what had transpired.

"If you've just tuned in, you're watching the latest breaking news here at Greater Metropolitan church in the heart of Philadelphia. It's reportedly one of the largest congregations in the city. Bishop Ellis Jones and a Minister Otis Simmons have just been arrested on a series of charges, including sexual assault and illegally selling pharmaceutical drugs. Ironically, this church was featured six years ago under very different circumstances. Many may recall Greater Metropolitan established a school for low-income families in the community. They've since won numerous state and local awards for academic excellence. This is truly a sad day for Greater Metropolitan and the surrounding community."

The reporter appeared distracted as he pressed his finger against the earpiece. "My sources are telling me police raided the church this morning based on an anonymous tip and that there are more charges yet to come. While standing here we've watched the police file out with boxes. I'm not sure what they've found, but I have to believe they're looking for drugs since the K-9 team is on the premise. This is quite a stunning set of events." The reporter paused again and began treading briskly. "Let's see if we can get in closer to Bishop Ellis Jones who is being led to a squad car," the reporter said directing his camera crew. "Let's hear what he has to say."

"I'm innocent. This is a gross miscarriage of justice and an insult to the house of God. Marching dogs throughout the church and disrespecting God's sanctuary. I'm innocent, and the truth will come out."

"Are you saying this is a mistake even though drugs were found on the premises?" another reporter called out.

"I'm saying God will deal with the perpetrators, the ones who have orchestrated this injustice."

"Well there you have it, folks; the leader of this church professing his innocence. This will prove to be an interesting story for weeks to come. Stay tuned as we bring you more feedback from onlookers here on the scene at Greater Metropolitan."

"Well, the day has finally come. He's in handcuffs and on his way to jail," Garrett told Maxwell.

"Yes, he is in handcuffs and that's an encouraging sight, but the real battle is just beginning. You know these charges won't equate to more than three to five years in prison at best, plus fifty or a hundred thousand in fines. And, that's if the racketeering holds up."

"And, that's a big if."

"You got that right. Any half-decent attorney can get him off, which is why I have to hit those pockets and cripple his defense funds."

"What else can you do?"

"Find more criminal charges, strengthen the civil complaint, and heck, I'll call the IRS if necessary. With so much dirty money floating around, some of it had to end up in the offering plate and violate their nonprofit status." Maxwell pulled a coin from his pocket, tossed it into the air and snatched it down. "Wow, what a setup. The church rakes in the cash that stuffs Jones's pockets so he can drive luxury cars, live in a fat mansion, buy property all over the city, wear tailor-made suits and not pay a penny in taxes. The IRS will be glad to crawl all over that."

"You probably have a point. What a tangled web the bishop has woven. With this much smoke, there's got to be fire somewhere. I think you got him," Garrett stated. "There's going to be too many charges for him to get off clean."

"We've got a long, hard trial process ahead of us before he spends more than a day or two in jail, let alone in prison. I have the civil case, but it's not enough. There has to be more tossed in to up the ante."

"I hate to bring this up," Garrett said, lowering his voice, which made Maxwell nervous. "What if it's true?"

"What?"

"Come on, you must have considered the possibility that the bishop is telling the truth," Garrett suggested. "What if he's actually innocent?"

Maxwell paused. He hadn't wanted to consider the possibility, but Garrett was right. The notion had popped into his mind, and he'd shoved it out. Waiting for vengeance his entire adult life justified the shove. He wasn't about to forfeit his victory on a minor technicality like truth.

"He's guilty of a long list of criminal acts spread over at least three decades."

"Maybe, but not this one," Garrett added.

"That's how twisted fate is. Remember when you were a kid. Sometimes you got a whopping for something you didn't actually do, but your parents felt justified. Mine did because they figured if the beating was in error, it only made up for something else I'd done and thought I'd gotten away with." Maxwell rubbed his hands together briskly. "It balances out in the end. Trust me, the bishop deserves exactly what he's going to get." Garrett kept quiet. "Remember, he cheated half the neighborhood out of their businesses. He's not innocent."

"You're right about the businesses."

"And, I'm not pumping that into the criminal case, because I prefer saving it for my arena—the civil courtroom."

Garrett chuckled. "I hear you."

"I'll catch up with you later," Maxwell told Garrett, then ended the call. Shortly afterwards, Maxwell picked up the phone to call the Pennsylvania attorney general, a buddy from law school. Fraud and money laundering had to be considered the same way it had for his parents. His next call would be to the IRS. He dialed rapidly as his adrenaline skyrocketed.

Maxwell wasn't completely ready to claim total annihilation. There remained many miles of this journey left in front of him. By the end of the day, with the evidence dredged up by Garrett and input from Deacon Burton, most of Bishop Jones's ministerial staff were arrested and hit with charges too. As far as Maxwell was concerned, they were guilty if for no other reason than being ignorant to the bishop's agenda. Everyone had to pay.

Deacon Burton stood in the living room of his home watching the TV screen come to life as the police raided his church. Five days later and the Greater Metropolitan arrests remained a leading story. Deacon Burton was tired of watching the local news channels recap the horrible event. There weren't any expressions that could show how distraught Deacon Burton felt at the precise moment when his handcuffed bishop was being escorted from the house of God and into the back of a squad car. He knew the charges were coming, but honestly, he hadn't been prepared for the arrests to play out like they had. The image replayed, rapidly, viciously, with no regard. He turned the television off and set the remote down. He'd seen plenty.

"Are you okay?" his wife said easing up behind him and placing her hand on his shoulder.

"No, I'm not, but God will work it out." That belief was his primary source of peace, that and the promise Maxwell Montgomery had made to keep him out of this fiasco. The deacon took comfort in his rapport with the attorney and embraced his wife. They were okay.

Ten minutes later there was a strong knock on the door.

"Are you expecting anyone?" Deacon Burton asked his wife. She told him no and continued drinking a cup of coffee while thumbing through a magazine. "Well, let me see who it is," he said, setting his word search booklet on the table.

The small house didn't require many steps to get from the kitchen to their front door. Deacon peered out the tiny peephole positioned in the middle of the door to see three gentlemen, none he recognized. "Yes, can I help you?"

"Mr. Steve Burton, we're Officers Kent, Craft, and Smith."

The deacon became edgy. He hadn't expected to give his testimony this early into the process. If he could only close his eyelids and wish the whole legal business away, he certainly would. He gripped the doorknob, certain that his purpose and role in this business had been established by God before his birth. He was predestined for this. He turned the knob, ready to tell the truth and get his testimony behind him.

When the door opened, he said, "Yes, Officers, how can I help you?"

They each flashed what appeared to be police badges. "Mr. Steve Burton, we have a warrant for your arrest," one officer said, handing him a piece of paper.

Deacon reached for the paper, but somehow his mind couldn't believe what he heard. "Excuse me," he said leaning against the door, "what did you say?"

"You're under arrest for fraud, the illegal distribution of drugs, and racketeering."

Deacon Burton's wife approached the front door. "Step back, ma'am," an officer said, drawing his weapon. The deacon's wife screamed and then clasped her lips shut.

"Is there anyone else in the house?" Neither Deacon nor his wife was composed well enough to readily respond. "I asked who else is in the house."

"No one else," Deacon blurted out, glad his children were at school.

In an instant, the officer had cuffs on the deacon. "Call Maxwell Montgomery," he told his wife. "Don't worry, honey, this is a mistake," he said. "I'll go down to the police station and get this resolved." His words seemed to comfort his wife. As he got into the car a flood of what-ifs drowned him. He blocked the flow of negativity. He'd made the right decision in reporting the bishop and Minister Simmons. There was no need for second-guessing. The truth was out in the open. He couldn't retreat, not now, not when the church needed at least one leader to step up and let righteousness prevail. It would only take one. He relaxed in the seat. He was that one.

Chapter 41

Pastor Harris had been at home in his study for over two hours. The songs of praise and worship were echoing softly. His wife had come to the door repeatedly to see if he was ready for a break. He read the morning paper, which was plastered with the continued headlines about Bishop Jones and his church. When Pastor Harris finally emerged from his study, the smell of coffee lured him into the kitchen. "That smells good," he told his wife, drawing in a big whiff.

"Dear, you look so weary," she exclaimed softly, turning away from the stove as he walked toward her. "Sit down, and I'll get you a cup of coffee and something to eat."

"Thanks, toast and coffee is fine. I just finished my three-day fast, and I don't feel much like eating."

"I know, you never do, but you have to eat something. You didn't sleep well last night either. So much tossing and turning, and I know you got up at four this morning and came downstairs."

"I didn't want to disturb you, but Greater Metropolitan is weighing heavily on my heart."

"There's so much talk going on," his wife said.

"I know, and for some reason, I can't get Maxwell Montgomery off my mind either. God is pressing me to pray for him and extend fellowship. I would rather have nothing to do with him and his obsession. He just seems like such a malicious man. Maybe I should say a troubled man." Pastor Harris turned up the cup and took a sip of his coffee while glaring out the bay window. The sun was shining brightly and a bird landed on the window ledge. Pastor Harris drew closer and the bird didn't move. It sat there completely unintimidated. The bird flapped its wings and flew near Pastor Harris, chirped and then flew away.

"I've got to call Maxwell Montgomery, and I've got to do it today," Pastor Harris said.

"If God has him on your heart, be obedient," his wife added.

Harris had only taken two bites of the toast when he got up and dumped it in the trash.

"Dear, you need to eat. I'll cut up some fresh fruit, okay?"

"I'll eat later. I've got to take care of God's business before I do anything else." He took her into his arms and held her tightly. "I thank God for blessing me with a loving supportive wife who I can always count on." In her arms he drew the strength needed to pick up the phone and make a necessary call. The cordless phone sitting on the island in the kitchen rang. "I'll get it," Harris told his wife, releasing his hold on her. "Hello, Pastor Harris speaking."

"Pastor, this is Sister Nelson."

"What can I do for you?" the pastor asked his long-standing member.

"Praise the Lord, Pastor. I hope you're praying for those folks over at Greater Metropolitan. What a mess for their bishop to be caught up in, selling drugs in the church; shame on him. That whole church is going to fall apart with the bishop in jail. I always knew something wasn't right over there. They're too big and have too much money from what I hear." She sighed and continued. "Anyway—"

Pastor Harris rubbed his forehead and sliced into his parishioner before she could go any further. "Sister Nelson, in a crisis like this we need to fast and pray for those of us who have made mistakes. None of us are perfect, and we all need God's strength and direction. When one church is under attack and falls, the entire body of Christ and the community is impacted."

"Oh, I know, Pastor. But—"

Pastor Harris cut her off again, determined to make his point. "Let's pray for Greater Metropolitan and its leadership. Pray that this situation will come to a quick resolution and those members and the community will hold on to its faith in God. I believe Bishop Jones has assigned one of his senior ministers to reside over Greater Metropolitan until this situation is resolved." Pastor Harris shot his wife a quick glance shaking his head in disappointment. "We cannot be part of the failure. We must stand together. I'm counting on you, Sister Nelson, to rebuke gossip and negativity about this situation anytime you hear or see it. I trust you will do that. I know you're calling to talk with my wife. She's standing right here. Have a blessed day, Sister," he rattled off, refusing to let her spew another word of frivolous religious rhetoric.

Pastor Harris handed the phone to his wife, kissed her on the cheek and retreated to the desk in his study. He panned his various pictures hanging on the wall. There were pictures of him preaching to large congregations, meeting with state dignitaries, but it was the one taken with Bishop Ellis Jones that resonated. Their churches and two others had held the largest recorded tent revival in the city's Fairmount Park several years ago. People were everywhere. Many souls had been saved.

Pastor Harris grieved for Bishop Ellis. Regardless of what he'd done, there had to be some godliness in him if he was leading people to salvation. The devil might get credit for doing many things, but saving souls from the pit of hell wasn't one of them. Only God got that honor, and praise be to those who were committed to sharing the good news of Jesus Christ with other people. Pastor Harris believed Bishop was in that group. He wouldn't judge another man's struggle.

Harris's thoughts shifted to Maxwell Montgomery and the comments he'd made about Greater Metropolitan in recent months. The harsh and unrelenting tone bothered the pastor. He understood the attorney had a job to do, but the bitterness behind his motives was troubling. Pastor Harris prayed briefly and then picked up the phone to his private line. His faith echoed that no man was beyond God's redeeming power.

He continued to pray as he dialed the phone. "This is Pastor Renaldo Harris. May I please speak with Maxwell Montgomery?" He didn't have to wait long before a man on the other end greeted him.

"Pastor Harris, good afternoon. What can I do for you?"

The pastor was surprised at the warm tone coming from the attorney. He felt God was already at work preparing a smooth path for their conversation. "Mr. Montgomery, thank you for taking my call." Pastor leaned forward planting his elbows onto his desk. "I called to thank you for your efforts in the community. It is imperative that there be integrity and accountability in the church. This is the only way the community will see the church as an oasis and a resting place."

"Thanks for the acknowledgment; just doing my job."

Pastor noticed another bird sitting on the windowsill as he listened to Maxwell talk about the widespread corruption in the church. Not sure if it was the same bird, he glided to the window. The bird didn't move, but it chirped as Pastor Harris saw a colorful rainbow gleaming beyond the bright sunlight. Inspired, he continued. "I would love to have you visit my church. I know you are a busy man, but I hope you take a Sunday off to stop in. I am sure you will be blessed."

"Hmm," Maxwell responded after a few seconds. "You could look up and see me in the audience one day. I just might find a reason to stop by."

Pastor Harris thought he heard sarcasm bubbling up in Maxwell's tone. He pressed forward anyway. "I certainly hope so. Actually, you've been on my mind quite heavily. I believe God wants to do something in your life. Heal something, restore something; God definitely has a plan for you. I will be praying for you, and I hope to see you soon."

Several moments of hush hovered then Maxwell's voice came forth. "Have a good day."

Pastor hung up the phone and slid to his knees in prayer. He could already tell that dealing with Maxwell Montgomery was going to require a heavy dose of patience and prayer. He hoped God would reveal a plan and show him what to do next. He believed God was going to deal with Maxwell Montgomery in some way. He didn't know when or how, but he was confident God was using him to reach the attorney. By faith he was ready for whatever lay ahead.

Chapter 42

Sonya was overwhelmed. There was a flurry of activity in the office. The phone was constantly ringing since the arrests had been made at Greater Metropolitan. Briefs had to be filed and depositions had to be taken. Thank goodness she'd gotten permission to hire a temporary office assistant who could help take calls, run errands, get documents to the courthouse, and do whatever else had to be done on short notice.

"Excuse me, Sonya," the temp said, sitting at a make-shift desk and call center. "There's a Steve Burton on line one."

Sonya was instantly nervous, searching the room to see if her boss was in the vicinity. She didn't see him and was slightly relieved but not totally safe. "I'll take the call in the library. Please forward the call in there for me." Sonya thanked her assistant and rushed to the phone. She entered the library as the phone rang and grabbed it right away. "Uncle Steve, why are you calling me here?" she said, basically whispering.

"They're only letting me make one call."

"Who?" she asked desperate to get off the line.

"I've been arrested. I'm in jail at the Roundhouse downtown."

Sonya gasped and dropped to a seat. "Oh no, Uncle Steve, what happened? What are you doing in jail?" Her uncle had always been a good, honest, churchgoing man. She couldn't imagine any reason for him to be locked up, none. "It must be some mistake."

"I sure hope so," he said.

"Seriously, what are you doing down there?" she asked.

"I was arrested along with the other church leaders."

"Those people were arrested a week ago. Are you telling me you've been downtown almost a week?" she said, no longer concerned with keeping her voice low.

"Oh no, I came down this morning."

"Wow."

"Look, I don't have much time. I'm calling because Mr. Montgomery agreed to help me if I needed it and clearly I do."

Sonya was sick at the thought of her dear uncle being locked up. She'd totally forgotten about her boss and all of his connections until her uncle mentioned his name. He was definitely the answer. He didn't handle criminal cases, but he could recommend someone who did. "Let me go get him. He has to help you, Uncle."

"Sonya," he blurted, "don't tell him we're related."

"I'm not worried about him knowing anymore. My top priority is getting you out. I don't care about the rest."

"I'll be fine, but I don't want you to lose your job behind this. Please, do me a favor and don't tell him we're related, please, niece."

"All right, I won't say anything unless I have to. Hold on before your call gets cut off."

She dashed from the room and went straight to her boss's office. Sonya knocked rapidly and repeatedly until Maxwell opened his door.

"Sonya, what's going on? Can I help you?" he asked clearly agitated by her persistence.

"Deacon Burton is on the phone. He's been arrested and wants to speak with you."

"Really, arrested. Hmm," he said seemingly surprised.

She was anxious to get him on the phone. Her uncle's call had probably ended already, but they could get him back on the line. Maxwell Montgomery had deep connections at City Hall, and she needed him to use each one to get her uncle out. He was an innocent man and didn't deserve to spend a second more down there. She knew her boss would take care of this and her disposition settled. "He wants to speak with you."

"Me?" he said moving away from the door and toward his desk.

"Yes, you," she said firmly. "He said you offered to help him."

Maxwell returned to his desk and began typing into his electronic tablet. "I don't know why he called me. I can't help him."

"What do you mean?" she asked becoming more antsy and irritated. For sure her uncle's call had been terminated by now. "He seemed pretty sure you could help him."

"I may have spoken hastily when I made the offer. Clearly Bishop Jones and his entire staff are dealing with a litany of charges. I couldn't help him if I wanted to. He needs an attorney who practices criminal law, not a civil lawyer."

"Will you at least take the call and give him some hope?"

"No, I won't, and why do you care so much about what happens to the deacon?"

This was her moment to come clean and let him know they were related. She was ready to open her mouth and let the truth soar, but her uncle's voice rang in her ear forcing Sonya to keep quiet on the matter. "He seemed to believe you made him a promise. I truly believe he's counting on you."

"Well, I'm sorry to hear that, but I can give you the name of a good defense attorney if it will help."

Her uncle wasn't rich. There wasn't money hanging from trees in her family. Where was Uncle Steve going to get big money for a real lawyer? Sonya was fuming. Mostly she felt guilty. It was her suggestion that he expose Greater Metropolitan. She was the one who pushed her uncle into meeting Mr. Montgomery and setting the legal action in motion. She winced at the price he was paying for being honest: a couple of nights in jail and no lawyer.

"Thanks," she said refraining from slamming the door off the hinges. She was steaming mad and practically running to the library only to find the line dead. She stood with the phone in her hand, pondering what to do. Her uncle needed her help and he'd have it; that was, right after she crafted her resignation letter. She'd start looking for a new job immediately. Once she got the new job, Sonya planned to hand this jerk her letter. She didn't give two hoots about the amount of work in the queue, especially the Greater Metropolitan civil complaint they were pushing to complete and get filed. There was no way he could handle the load without her. Too bad for him. He'd better work it out with the new temp who came onboard yesterday. His needs were no longer her concern.

She relished the image of informing him about her resignation. Then he'd get a taste of what it felt like to need help, expect it, but not get it. *He'll get his,* she thought, placing the phone receiver back into its base. Not today, maybe not tomorrow, but soon.

Maxwell wanted to bask in glory after Sonya left his office. The bishop and his ministerial staff were eventually going from jail to prison for a few years. He wanted to be ecstatic, truly Maxwell did, but the joy wasn't rising. He actually felt sorry for Deacon Burton. From what he could tell the man appeared to be pretty decent. It was as if the deacon was plastered in his mind. The image wouldn't dissipate. Although he wasn't happy about the predicament, Maxwell knew he couldn't offer any assistance to the deacon without compromising the entire case and creating a conflict of interest. He'd worked too many years and had given up too much to lose perspective now. Maxwell kicked Burton out of his conscience and attempted to get back to work.

He sighed poring over his laptop not making much progress. He was bound by the past and the grip was tightening. His father had been a decent man too, but it hadn't saved him from prison. He scratched across his forehead with eyelids shut. Where was the help when his parents were facing prison time? No one stepped in and rescued them just because they seemed to be good people. Nobody cared about the two children they were leaving orphaned at home. Well, practically orphaned. They had no choice but to live with an aunt until their mother was released. His aunt wasn't nurturing. He and Christine didn't go off to school with a hug and kiss, the way their mom had sent them out of the house each morning. Their aunt didn't have much patience or money and the stench of her cigarette smoke and beer bottles made living with her unbearable. Maxwell drew in a gasp of air. To heck with Greater Metropolitan; he didn't owe any of them a single act of kindness. Let them reap precisely what they'd sown: zero compassion.

The only victims truly worthy of his help were people like Jill and the business owners who were unfairly rezoned from their property. They rightfully deserved substantial settlements, which were expected to bankrupt the bishop. Maxwell had no problem relying on favors when he'd asked that Jill's involvement in the prescription drug scheme be reduced to a low-grade misdemeanor with five years probation, no fines, and no jail time. In exchange, Maxwell turned over every shred of evidence he and Garrett had gathered, saving the prosecutor months of work. Maxwell didn't hesitate in securing the deal for Jill, although he felt the city was getting more than they deserved. He didn't care. Jill was worth saving. He would take care of her on the civil case too. If Maxwell had his way, her restitution would also cover her stay at the best rehab facility in North America. More than getting a fat paycheck, he wanted Jill to get her life back. He made a mental note. Regardless of what happened in court, he would make sure she got treatment on his nickel for her kid's sake. If he could save one child from being separated from a parent who actually cared, then his effort had paid off by the billions.

Sonya knocked on the door breaking his concentration. "Yes, what do you need?" he asked somewhat agitated, flopping back and forth from the tablet to his laptop. He wasn't interested in bantering about the deacon again and hoped she got the hint.

"I'll be out for the afternoon."

"Seriously, we have a boatload of work to get done."

"The temp will be here. Maybe she won't mind picking up the extra hours," Sonya said with a weird tone of complacency.

"Is she a paralegal? Exactly how much can she do without your direct supervision?"

"I don't know," she said without elaborating.

"Is there any way you can stay until three or so?"

"Nope," she said leaning on the doorknob. "I have a family emergency that's going to take most of the afternoon to handle. Nothing is more important to me right now, nothing."

"All right then!" Before she left he asked, "Can I help?"

Sonya turned toward him and with a staunch deposition responded, "I don't think so," and walked out of sight.

Maxwell couldn't pinpoint the source of their discord, but something was going on with Sonya. Unless his imagination was completely out of whack, it felt like she had an attitude. He wondered what was giving her angst and racked his brain trying to think of anything else that might have upset Sonya in his office. It couldn't possibly be related to the conversation about that Deacon Burton and the Greater Metropolitan business. But, she was a member of the church and most likely had loyalties to a few of the criminals arrested. Oh well, he'd let it go declaring her attitude was exclusively related to her personal emergency. He resumed typing on the laptop. Whatever was bugging her he hoped was fixed before she got back. Distractions weren't welcomed.

Chapter 43

Bishop Jones closed his prayer time with, "In Jesus' name. Amen." He'd been on his aching knees asking God for mercy and direction. He prayed as sincerely and intensely as a jail cell allowed. The concrete floor lacked the plush comfort his thick-carpeted sanctuary, church office, and home provided: the places where he was accustomed to praying. A loud grunt escaped his lips when he pressed down onto the steel cot and braced himself to get up from the cold floor. Standing in the middle of the jail cell, he couldn't believe his current circumstances. His eyes glazed over the stainless steel commode. The steel sink counted seconds of each hour with endless dripping. There was an upper and a lower bunk. As of now, he did not have a cellmate. The bishop combed the width of the six-by-eight jail cell from one side to the other counting aloud each of the twenty-one bars that held him captive.

He sat on the bottom bunk, laced his fingers together, and dropped his head. He didn't have long to sulk in his cold corner of the world before someone spoke to him.

"Bishop Jones, you have visitors." The guard's snicker coupled with the jingling keys mocked Bishop as he stood. He schlepped over to the cell door, pushed his hands through the small open slot and felt the handcuffs grip his wrists tightly. "You know the drill by now. When you get down to the visiting room, keep your hands visible once you initially greet your visitors."

In silence, Bishop Jones watched the cell doors open. He stepped out of his small, confined area and into the open space. He looked back at the cell, happy for the wide berth that now stood between him and his pit, though it would be short-lived.

He arrived at a private visiting room he'd been in twice since his arrest several weeks ago. He peeked through the small square glass on the door. There was his wife. Her face was filled with worry and weariness. His lawyer was there, too. The officer unlocked the handcuffs and opened the door, nodding for him to walk through the doorway. The bishop rubbed at both of his wrists and stepped inside the room. Doors had often been opened for him. Usually applauses and crowds of people anxious to hear him preach were on the other side. Not today.

"Ellis." His wife's greeting reached him before he could make it across the room to her. She stretched out her arms latching on to him the moment he was within her reach. "Ellis, are you okay?" When she released her hold, she checked him from the top of his head down to his feet. She covered her mouth with both hands then patted her tears before they could fall.

"I'm okay, sweetie. I'm okay. Don't worry about me. Please don't worry about me." He glanced back at the officer, wanting to embrace his wife again, but he knew the rules. He took her hand into his, squeezing it tightly, and turned to his lawyer and gave him a strong handshake. "Thanks for coming. I was hoping to see you soon."

The three sat and the bishop's lawyer gave him an update on his case. "We have good news. After the money laundering and fraud charges were added last week, there haven't been any other charges presented. I'm still working on getting your assets freed up, but that will take some time, especially with the IRS getting involved." The bishop grimaced. "Be patient. We have a lot to work with, but you're innocent. We'll get you out soon."

Bishop just shook his head. "I see."

The lawyer informed Bishop that Councilman Chambers had also been charged with fraud and racketeering. The defense attorney was concerned that Councilman Chambers would cut a deal and be called as a witness for the prosecution. He laid out his defense strategy and worked on a list of character witnesses with the bishop and his wife.

"We need to talk about your involvement. I have to review what you knew and when."

"I'll gladly tell you what I know," Bishop responded.

"First, I have to ask Mrs. Jones to leave the room."

"No, I want to support my husband. No matter what he's done, I'm standing with him."

"That's great, but I have to talk with him privately. Any information you hear could be used against him during cross-examination if we decide to use you as a character witness," the lawyer stated.

"Oh, I see." She fumbled with her hands. "I'll go, because I don't want to do anything that's going to hurt you, Ellis."

"I'm going to be all right," the bishop told her, not totally sure.

Once she'd left the room, the lawyer began his questions. "I need you to tell me again exactly what you knew and how you found out about the prescription drugs being sold by Minister Simmons."

Bishop Jones recalled the talks with Simmons and Jill that had now turned into the nightmare he was living. Once he'd heard his own voice describe the course of events and the lawyer had picked his story apart, question after question, he felt spent, disappointed, and remorseful.

"I can't believe I'm in jail and up against such ugly charges."

"It's absurd for your bail to be set so high for these types of charges. One and a half million dollars is steep," the attorney stated peering at Bishop. "But there's tremendous pressure coming from the public; add a zealous prosecutor, and this is where we are."

"This is killing my family and the church. I need a lower bail."

"As of now you're being considered a flight risk, but I've petitioned the court for another bond hearing."

"Where would I go?" he uttered letting his voice rise until the guard eyeballed him.

"Don't worry. My job is to get you out of here and back home as quickly as possible."

Bishop's gaze plummeted. "I don't have any money to make bail, not with them freezing my accounts and assets based on the money laundering and fraud charges. We probably can't get any money on the house either with my name on the deed."

"What about support from the church?" the lawyer asked. "I've spoken with the heads of both the deacon and trustee boards. There was some resistance, but they've offered to assist in your bail."

"No way," Bishop roared, calming down when the guard stared at him again. "I'm not dragging the church any further into this. No way. I'd rather sit in jail than to let Greater Metropolitan bail me out. If I'm getting out, it will be up to God." His body felt limp thinking about the financial nightmare his wife might endure without him being at home to take care of matters. He was grieved beyond comfort. "This is a disgrace," he cried out. "I can't even pay you."

"Let's get you out of jail first and then tackle other matters," the lawyer said latching his fingers.

Bishop Jones wasn't comforted. "This is too much. I can't handle this."

"Yes, you can, and you will. There are people counting on you."

"I've failed God's calling on my life. When I found out what Simmons was doing, I told him to stop. I was very clear when I said he would not remain on staff at the church if he continued. I even had a second conversation with him in the sanctuary, challenging him to make sure he had put an end to this drug thing." Bishop glanced over at the guard then back at his lawyer. With a glossy gaze that clouded his vision, he pushed his words out past the tightness in his throat. "I should have done more to stop Simmons. Because I didn't, I've ended up hurting us all. I've made some huge mistakes. I didn't steer Simmons away from his involvement like I should have. It was obvious that the money and power was too much for him to give up. Now, his sin and my negligence has cost us dearly, especially me, my family and the church. May the Lord forgive me for my part."

"Did you ever give Simmons the okay to proceed with selling the drugs on behalf of you or the church?"

"Absolutely not; I admit that at first I considered it, but God got a hold of me and got my mind right. No, I didn't approve, and Simmons knew I didn't. Like I said, I told him more than once."

"Why did you consider it at all?" the lawyer asked.

"Because we needed the money. I got the church into a tough spot. I was filled with pride. I was too aggressive with my plans to build a mega ministry. It was indeed God's direction, but I took some short cuts along the way, short cuts that hurt people. In doing so, I became unworthy." Bishop Jones glanced down at the state-issued shoes that were pinching his toes. They were miles away from his soft Italian leather footwear, which felt as soft as socks. Being out of God's will wasn't a desirable place to be; everything was hard.

"Pride may not be a redeeming quality, Bishop, but it is definitely not a crime," the lawyer echoed. "I'm only concerned about your defense, and right off the top, I'm confident the racketeering charges will be dropped. There's no evidence against you, and the fraud we can handle too."

"What about the drug charges? They found bags of pills in the church."

"Dispensing drugs is at most a year of jail time and a fine. I should be able to get the sentence reduced to time served on that one."

"I'm not so sure," the bishop uttered in a sullen tone.

"I have to ask again, are you sure you didn't sell drugs or help anyone else do so?" the lawyer asked.

"I absolutely did not have anything to do with selling prescription drugs, certainly not stashing them in the church and coercing poor Sister Jill into helping."

"Now, she's going to be our challenge," the lawyer said wringing his hands. "We have to deal with the sexual assault head-on."

Bishop began perspiring profusely. He brushed the palm of his hand across his forehead. "I didn't touch her," he spewed not necessarily at his lawyer.

"I understand, but as the senior leader at Greater Metropolitan, the prosecutor and some in the public will want to make you culpable."

Stress ensued. Over the past few days, Bishop Jones could feel his orange jumpsuit fitting looser than it had when initially issued to him. His presence faded under the avalanche of emotions that came along with his repentance.

Time passed and Mrs. Jones was allowed back in. She reclaimed the seat next to him. Getting as close to her as allowed, he spilled out the last little core of his heart. "I'm so sorry for the embarrassment this has caused you. I'm sorry this has hurt the church we've labored over for so many years." He swallowed down the emotion that was clawing at his throat with an audible grunt. "I'm sorry for hurting you and causing the pain I see in your eyes. I am not guilty of these charges against me. This thing is some type of persecution. Not just a personal attack on me but on the church too. But, I won't be defeated. I know the power of prayer, and I will trust and hold on to my faith that God will make everything right in His time." Bishop Jones tried hard to block out doubt, desperately wanting to believe his statement was true.

Chapter 44

Nearly four weeks had passed since the arrests. Maxwell was euphoric, having filed the class action suit less than an hour before the courthouse closed today. Typically he would have closed out the civil case and then let the prosecutor have at the perpetrators in criminal court. Having both the civil and criminal cases going on simultaneously wasn't his preference. He sailed toward the courthouse doors, eager to get back to his office and prepare for trial. Reality was that he never expected the civil case against the bishop and his cohorts to gain traction. By now, Bishop Jones and the rest of his foot soldiers had probably lawyered up and cut heavily into the bucket of funds available for the lawsuit payout, which was why he was going after the church as a secondary option. In this case, Maxwell had to take what he could get. As he drew closer to the exit, his steps became more pronounced. Unfortunately, the poor plaintiffs didn't know what he expected, but there were instances when sacrifices from a few had to be realized for the greater good. He straightened his tie and shifted his suit coat so it hung perfectly.

He pushed the revolving door slowly, savoring the taste of victory. He hadn't won the case yet, but the satisfaction of having the bishop cuffed and paraded across the television like a common criminal was a win in itself. The rest was gravy.

The sunlight glistened across the pavement as the camera crew descended on him. Microphones and cameras were everywhere. Some would have been intimidated and darted from the madness in a cowardly fashion. Not Maxwell; this was the forum he craved. This stage called out to him. *Showtime.*

His name was shouted from multiple directions. One aggressive reporter pushed up front and shoved the microphone close to his lips. "Mr. Montgomery, how strong is your civil case against Bishop Jones and the Greater Metropolitan Church?"

Maxwell loved the spotlight but was smart enough not to compromise his case by giving away too much too soon. Most likely the case would be settled out of court, and he'd have a gag order slapped on him prohibiting Maxwell from talking publicly about the details. He stretched his sleeves out and shook his cuff links. What the heck, he didn't care. This case was too big and meant too much for him to be silenced, not this time. "I've handled many cases in my fifteen years of practicing law, but this is the worst I've seen. It's a classic case of arrogance and a flagrant abuse of power. What's worse is that this case takes on a sinister component when the ringleader is a bishop, a man charged with helping people. Every occupation has worth, but some jobs have a greater level of accountability."

"So, you believe Bishop Jones will be found liable?"

Maxwell grinned. "Our legal system entitles everybody to a speedy and fair trial, even the most despicable criminals with multiple cases pending."

"Are you calling the bishop a despicable criminal?"

Maxwell pulled a pair of Ray-Ban shades from his inner pocket and slipped them onto his face, grinning all the while. "Let the bishop have his day in court, and I'm confident he will get exactly what he deserves. Actually, I should say both days in court," he said with satisfaction as his grin widened.

"That sounds personal."

Maxwell stared directly into the camera. "You're right, it is," he declared and pushed through the crowd, pleased the man responsible for destroying his family was finally where he belonged—as close to hell as he could get on earth.

Garrett's words popped into his head as he strutted to his Porsche. What if the bishop was innocent and had no direct involvement in the drug trafficking or the sexual harassment? The question left his head as quickly as it had entered. Bishop Jones's innocence was irrelevant. He was guilty of many sins. It didn't really matter to Maxwell which act landed the man in prison for a few years, so long as that's where he landed.

Maxwell got into his car, dropped the convertible top, and sped off feeling as jubilant now as he had upon exiting the courthouse. He couldn't imagine anything changing his mood. His phone rang, but he ignored it wanting to bask in the moment for as long as possible. When the phone rang again and again, he pulled to the side of the road and took a quick glance. The digits weren't familiar, but whoever it was had better have the wrong number.

"Maxwell Montgomery here," he said with a snip of bitterness.

"Maxwell, it's me."

His sister's voice was faint but recognizable. "Christine, I didn't expect to hear from you." Before he could ask why she was calling, Christine chimed in.

"I'm sorry to track you down like this, but it's Dad."

"What about him?"

"He's had a massive heart attack. The ambulance is rushing him to the hospital."

"Heart attack? I thought he had cancer."

"He does but Mom and Dad have been watching the news every day since Bishop Jones was arrested. When he saw you a little while ago on the TV, I honestly think it became too much. He bent over clutching his chest and lost consciousness."

Maxwell sat on the side of the road, speechless. He'd just experienced the most gratifying moment of his adult life, watching Bishop Jones get his due justice. To believe his joy was predicated on his father's pain didn't make him feel good. He had a sinking angst that wasn't budging. "Where is he now?"

"In the emergency room."

Maxwell stumbled terribly over his words unable to coherently process Christine's revelation. He took a deep breath and pulled out a pen from his leather-bound pad. "What's the name of the hospital?"

"Oh my goodness," Christine belted out, crying. "It would mean the world to Dad and Mom to see you."

"Sis, I'm not making any promises, but I'll do what I can."

"Maxwell?"

"What?"

"Don't wait too long, not if you want to see Dad alive." He heard her and understood. "It may be too late already."

Maxwell got off the phone but sat there for a long while, not sure what to do. If he went today, and his father lived, what was he going to say to him? If he didn't go, and his father died, how was he going to feel tomorrow? His emotions were torn.

After a few minutes, which seemed like hours, he maneuvered from the shoulder into traffic, not sure if he was making a right at the next light to go home or turning left to hit I-95 South toward Delaware. In thirty seconds his decision would be made. Until then, he let the wind graze his face and provide a brush of peace, a sensation he didn't expect to feel for a long time after he reached the light. No matter which way he went, Bishop Jones had won, again. He might be headed to prison, but Bishop Jones was dragging his father's heart with him. When would the torment end?

Maxwell reached the stoplight. He hesitated, and then darted into the left-turn lane. He hit the highway, deciding not to think too much. The plan was shaky and any heavy contemplation would have him back in downtown Philadelphia, pulling into his garage. He pressed the gas pedal, letting the car cruise around ninety miles an hour. He had to get to Delaware before he changed his mind.

Chapter 45

Maxwell turned on the radio and scanned for a soft jazz station. Any soothing background noise would do. Just as he was settling down, the phone rang startling him. Maxwell tensed. Anxiety stifled him instantly. Many emotions tackled him. It had to be Christine. If she was calling back this quickly, it couldn't be good news. Could his father really be gone—dead? Maxwell wanted to scream, but who would hear him? Who would care about his ache? In that split second, the anger he'd harbored toward his father was empty.

The phone rang again. He answered the call while finagling his car to the shoulder. Maxwell cleared his throat in a fruitless attempt to brace himself for the news he wasn't prepared to hear. "This is Maxwell."

"Mr. Montgomery, this is Pastor Harris."

"Pastor Harris?" Maxwell repeated, not sure if he should be frustrated for having to pull off the road for a nonemergency, mad about the temp giving out his private number, or relieved that it was not his sister relaying bad news about his father's condition. Sentiments were mixed, and he'd sort them out later. For now he wanted to pull off and get to Delaware as soon as he could.

"Is this a good time to talk?"

"Not really. I'm on the highway."

"Oh, I'm sorry. I can speak with you later."

"I figure your call must be important if you've tracked me down on my private line."

"I had no idea this was your private number. I saw you on the news and felt led to offer you a word of encouragement. When I called your office they gave me this number. I apologize for any inconvenience I've caused you."

Pastor Harris's gracious tone humbled Maxwell. His desire to get on the road hadn't diminished, but he could spare a second of courtesy. "It's no problem. I have a new assistant in the office, and she's learning her way around. It's not your fault she gave you this number."

"I just hope it doesn't cause a problem for her."

"It's fine, really, don't worry about the phone. How can I help you?" Maxwell adjusted his headset while peering into his side mirror, waiting for the perfect time to bolt into traffic.

"Like I said, I saw you on the news and felt led to call."

"You can imagine how surprised I am to hear from you."

"I don't know why," Pastor Harris said.

"Because, I was instrumental in bringing down one of the most powerful ministries in Philadelphia. I'm not exactly the most revered man in the religious community. You know what I do, and I know what I do. So, it's no surprise my circle of friends doesn't include too many of your colleagues."

"I can't speak for every man of the cloth, but I will say that those who seek after truth and righteousness will be rewarded. I am certainly not one to judge anybody, especially someone who believes they've been called by God to preach. Their walk and decisions are solely between them and God," Pastor Harris proclaimed.

Maxwell didn't agree. Leaders were accountable to others, and ministers were no exception. He reared the engine to a cruising speed of eighty to wipe out the last seven miles separating him from the highway exit. "Pastor Harris, thank you for the call, but I'm in the midst of handling a personal crisis. My father is in the hospital."

"Oh my."

"He had a heart attack, and I'm trying to get there before anything happens."

"What's your father's name? I'd like to pray for him."

Maxwell wasn't big on prayer, but it wouldn't hurt to get some for his father. "Sure, it would be nice," he said, shocked to hear those words roll across his lips. "His name is Paul." He paused taking in the gravity of his father's name, the one he bore but didn't use. "Paul Montgomery Sr. would appreciate your prayer and so would I."

"Consider it done. I will be lifting up your entire family and believing God for strength and direction. Be safe my friend and maybe I'll see you at Faith Temple in the near future."

"You never know, maybe."

Maxwell ended the call and for an unexplainable reason, he felt a sense of peace that wasn't present earlier. He didn't believe in religious mumbo jumbo. So, his initial instinct said his sensation had no connection with Pastor Harris, but Maxwell took pride in being a sensible man. Two plus two was four, one plus one was two. It would be plain silly to ignore the obvious. Maxwell had noticed an element of sincerity each time he'd interacted with the pastor. He signaled to change lanes as the exit approached. Could it be possible? Could he have found the one legitimate minister in the whole of Philadelphia? He'd find out soon enough, but not right now. Zipping off the exit, his hope was high, miles left to travel were few, and the minutes were short. There was an old man clinging to life who took precedence and with any luck or help from the pastor's prayer, Maxwell would arrive at the hospital in time to make peace with his father while it counted.

Chapter 46

Maxwell pulled into the first available parking space thrusting the gearshift into park. Hustling at a brisk pace, his focus latched on to the silver letters on the building that spelled out Wilmington. His father had been sick for a while. Maxwell hadn't expressed any concern or even made a follow-up call when Christine told him his father may have cancer. Now he was eager to see his father after years of estrangement.

The piercing sound of an ambulance's siren sent a wave of anxiety cruising through Maxwell's body. He squeezed his fist tightly, quickly sensing the fingernails boring into his palm. Just as he pushed the cell phone into his pants pocket, it rang. Maxwell couldn't talk and would send the call to voicemail. His focus wasn't on Bishop Jones or anything work related. He glanced at the screen. After it stopped, the phone rang again. It was Christine. He froze instantly, and stood staring at the phone. Maxwell was numb as emotions and regrets tackled him. Was his father dead? He wasn't sure, but he didn't want to take the chance of hearing those words on the phone. Maxwell silenced the ringer and burst through the double doors of the hospital.

Maxwell stopped at the information desk and was told his father was upstairs in intensive care. The elevator moved in slow motion. He counted the floors with every number that lit up above the elevator doors. Finally, the elevator bell chimed, and the doors opened to the fifth floor. Maxwell took long strides that got him to the nurses' station in seconds. "Paul Montgomery, my father, he's here in intensive care. May I see him?" Maxwell's words, *my father,* echoed in his mind. He wasn't sure if those words had been uttered out of an abundance of compassion, concern, or fear.

"Sir, the doctor and his wife are in with him now. There are other family members in the waiting room around the corner, second door on the left. Have a seat in there, and you'll be able to see him shortly."

"Thank you," Maxwell responded pulling his hands back from the countertop. The nurse's proclamation about other family members put a chokehold on him preventing Maxwell's feet from moving. He hadn't seen his family in years. How much had his mother changed? Did she keep her hair thick and long? Maxwell shook his head forcing out the taunting images. Two more steps and he turned the corner. Six steps and he was standing in front of the waiting room door. Maxwell gripped the knob tightly, counted one, two, three and pushed the door open. He didn't have to scan the room for his family. Immediately, a voice drew his attention and pulled at his heart.

"Uncle Max." Tyree ran across the room and jumped into Maxwell's arms. "Hey, Uncle Max," he said, throwing his arms around his neck and squeezing.

"What's up, little man?" Maxwell was comforted by Tyree's hug.

Christine rushed over and swallowed Maxwell and Tyree up into a single embrace. "I'm so glad to see you."

Maxwell waited for her to release her hold. He was glad there was no one else in the waiting room. "How is Dad?"

Christine's arms fell to her sides. Her puffy red eyes gave Maxwell a hint at the answer. "He's not doing well at all." She glanced at the clock on the wall. "Mom and the doctor are in with him. They've been in there fifteen minutes already." She lifted Tyree from Maxwell's arms. "Sweetie, go sit down. I need to speak with Uncle Max for a minute."

"But, Mom, I need to tell him about my birthday party. Uncle Max didn't come, remember?"

"You'll get to talk to him. He's not leaving." Christine glanced up at Maxwell for confirmation. "Right?"

"Right," Maxwell assured Tyree peering past Christine to witness the delight on his nephew's face.

Christine latched on to Maxwell's wrist and led him across the room near the door. Her nails dug into him and her voice trembled. "What if he dies?"

He had wondered the same thing but for probably different reasons. Maxwell wasn't sure of the exact moment when his perspective had shifted, but he didn't want his dad to die without having a chance to build a bridge over the empty valley of sorrows between them. Maxwell could feel the sharp, pointed needles of regret poking at him. But how could he make it right? Maxwell was a grown man. His father was an old man. Both had their way of being.

"Maxwell, do you hear me?" Christine tugged hard at the lapel of Maxwell's suit jacket. "Don't you care?"

"He won't die, Christine. He just can't." Maxwell thought about the Father's Days, holidays, and birthdays that had passed by without him contacting his dad. There was so much lost time with his father that he couldn't restore. It was gone forever. In the courtroom he had some power. In this situation, he could only hope for the best.

Maxwell and Christine lingered in the waiting room, along with Tyree, who had fallen asleep. Thirty minutes had passed and their mother hadn't returned with an update. Maxwell rubbed his hand across the top of Tyree's soft hair. "I'll go find out what's going on. It's been long enough. Someone should be able to tell us something by now." A commotion in the hallway swept past the waiting room on the heels of Maxwell's comment.

Two nurses and a doctor hustled by the waiting room. Another person whisked by hurrying in the same direction. Christine sprang from her chair. "It's Dad. I know it's Dad. I can feel it." Six wide steps and she was at the door pulling it open with such force, the door slammed into the wall. A loud female voice could be heard around the corner.

"He's coding. I've got a code in five ten."

"Code blue, stat," rang out over the intercom.

Maxwell swept up Tyree and rushed down the hallway behind Christine. He stopped when he saw his mother standing outside of a room with her hand pressed against the thick glass window. The curtains were closed, but the noise and voices inside spilled into the hallway making it clear there was trouble inside.

The louder the ruckus on the inside got, the softer Ethel prayed. With tears crawling down her face and hands planted on the window, she began to tremble. There she was, Maxwell's mother. He couldn't remember when he'd last seen her. She was thinner. Her hair was much shorter and hands covered with wrinkles. Her prayer was transforming into inaudible moans. "Mom," Maxwell called out softly.

Ethel opened her eyelids and spoke her son's name: "Paul, oh my God, Paul. You're here."

Maxwell didn't correct her. This time being called Paul wasn't irritating. He knew his mother would try to hug him as she made her way toward him. Before he could decide if he would allow the connection to happen, or not, another wave of panic roared through ICU. A thick voice inside senior's room could be heard by Maxwell and his family.

"We're losing him," a man yelled out. The sound of movement and calamity inside the room drew everyone's attention. The same male demanded, "Clear, hit him again."

Maxwell's mother clung to him with her arms wrapped around his waist and her head buried into his chest. She prayed through her sobbing. He couldn't push her away. She was emotionally fragile and needed him. Her embrace couldn't be denied. Christine tried comforting Tyree, who was now crying, while moving as close to Maxwell as possible. "Paul, we can't lose our father," she told him laying her head on her brother's shoulder.

Maxwell's personal space was completely gone. His safe distance maintained by keeping miles between him and his family were instantly removed by the crisis at hand. In the moment, he couldn't deny his family. Their touch, the smell of perfume, their fear was all tangible as they leaned on him for support. Maxwell's focus darted to his father's door. After what seemed like an eternity, medical staff trickled out.

"What's going on?" Maxwell demanded.

No one answered him except a nurse who told Maxwell the doctor would be out soon.

There weren't any loud shouts spilling into the hallway. It was too quiet. Maxwell's mother and Christine were both mumbling almost in unison. He was pretty sure they were praying. Tyree had quieted. Just as Maxwell was pulling Tyree closer, his father's door opened. A short olive-skinned man emerged from the room.

With her hand pressed flat against her chest, Ethel asked, "Doctor, what's going on? How is my husband?"

"Is he all right? Tell me he's all right." Christine blurted out with a trembling voice.

The doctor ushered them down the hallway a few steps. Maxwell assumed leadership. "Just tell us what's going on, Doctor. How is he?" Maxwell took a step closer to the doctor.

With a thick accent, the doctor replied, "Mr. Montgomery has suffered a massive heart attack. He is stable for the moment. However, that could change quickly. His heart stopped twice. He was out for a little over two minutes the first time and just over a minute the second time." The doctor removed his glasses, allowing his intense stare to pass over each of their faces. "We can't determine if there is any permanent damage to his heart or his brain without running some tests. He's too weak for that right now. Tell me, has he been under any stress lately?"

Maxwell heard his mother tell the doctor yes. He halfway expected her to look his way when she answered. Ethel didn't, but she did say he hadn't been sleeping well. His blood pressure had been consistently too high and there were family issues constantly worrying him. Maxwell listened intently at the exchange between his mother and the doctor before interjecting. "Will he be all right?"

"It's too early to tell. Let's get through the night. We will run some tests in the morning and hopefully have a better idea of what we are up against. The stress along with the cancer treatment has put a strain on his heart. We are doing the very best we can for him. His regular doctor will be here in the morning and will take over his care," the doctor answered with his gaze holding on to Maxwell.

"When can I see him?" Ethel asked, patting Maxwell on his arm.

"Let him rest tonight. The nurse will let you know when you are able to see him," the doctor answered, putting his glasses back on. "Go home, get some rest. There's really nothing more you can do here tonight."

"Doctor, I'm not leaving my husband's side. Now I can sit quietly in his room and not make a sound."

"I understand your concern, but ICU rooms aren't set up for overnight visitors."

Maxwell could tell his mother wasn't giving in. "Mom, why don't we sit in the waiting room together for as long as you want. You'll be right down the hall from Dad."

She seemed to contemplate his suggestion and finally agreed.

Christine told her mother and Maxwell she would be back at the hospital as soon as she got Tyree settled with a sitter. She tried to convince her mother to go home with her and they could come back together. Ethel was determined not to leave her husband's side or let her son out of her sight.

Maxwell and his mother took a seat in the waiting room. His mother talked, he listened. She talked about when he was a little boy, how cute and smart he was. She told him how much she'd missed him and that God answered her prayers by allowing her to see him after so many years.

Maxwell didn't want to dwell on the number of years. The tiny age lines that sprouted from the corners of her eyes and the strands of gray that streaked her hair wouldn't let him ignore the fact that so many meaningful years had slipped by. His mother told him how much she loved him and that everything happens for a reason. Listening to her, he knew he had to talk to his father.

Chapter 47

A few days in jail was as much as Deacon Burton could handle. Getting out on bail was a blessing he didn't take lightly. He was home and there was nothing better. The sound of a basketball hitting the pavement was loud going through the net as Deacon Burton scored on his thirteen-year-old son. He slapped his sixteen-year-old a high five sealing his victory. "You guys keep playing. I'm going into the house to get a drink. These old knees need a break."

His youngest son, a chiseled image of him, stopped Deacon Burton before he got to the door.

"Hey, Dad, can I ask you something?"

"Sure, what is it?" Deacon Burton turned to make eye contact with his son.

"Are you going to prison and leave us?"

His droopy, light brown eyes burrowed right into Deacon Burton's heart. "No, I would never leave you guys. You know I love both you boys and your mother very much. I—"

His son flung his body into his dad's and clutched his neck. "The kids at school keep saying you're going to prison, and I'll never see you again."

"Listen, we believe and trust God, right? God will work this thing out. It's just a mistake, and it's not for you to worry about. I don't even want you to think about it. That's my job. You keep going to school, having fun, and don't think about what people say. You listen to what I'm telling you. Okay?" Deacon Burton brought his son close. They pounded fists and then both snapped their fingers representing the special handshake they'd concocted when his son was a little boy.

Standing in the kitchen, peering out of the window at his boys, Deacon Burton considered his son's question with a heavy heart as he grabbed the container of juice sitting on the counter. The high-pitch shrill of the phone on the countertop broke his concentration. He considered not answering it. He knew it wasn't someone from the church calling. His role as a deacon was suspended until this mess was cleared up. He was told the decision wasn't personal; it was just the best thing for the ministry in light of the publicity. Yet, the call could be important. So, he picked up the cordless phone and greeted the caller.

"Deacon Burton, I'm glad you answered. I called earlier this morning and didn't get anyone."

"Attorney Hayes, sorry about that; I was outside with my boys. What's going on? Is something wrong?" the deacon asked in a deeper tone.

"I know you've been unsuccessful in contacting Max-well Montgomery, but I really need you to try again. He's critical to your defense. He can establish you as someone who helped him bring this case to justice instead of being one of the guilty parties. With you holding a key role in the ministry and having signed tons of financial docu-ments, it will be a real challenge to prove you didn't know anything about the zoning violations or any of the other criminal actions."

Deacon Burton stopped pouring orange juice and schlepped from the kitchen into the half bathroom around the corner. He closed the door. After a quick peek out the window to ensure that his boys were still outside, he responded. "I've called his office constantly. He hasn't returned my calls. I've gone to his office twice, and I was told he was in a meeting both times. I don't know what else to do about him. Mr. Montgomery told me he would help, and I trusted him." Deacon Burton pushed out a heavy sigh, closed the toilet lid, and dropped down to sit. "My wife and I put up our house to come up with my bail money and your fee. We can't afford to pay Mr. Montgomery and you too. Maybe that's what he wants, money. I don't know, but I can't go to prison. I just can't."

"I strongly suggest you keep trying. Maxwell Montgomery is an influential man in this city. If he'll speak on your behalf, I'm confident you can avoid jail time. You have to find a way to reach with him. I'll be in touch."

Deacon Burton yanked the phone from his ear and pounded it into the palm of his hand. He trudged from the bathroom to his family room. Focused on his boys playing outside, he began to calm down. He scanned the wall plastered with pictures. His wife called it the family wall of love. He moved closer and relived every memory. With his fingertips, Deacon Burton traced the edges of the frame holding his wedding picture. He didn't want this legal problem hanging over his head and hurting his family. There had to be a way to reach Mr. Montgomery. His eyelids were pinched together tightly as he prayed silently. A few minutes later an idea offered him a bit of hope. His gaze combed the room for a notepad with no luck. He hurried to the kitchen and ravished drawers until he found a pen and paper.

Deacon Burton put on his reading glasses, sat at the table and his ink pen soared across the paper. He now had a two-page letter conveying his desperate message to Maxwell. After reading the letter over and over and making changes, it was ready.

When he wife arrived home later that afternoon, he approached her. "I wrote a letter to Maxwell Montgomery. You know the attorney Sonya works for, the one who said he would help me. Tell me what you think. I don't want to come across angry or demanding. Though, I do need his help." Deacon Burton didn't want to worry his wife so he didn't tell her about the call from his attorney. He adjusted his glasses on the bridge of his nose and began to read:

Mr. Montgomery,

I'm writing this letter because I've called your office multiple times to speak with you about some serious charges I'm facing. Each time I attempted to reach you, I was told you weren't available. I realize you're very busy, but it is imperative that I speak with you.

You told me the information that I provided about Greater Metropolitan, Bishop Jones, and Minister Simmons was helpful. You also told me that if I wasn't involved in any wrongdoing, you would help me. Actually, you told me I could get immunity from the criminal charges. Mr. Montgomery, I came to you, because you have a reputation for being diligent, thorough, and fair. I took you to be a man of integrity. I've heard you speak on T.V. about restoring integrity and accountability in the community and the church. You are accountable for your actions and your words too. You were diligent in your efforts to expose corruption in Greater Metropolitan. You've been determined to make the guilty pay for their actions. I expect you would want to ensure the innocent don't suffer an underserved prison sentence, too.

Please contact me. I don't know if you have a wife or children who depend on you. I do, and my family is my treasure. Some people strive to have lots of money and fame. None of that means anything to me. My family is what matters most to me. I'm just trying not to let this trouble I've gotten involved in hurt my family. If you are indeed a man of integrity and care about justice, you will honor your word and help me. I hope to hear from you soon.

Deacon Burton's attention left the paper and dashed straight to his wife's eyes. He tried to offer her confidence with his calm demeanor.

"It's a good letter," she said. "But—"

"But what?" he asked.

"Well, it sounds like you're desperate." He could no longer look upon her worried countenance.

"Maybe I am."

"What's going on with the case, Steve? What aren't you telling me?" his wife asked touching his arm.

Chapter 48

Pastor Harris turned into his driveway and used the remote control over his visor to open the garage door. Headlights shined on the door as it slid up. He sat in the car staring at the neatly organized garage with his fingers gripped firmly around the steering wheel. Five minutes passed, and he hadn't moved. His wife opened the kitchen door leading into the garage and calling out to him. "Renaldo, what are you doing? Park the car and come on inside. It's getting late."

Her voice yanked him out of his trance, though his brain didn't process what she was saying. He took his foot off the brake and let the auto roll into the garage. Once inside, he stopped at the kitchen countertop and scooped up the mail. He sifted through it on his way to his study where he dropped down into a chair. His wife joined him minutes later with a jeweler's catalog in hand.

"I finally found the new wedding set I want." She gave a slight grin. "I think I'm worth the upgrade after ten years," she stated and tapped her finger on the rings that had captured her interest.

"Good, sweetie," Pastor Harris replied without glancing at the catalog. He peered straight ahead while he rubbed the tips of his fingers back and forth over his chin.

"What's wrong?" She closed the catalog and set it on his lap.

Pastor Harris's hand fell from his chin to the catalog. He glanced at his wife in silence and then shared what was tugging at his heart. "I drove by Greater Metropolitan tonight on the way home. Their Wednesday night Bible class used to be just as packed as Sunday morning service; not tonight or last week either. The parking lot wasn't overflowing. There weren't any parking attendants directing traffic and only one section of their multilevel parking lot was sparsely occupied."

"I heard a woman at the beauty shop today talking about how many members have left the church. They've gone from multiple services on Sunday with thousands to holding one service that isn't full," his wife replied.

"The Citywide Ministers Council met today. The interim senior minister at Greater Metropolitan told us the church has suffered a devastating split in membership. They're fighting over this and that. When a shepherd falls, the sheep run astray, lost. Half of his church has given up on Bishop Jones."

"The other half is staying loyal to him and the ministry. Either they don't believe the charges or they're going to support their pastor no matter what he does," his wife interjected. "You just don't know what to believe. It's awful."

Pastor Harris rolled a pencil back and forth between his fingers. "The gossip is swirling about other things that might have been going on but weren't uncovered. Sadly, Bishop Jones's arrest was enough for many to deem him guilty." Harris snapped the pencil in half. "This situation will have a devastating effect on the church and our community."

"I want you to hear something." His wife reached across the desk for the phone, dialed into their voicemail, and pressed the speaker button.

"Pastor Harris, this is Sister Lisa Houston. I was a member at Greater Metropolitan until recently. I can't believe the den of iniquity that was brewing over there. I know the case hasn't gone to court yet, but the fact that drugs were found in the church is just too much for me. I find it hard to believe Bishop Jones didn't know what was going on with those drugs and swindling those folks out of their businesses. He has his hand in every aspect of the ministry. It's a shame. Anyway, after twelve years of being a faithful member, I was so distraught over this craziness; I had to take a couple of weeks off. I just didn't want to go to—" A sharp beep cut off the message. Pastor Harris looked up at his wife with a pinched brow.

The bubbly female voice came to life again. "Oh, I guess my message was too long. Well, anyway, I've been out of church a few weeks now. I seriously considered just being done with church. I mean, if you can't trust a bishop. This whole thing just snatched the taste buds right out of my mouth. I couldn't even eat. Anyway, I'm looking for a new church home. Please call." She rattled off a phone number. "I've known your wife for years, and I've heard nothing but good things about your ministry. I'd love to hear from you."

Pastor Harris pushed himself up from his chair and sat on the edge closer to his wife. "I'm glad she didn't just give up on church. That's one of my biggest concerns about this chaos. I don't want people to be soured on church in general. Yes, people make mistakes, but we can't judge a whole institution based on one individual's shortcomings," Pastor Harris told his wife dropping his head.

"I know, hon," she offered, sliding her hand over the top of his while rubbing a small black mole as she often did. "Who's taking over the pastoral role permanently?"

"There is so much internal conflict among the assistant ministers for the position that it has caused more dissention in the church. The situation is disheartening and shameful. If Bishop Jones is found guilty, someone within his church organization will step in and make that decision. From what I hear the governing church body over him is reluctant to name anyone from that church to the position. I think they may want someone with a fresh perspective from outside Greater Metropolitan."

A loud ding sounded off in the kitchen. "I hope you're hungry. I warmed up your dinner," she told him as she stood.

"I am, but let's pray first. I know God is going to step in and heal this situation at Greater Metropolitan and its congregation," Pastor Harris stated, taking his wife's hands. They prayed that God would intervene and show forth His power, grace, and mercy. They asked that the ugly shadows of sin wouldn't have a lasting impact on the body of Christ. Pastor Harris closed his prayer gripping his wife's hands firmly and hoping Bishop Jones hands were clean. "Lord, strengthen Bishop Jones and his wife. Encourage their hearts and be their source of strength. As leaders, we are held to a higher level of accountability. And that is a level only you can judge. Amen."

The scripture in Matthew chapter seven came to mind and he couldn't shake it. There were many who claimed to know the Lord and to do works in His name, but in the end Jesus said, "I never knew you. Depart from Me, you lawbreakers!" Bishop Jones and the other leaders from Greater Metropolitan were in God's hands now and He knew the whole truth.

Pastor Harris washed his hands at the sink. "Honey, I'm hungry. Let's eat."

Chapter 49

It was day three in the ICU for Maxwell's father. The unit was a cold, quiet place unless someone was coding. Maxwell walked through the glass double doors as they slid open for him. He'd stayed overnight in the hospital waiting room with his mother and sister since the day his father was admitted. The second day was more of the same. The ladies had seen him, prayed for him, and kissed him good night. Not Maxwell; he had remained close by but hadn't mustered sufficient courage to see his father. He was headed back to Philadelphia today. Having said good-bye to his family, Maxwell had to get back to the legal arena, but not before he talked with his father.

He stopped outside the nurses' station, a few feet from his room.

"Good morning. How is . . . Mr. Montgomery, today?" Maxwell stumbled almost saying, "my father," but swallowed it.

"There's a slight improvement, but the good news is that he's holding his own. His blood pressure is quite high this morning. We'll keep a close watch in order to get it down to a safe level."

"Is he on any life preserving equipment?"

"Nothing major; he's still on a heart monitor. We also put him on oxygen since he has been experiencing some trouble breathing. He seems comfortable."

"I'm going in to see him."

"He's very weak. So, please keep your visit brief," the nurse requested with the corners of her lips halfway turned up. "He's sleeping; try not to wake him."

Maxwell nodded and headed toward his father's room. He stopped in front of the door and peered into the dim room through the thin panel of glass. A minute later, he pushed the door a quarter of the way open and assessed the man in front of him. There was Paul Montgomery, Sr. lying there, helpless. His eyelids closed, oxygen tubes in his nose and several wires sprouting across his silver-haired chest. He entered the room and stepped to the bedside. The salt-and-pepper hair, thin frame, and wrinkles spoke to the transformation effect of time, which made Paul Sr. look like a stranger. The tiny apple-shaped birthmark on the left side of his neck told Maxwell the man in front of him was indeed his father.

Maxwell pulled the chair from the corner up a couple of feet near the bed. Sitting down, he looked up at the monitor. Red lights, numbers, and squiggly lines were outside Maxwell's comfort zone. He was just as uncomfortable speaking to his father. Lacing his fingers together, Maxwell leaned forward, planting his elbows into his knees. His heart searched for the appropriate words.

His elbows were needles stabbing his knees. He wasn't sure how much time had passed, but he didn't know how to start the necessary conversation with his father. The quiet was sliced away by a strange sound.

"Son, my son." The weak voice and the words caught Maxwell off guard.

"Hi, how do you feel?" Maxwell muttered, getting up from the chair.

His dad coughed and grunted a couple times. "I'm alive, thank God," he whispered.

After watching his father lick his lips and swallow down a gulp of air, Maxwell replied, "Yes, you are."

Their gazes were locked on to each other. Neither said a word for a long minute. Then Maxwell noticed a tear fall from the corner of his father's eyelid and slide down into his ear.

"Son, I'm sorry. I made a mistake that hurt you badly." His eyelids opened and closed as he spoke. "It cost you so much, and it cost me a price I didn't know I would have to pay." His voice was low, his words spaced out too far apart. "It cost me . . . my son."

Paul Sr. coughed seeming to struggle for his next breath even with the oxygen intact. "I'm so sorry."

Maxwell was quiet. He hadn't expected a remorseful and apologetic start to their conversation. He expected his father to be firm, unregretful. Had the years lost between them or the near-death experience changed his father? Maxwell didn't know. Something was different, and it wasn't just the weak voice delivering his father's words. He'd never seen his father shed one single tear.

Paul Sr. inched his hand toward the edge of the bed, motioning for his son to move closer. Maxwell stood there, one hand shoved into his pants pocket. He wasn't sure if he wanted to move. He could see his father just fine. Coughing and sucking in hard for air, his father beckoned again for Maxwell to move closer. Maxwell's feet felt like they weighed a hundred pounds as he shuffled them within inches of the bedside.

"Don't punish your mother for my mistake. You've stayed away long enough." His voice stayed low and words still spaced too far apart.

Staring down at his father, Maxwell's thoughts took him back in time. He remembered loving his father and wanting to tag along behind him as a little boy. Like a whisper in his ear, Maxwell could remember his father saying, "You're going to be a great man one day. Be a godly man as well, and don't carry bitterness in your heart." Growing up, his father said those words to him often. The hallway outside the door came to life with a gush of panic sweeping Maxwell's thoughts back to the moment.

Voices, people scurrying called Maxwell's attention to the door. A nurse pushing a small cart and a doctor both whisked by. In that moment, the door opened and the bright light from the hallway spilled into the room, blinding Maxwell for a few seconds.

"Sir, Mr. Montgomery needs to rest," the nurse advised.

"Sure," Maxwell responded, squinting his eyelids to regain his focus. He turned to see tears streak down the side of his father's face. Maxwell pondered the moment. A man he'd never seen cry before, and today there it was. Without thinking about it, Maxwell rested his hand on top of his father's. Paul Sr.'s eyelids parted halfway. He gazed up at Maxwell.

"I'll see you soon," Maxwell said squeezing his father's hand. He didn't know how to bridge the valley of distance. How could they fill in all the missing years and create a father-son relationship where one hadn't existed? He didn't know. The gnawing ache crawling around in his belly, and the clarity he now saw his father with, infused him to consider the possibilities.

Chapter 50

It was early afternoon by the time Maxwell left the hospital and steered his car into his private parking stall at the office. Over the past three days in Delaware, his thoughts had weaved in and out, up and down. Maxwell considered his father's heart attack and the expression on his mother's face when she saw him at the hospital. Christine's words echoed in Maxwell's mind with an annoying frequency. "It's a shame it took a life and death crisis to get us all in the same city."

The distance between Philadelphia and his past no longer felt like thousands of miles apart. The ding of the elevator, when Maxwell reached his office floor, flipped a switch in his mind. He stepped out of the elevator and headed toward his office. His energy, passion, and drive were rejuvenated just by entering his corner of the world.

"Mr. Montgomery, you're back," the receptionist announced, standing.

"Yes, and I need to get caught up quickly. Hold any calls for the next couple of hours," he directed never breaking his stride. He passed her and around the corner Sonya was in his sights.

"Good, you're back. I've got a list of questions about the Greater Metropolitan civil suit and some mail you need to see right away."

Sonya moved and talked at Maxwell's speed. She was the only paralegal who worked at his pace, able to anticipate his needs, and knew his priorities. He'd gone through plenty before hiring her. Maxwell forged into his office with Sonya on his heels. "Have a seat and let's get right to it," he told her, tossing his leather briefcase to the side and claiming his high-back chair. "Bring me up to speed."

Sonya spent forty-five minutes briefing Maxwell on everything that had taken place in his absence and gave a thorough update on the Greater Metropolitan case. She handed him a blue stack of small papers. "Here are your messages. They're sorted by priority. The first eight will need your attention ASAP. By the way, the temp told me about the personal emergency you had the other day. Is everything okay?"

Maxwell glanced up at Sonya then back at the messages, continuing to sift through them. "Ah, yeah, I think things will be okay. I'll just have to wait and see." Maxwell kept sifting through the papers. "Anything else I need to know about?"

"Yes, one more thing." Sonya pushed a pile of mail bound by a thick rubber band across Maxwell's desk.

Just as he picked up the bundle, Sonya announced, "You might want to read this one right away." She held a single white envelope in her hand. "It's a letter from Deacon Steve Burton at Greater Metropolitan." Sonya stretched her arm across the desk almost shoving the envelope at him.

His gaze swept over the name on the envelope; then he placed it next to the other mail. "Okay, I guess we're done for now. I may need you to take some notes later."

"You're not going to read it?"

"I'll get to it later." Maxwell riffled through the other pieces of mail.

"Deacon Burton keeps calling, and you know he dropped by the office before you left town. It seems like he really needs to speak with you."

"Okay, okay. I've got to get caught up first." Maxwell handed Sonya a piece of paper from his briefcase. "Can you check on the case law surrounding these charges and the precedents for monetary awards?"

"Sure," Sonya answered getting up to leave. She had to calm herself and be realistic. He'd been out of the office and needed to get his head around things. He'd read the letter, commit to helping her uncle, and then she could continue working for this man. Her patience was nearly depleted.

She'd kept busy, but time seemed to inch by, while she struggled not to bolt into her boss's office and ask, "Did you read Deacon Burton's letter yet?" Hours had passed and Sonya couldn't wait any longer. She needed to know and only Maxwell Montgomery could satisfy the aching curiosity slithering through her body. With a manila folder in hand, she rapped on his office door.

"Come on in," she heard.

Sonya entered Maxwell's office hopeful and with a pleasant countenance. "I have the case law and information you asked for earlier."

"Thanks; just put it on top of the pile."

As she did so, Sonya scanned the desk for her uncle's letter. It wasn't in view. "So, did you find out what Deacon Burton wanted?"

"Ah no, not yet." Maxwell didn't take his eyes off the document he was working on.

"He might be trying to tell you something about the case. I mean, you never know." Sonya fidgeted with the bangle bracelet on her wrist as she stood with her hands behind her back.

Maxwell stopped writing instantly. "That's a thought," he said glancing up at Sonya. He pulled the letter from his desk drawer and ripped into it. Sonya watched his head move from line to line. Halfway through the letter

Maxwell sounded off with a loud grunt. Sonya anxiously waited as her palms sweated.

Maxwell read the last few lines and folded the letter. She was stunned when he stuffed it in the envelope and dropped it into the trashcan beside his desk. He looked up at Sonya. "More of the same; he wants my help to get out of this jam he's in."

"Didn't you promise to help him?" Sonya's hands fell to her side.

"Why would I? He's not my client."

"He's been trying to reach you for weeks now. He seems to think you promised him your help, and apparently he needs it." Sonya folded her bottom lip in and filled her lungs with a deep breath. She turned away from him, marching toward the door.

Maxwell's words pierced her like a dagger. "Why are you so concerned? He's just another criminal. He'll have to pay the cost for his sins just like the rest of the bunch."

Sonya spun around abruptly almost losing her balance. "My uncle is not a criminal." The retort flew out of her mouth with no filter.

Maxwell fell back into his chair. "Your uncle?"

"Yes, my uncle. When he told me about his suspicions at Greater Metropolitan, I told him to call you. I believed you would get to the bottom of things, and he could trust you. I had a lot of respect for you. I saw you as a man of integrity. I thought you genuinely cared about the truth. Now I—"

"Sonya, what in the world are you rambling about? I had no idea he was your uncle. Another little something you weren't completely honest about," he said pressing his thumb and index finger into his temples with eyelids shut tightly. "And, I don't care who he is, guilty is guilty. That's what I do: uncover the corrupt actions of snakes lying beneath the surface." He stared at her harshly.

"Don't blame me because your uncle got swept up in the net when arrests were made."

"You promised to help my uncle avoid criminal charges if he told you what he knew. He helped you build a case against the bishop and the other people. You didn't have a case before he got involved," she snarled. "Now thanks to you, my uncle was arrested for something he didn't do." She stepped closer to Maxwell's desk. "He and my aunt had to get a second mortgage on their house to bond him out of jail." Her nostrils were flaring in and out to the rhythm of her heartbeat. "This is crazy, and it's just wrong."

"Young or old, the guilty parties have to suffer the consequences of their actions. I didn't make out the arrest warrants. If he's in jail then the authorities must feel he deserves to be there."

"That's just it; he doesn't deserve to be there." Sonya snapped back with her head wobbling. "You make me sick standing there in your tailor-made suit. I can't believe I admired or respected you," she told him with a creased brow and narrowed eyelids. "What was it you said in one of those ridiculous interviews of yours? 'Work together to restore the integrity of the community and the church.' Yeah, right. That's what my uncle was trying to do and look where it got him." Sonya turned around in a full circle, taking in a panoramic view of his fancy office, and pointed her finger at Maxwell. "I see how you got to where you are, railroading innocent people into prison."

Maxwell leaned forward, pressing his palms hard into the top of his desk. "Just who do you think you're talking to? Obviously, I should have fired you when I found out you didn't tell me about your membership at Greater Metropolitan. You can believe—"

This time it was Sonya's strong voice taking charge. "Oh, you don't have to worry about it. Unlike you, I have a life and family outside this place. My family means more to me than this job." Sonya shoved her hand down into her skirt pocket and yanked out her office keys. She flung them onto Maxwell's desk. "You can have this job. My loyalty and integrity aren't for sale." Shaking her head, she said, "I feel sorry for you. Your life is defined by what you do for a living. You don't have any family or friends who want to have anything to do with you. That's why all you have is your relentless and heartless attack on churches." Stabbing the air with her forefinger, Sonya shouted, "My uncle isn't guilty of anything but the poor judgment of trusting you." She bolted from Maxwell's office leaving his door standing wide open.

Maxwell scooped up Sonya's keys and tossed them into the air. Then he pulled out his desk drawer and threw them inside, slamming the drawer shut. Mechanically, he moved to the door, closed it, released a frustrated breath that filled his cheeks, and then counted to ten in his head. He trekked to the trashcan and fished out Deacon Burton's letter, rereading it. Now standing at the window, Maxwell stared off into the distance not really pinpointing anything with the letter crumpled up in his hand.

Had he done the right thing by not helping Deacon Burton? Was he just an innocent bystander who was caught in the crossfire of corruption around him? Maxwell thought about his parents, their innocence, and the price he and his family paid for his father's efforts to do the right thing. He unrumpled the letter and ripped it into small pieces tossing them into the air. The pieces of paper lay scattered on the floor about his feet. Deacon Burton would have to pay the cost. He would get no more mercy than Maxwell's father had received. The decision was made and there was no turning back as long as Maxwell had anything to do with it. He'd had the last say thus far . . . or was God about to show His hand? Only time would tell.

Readers' Group Guide Questions

Makes you go "hmmm!"

Now that you have read *Relentless,* consider the following discussion questions.

1. As head of Greater Metropolitan, was Bishop Jones rightfully or wrongly charged? Were any, all, or none of the charges appropriate?
2. Is Maxwell justified in wanting Bishop Jones to be held accountable for wrongdoings in the church?
3. Maxwell seems to be softening regarding his family. Do you think he will forgive his parents and fully reconcile? Is this important? If so, why?
4. Will Nicole really give up on Maxwell and move on?
5. Sonya seems pretty mad. Since she's been exposed to unlimited amounts of confidential information in Attorney Montgomery's firm, do you think she'll use any of it to get even?
6. The phrases "what goes around comes around" and "you reap what you sow" are typically used when a person is perceived to deserve a setback. Do you see the current set of events as Bishop Jones's past catching up with him? If so, why? If no, why not?
7. Was Deacon Burton misguided in taking his suspicions about Bishop Jones and Minister Simmons to Maxwell? Why? If yes, what should he have done instead?

8. Paul Montgomery Sr. was a seasoned Christian. How did he end up convicted of a crime he didn't intentionally commit?

9. Forgiveness is a key element in our Christian walk with the Lord. Maxwell's father allowed many years and old issues to keep them estranged. Does this affect your opinion of his Christianity or is it just his humanity?

10. What similarities do you see between Maxwell Montgomery and the Apostle Paul?

11. How does a church survive the type of crippling scandal Greater Metropolitan was faced with?

12. What impact does this type of scandal have on the communities' view of church and organized religion as a whole?

13. Bishop Jones entertained the thought of partnering with Simmons and his drug scheme because he needed money for his church expansion project. Though he decided that wasn't the right thing to do, how do you feel about his considering the possibility?

14. Maxwell refused to believe that Jones was innocent of any of the charges against him. Even when Jill was insistent that the bishop did not sexually harass or assault her, Maxwell refused to believe her. Did Maxwell take any shortcuts or skirt too close to illegal activity when gathering evidence against the bishop? Is it okay to bring someone to justice by any means necessary even if it's illegal and/or immoral?

15. If all the charges were true about Bishop Jones (they're not but for discussion purposes let's say they are), should Bishop Jones's wife stand by him? Why or why not?

Note: The *Redeemed* drama series is loosely based on the biblical leader Apostle Paul. Originally named Saul, he was known as someone committed to persecuting the church. It seemed that would be his legacy, but God had other plans for him. Saul had an encounter with God on the road to Damascus and his philosophy converted, and he became a faithful believer. His name was changed to Paul and he repented. He spent the rest of his life preaching the good news of salvation and deliverance, through the acceptance of Jesus Christ, to a list of struggling churches (New Testament).

Acknowledgments

We are grateful for each reader who has graciously allowed us to entertain them with our new *Redeemed* series, beginning with *Relentless*.

We must thank Joylynn Ross for taking on this project with us. We couldn't ask for a more supportive, insightful, and inspiring editor. Many blessings to our dear sister as God continues to use her literary gifts in many ways. We also have to thank our agent, Andrew Stuart, who goes the extra step to do all that he can on our behalf. You've made the business aspect easy. We give a big shout out to the Urban Christian production team, especially to Smiley Guirand who designs great covers. Finally we give a huge thanks to Emma Houston Foots for the encouragement and amazing editorial feedback she provided on this manuscript. Blessings to you always.

From Patricia

I will also thank my family, daughter, parents, brothers, friends, advanced readers, spiritual parents, church family, prayer warriors, Delta Sigma Theta sorority sisters, booksellers, book clubs, and so many other well-wishers. I especially thank my dearest husband, Jeffrey Glass, the man who keeps me laughing, inspired, and reminded of how truly blessed I am. I am grateful and honored to do this project with Gracie Hill, my high school friend and sister in Christ. To God be the glory in my life as I fulfill the purpose for which He created me.

Acknowledgments

From Gracie

I thank God for all of His rich blessings unto me. I also thank my family, friends and my loyal readers who have supported and encouraged me with each book that I released. I am so appreciative of my loving church family, Promise of Life Ministries; you are a blessing in my life. I thank God for Patricia Haley-Glass for including me in this awesome literary journey.

Authors' Note

Dear Readers:

Thank you for reading *Relentless*. We hope you were entertained by this first installment in the *Redeemed* Faith-Based Drama Series. Look for *Redeemed,* the second book in this saga.

We look forward to you joining our mailing lists, dropping us a note, or posting a message on our Web site. You can also find each of us on Facebook at Patricia Haley-Glass and Gracie Hill.

As always, thank you for the support. Keep reading, and be blessed.

www.graciehill.com
www.patriciahaley.com

UC HIS GLORY BOOK CLUB!

www.uchisglorybookclub.net

UC His Glory Book Club is the spirit-inspired brain-child of Joylynn Ross, an author and the acquisitions editor at Urban Christian, and Kendra Norman-Bellamy, an author for Urban Christian. It is an online book club that hosts authors of Urban Christian. We welcome as members all men and women who have a passion for reading Christian-based fiction.

UC His Glory Book Club pledges its commitment to providing support, positive feedback, encouragement, and a forum whereby members can openly discuss and review the literary works of Urban Christian authors.

There is no membership fee associated with UC His Glory Book Club; however, we do ask that you support the authors by purchasing their works, encouraging them, providing book reviews, and, of course, offering your prayers. We also ask that you respect our beliefs and follow the guidelines of the book club. We hope to receive your valuable input, opinions, and reviews that build up, rather than tear down, our authors.

What We Believe:

—We believe that Jesus is the Christ, Son of the Living God.

—We believe that the Bible is the true, living Word of God.

—We believe that all Urban Christian authors should use their God-given writing abilities to honor God and share the message of the written word that God has given to each of them uniquely.

—We believe in supporting Urban Christian authors in their literary endeavors by reading their titles, purchasing them, and sharing them with our online community.

—We believe that everything we do in our literary arena should be done in a manner that will lead to God being glorified and honored.

We look forward to online fellowship with you. Please visit us often at www.uchisglorybookclub.net.

Many Blessing to You!

Shelia E. Lipsey,

President, UC His Glory Book Club

ORDER FORM
URBAN BOOKS, LLC
97 N18th Street
Wyandanch, NY 11798

Name (please print):_____

Address: _____

City/State: _____

Zip: _____

QTY	TITLES	PRICE
	3:57 A.M Timing Is Everything	$14.95
	A Man's Worth	$14.95
	A Woman's Worth	$14.95
	Abundant Rain	$14.95
	After The Feeling	$14.95
	Amaryllis	$14.95
	Anointed	$14.95
	Battle of Jericho	$14.95
	Be Careful What You Pray For	$14.95
	Beautiful Ugly	$14.95
	Been There Prayed That:	$14.95
	Betrayed	$14.95

Shipping and handling-add $3.50 for 1st book, then $1.75 for each additional book.
Please send a check payable to:
Urban Books, LLC
Please allow 4-6 weeks for delivery

ORDER FORM
URBAN BOOKS, LLC
97 N18th Street
Wyandanch, NY 11798

Name(please print):_____

Address: _____

City/State: _____

Zip: _____

QTY	TITLES	PRICE
	By the Grace of God	$14.95
	Confessions Of A Preachers Wife	$14.95
	Dance Into Destiny	$14.95
	Deliver Me From My Enemies	$14.95
	Desperate Decisions	$14.95
	Divorcing the Devil	$14.95
	Faith	$14.95
	First Comes Love	$14.95
	Flaws and All	$14.95
	Forgiven	$14.95
	Former Rain	$14.95
	Humbled	$14.95

Shipping and handling-add $3.50 for 1st book, then $1.75 for each additional book.

Please send a check payable to:

Urban Books, LLC

Please allow 4-6 weeks for delivery